"I loved this hot little sexy story and can't wait for the next installment. Sawyer Bennett is awesome."

—Monica Murphy, *New York Times* and *USA Today* bestselling author

"Like an episode of *L.A. Law* with a side of orgasm and a glass of hilarity."

—Lauren Blakely, *New York Times* and *USA Today* bestselling author

"I always enjoy Bennett's writing, so I expected to enjoy this. What I truly adored about *Objection* is the fun and slightly snarky tone. *Objection* is very different from Bennett's previous books, and you can just tell that she had an absolute blast creating Mac and her crazy fun story."

—Andrea, The Bookish Babe

FRICTION

ALSO BY SAWYER BENNETT

The Off Series

Off Sides

Off Limits

Off the Record

Off Course

Off Chance

Off Season

Off Duty

The Legal Affairs Series

Legal Affairs Boxed Set

Confessions of a Litigation God

Clash

Grind

Yield

The Last Call Series

On the Rocks

Make It a Double

Sugar on the Edge

With a Twist

Shaken, Not Stirred

Carolina Cold Fury Series

Alex

Garrett

Zack

Ryker

Stand-Alone Titles

If I Return

Uncivilized

FRICTION

A LEGAL AFFAIRS NOVEL

SAWYER BENNETT

Montlake
Romance

Text copyright © 2015 Sawyer Bennett

Published by Montlake Romance, Seattle
www.apub.com

Amazon, the Amazon logo, and Montlake Romance are trademarks of Amazon.com, Inc., or its affiliates.

ISBN-13: 9781503947900
ISBN-10: 1503947904

Printed in the United States of America

To all my legal peeps. I miss you every day!

PROLOGUE

Five Years Ago

I can't control the way my legs are shaking, so I sit back in my chair and cross one leg over the other, hoping the weight and position will still the trembling.

You've got the job, Leary. Nothing to be nervous about.

Glancing out the lobby window to my left, the sun is breaking high over the downtown Raleigh cityscape with clear blue skies and fluffy white clouds. It's a bright, cheerful scene and yet I'm filled with oily dread.

Today is my first day of work with the law firm of Knight & Payne, and I don't know why in the hell I thought that I'd be cut out for a job like this. I'm waiting in their massive lobby on the twenty-seventh floor of the Watts Building. The firm is so big it actually has two lobbies: one on this floor for the civil litigation department, and another on the twenty-eighth floor for the criminal department. Exposed black-iron beams above and rough-hewn wooden floors below lend the decor an intimidating air. The raw nature of the industrial design is tempered with sleek leather furnishings in shades of cream and taupe, which screams money and power—two words that would never be used to describe Leary Michaels.

As one of only two incoming associate attorneys for the year, I'm still convinced they made a mistake in offering me so highly prized and coveted a position. I didn't think my interview six months ago was anything special, and while I graduated in the top ten percent of my law class at Stanford, firms like Knight & Payne usually only accept the top one percent.

Still . . . I wanted this position badly. It was something I'd set my sights on early.

Even though I went to law school on the West Coast, I always knew I'd come home to North Carolina to practice. More important, I wanted to be the type of lawyer who made a difference in an ordinary person's life, and in my mind, the best place to accomplish that was with Knight & Payne.

The law firm is massive, employing sixty-three lawyers, twenty-nine paralegals, thirty-six secretaries, and two receptionists, one for each floor. It's an institution in North Carolina, sought after by every top-ranked law school graduate, because the pay is legendary, the benefits are beyond belief, and the work environment is cutting-edge. But that's not why I wanted to come here.

I wanted to be a Knight & Payne attorney because the firm's entire practice was built upon helping individuals. You won't find any corporate lawyers here representing banks insistent on foreclosing on poor, unfortunate fools. You won't find a single insurance company represented in these halls. Big business is the devil within this institution.

No, the founding attorney, Midge Payne, has it clearly written on her website for all to see that she represents only the downtrodden.

Come, any poor soul needing help.

That's her freakin' tagline.

It's like an open-door policy for every miscreant and shiftless bum to seek help from the best attorneys in the state. We're talking the dregs of society . . . drug dealers, pimps, prostitutes, homeless people, deviants, assholes, and various other scum. Some of these people are so vile most people would shun them. Many attorneys would refuse to help them, forgetting the fundamental concept that everyone deserves a fair shot at justice.

Don't get me wrong—the firm represents ordinary citizens who need legal help, too, but the point is Midge Payne does not discriminate, other than she'll only represent people, not corporations. She isn't afraid to get her hands dirty, and that's what I wanted in my law practice. I want to help those folks who need help lifting themselves out of the filth and grime of unfairness.

"Miss Michaels," I hear from my left.

Turning my head, I see Danny Payne walking toward me. He conducted my interview all those months ago, and he still looks as sleazy as ever. Oh, he's dressed impeccably enough, in a custom-tailored suit that perfectly fits his five-foot, six-inch frame. I tower over him by four inches, thanks to having a tad more height and sensible three-inch pumps.

Danny is dressed to the nines, but he looks like slime oozes out of his pores. It's the way his eyes appraise you . . . like he's trying to figure out how he can best use you or one-up you. It's a calculating look, which makes me shudder slightly, but it in no way turned me off from working here. I was coming for the reputation of the great Midge Payne, not her lackey cousin who manages the firm.

Danny Payne is a conundrum, and not much is known about him publicly. He graduated from some law school I'd never heard of out in Idaho, and rumor has it he didn't really pass the bar exam. The dirtiest of rumors say that his degree is forged, but I don't buy it for a second. I doubt that Midge would let that occur in her firm. What I do know is that Danny doesn't actually practice law but rather runs the firm for Midge. He handles all the glorious duties of the day-to-day operations: human resources, marketing, growth and development, yada, yada,

yada. Sounds boring to me, actually. I went to law school so I could change the world, not sit behind some desk and figure out payroll.

Standing from my chair, I wipe my moist palms on my skirt and hold out my hand. "Mr. Payne, it's a pleasure to see you again."

He gives me a look that could be a leer, or maybe it's just a conspiratorial gesture of welcome, but he shakes my hand enthusiastically. "Come . . . Midge wants to talk to you."

My breath hitches in my throat, and my nervousness ramps up tenfold. "Ms. Payne wants to see me?"

"It's Midge," he says with a smarmy grin. "We're all on a first-name basis here. So it's Danny . . . not Mr. Payne."

"Um . . . okay. So, Midge wants to see *me*?"

This is unheard of. No one—and I mean no one—gets to see Midge Payne. She's like the great and powerful Oz, hidden in a bejeweled tower, protected by the fiercest of dragons. It's rumored that she comes in to work at 4:00 a.m. and doesn't leave until after 9:00 p.m. She supposedly has a private elevator that takes her to the parking garage, and you get admittance to her office only by papal decree or something.

If Danny Payne is a conundrum, Midge Payne is an absolute enigma, perhaps slightly less mysterious and elusive than Bigfoot or the Loch Ness Monster. While she was a powerhouse in the courtroom in her day, she hasn't seen the inside of a courthouse in more than two decades, preferring to work behind the scenes. She still handles cases and does consultations with other law firms, but she does it all from behind her desk and is considered a virtual recluse. There isn't even a picture of her on the firm's website, although I have seen an old photograph. When I was researching this firm before sending my résumé, I went to the library and looked at old newspaper articles. Midge was a pioneering civil rights attorney in the late seventies, early eighties, championing women's and gay rights in rural, southern North Carolina, where said groups were considered third-class citizens. In one photo she was walking out of the court of appeals building after having argued a discrimination case. She was beautiful, with her shoulder-length pale-blonde hair, her face regal and determined. Looking at her, I saw greatness.

She's what I aspire to be, and I hope I don't let her down.

Danny turns to walk through monstrous double doors. I know from my prior interview that this hallway leads from the lobby into the main work area of the twenty-seventh floor. "Yes. She's looking forward to meeting you . . . to talk to you about your role in our firm."

My head is spinning. I'm getting ready to meet Midge Payne, my legal hero, and suddenly I feel like ten times the fool for even applying to a firm like this. The cheap black suit I bought at Walmart—because that's all I can afford with the law school debt I accumulated—is made of polyester and swishes against my taupe nylon stockings, which suddenly look too dark against my pale skin.

She's going to see me for the fraud that I am.

Danny leads me through the Pit, an open work area that takes up the entire interior of the twenty-seventh floor, so called because that's where a lot of the "dark and dirty work" takes place. Most of the attorneys and staff work here, with no walls or offices to separate them. Client meetings are held in conference rooms bordering the exterior of the work area along with the partner offices. All of the exterior rooms are walled with glass, so every office is open to the eye, which makes the work area seem immense. There's no privacy to the outward gaze, however, I happen to know the exterior offices and conference room have double-paned glass, and if you want a measure of concealment, you simply push a button on your desk and a thick, dark-gray smoke filters in between the dual panes, coating the glass walls and giving the people within absolute confidentiality. When you're done, you simply push the button again, and a vacuum sucks the smoke out, leaving clear glass once again.

I want one of those offices one day.

As we walk across the Pit, I get several smiles and nods from my new colleagues. Everyone is dressed differently. Some wear high-powered suits, while others wear jeans and T-shirts. It's one of the perks of working here—absolute autonomy in how you dress . . . how you look. I don't bat an eye at one woman with pale white hair streaked with blue and her face covered in piercings, who sits at her desk smacking on bubble gum. She's wearing a low-cut, shredded T-shirt and black leather pants with knee-high boots. She's talking to a middle-aged man in a three-piece suit, who I assume is an attorney, but you never know. Hell, for all I know, she's the attorney and he's the secretary, which is what makes this firm so unique. Maybe my cheap suit won't be so out of place, since we're allowed to wear whatever we want unless we're going to court or meeting with a client who might have tender sensibilities. Regardless, Danny leaves it up to everyone's smarts and discretion, and he told me during my interview he's had to reprimand someone only once for what they chose to wear. It was apparently a guy who showed up to work one morning after a hard night of partying and still had vomit on his Mötley Crüe T-shirt. Danny told me it wasn't the Mötley Crüe T-shirt he had a problem with.

Only the vomit.

We reach the southwest portion of the Pit, and Danny takes me to the corner office. With its dark-paneled mahogany walls and thick wooden door, this is the only office that varies from the open transparency of the Pit.

Midge Payne's office.

A middle-aged woman sits out front at a small desk with a tiny laptop on it. She has a wireless earpiece and is flawlessly attractive and elegantly dressed.

"She's expecting you," the woman says to Danny and gives me a warm smile. "Welcome, Leary."

"Thank you," I tell her with a backward glance, because Danny is leading me into the inner sanctum of Midge's kingdom. He steps inside her door, ushers me past him, then turns to leave. When the door shuts behind me, I turn to face my hero.

Words can't describe my first look at Midge, and I only hope she can't hear the frantic beating of my heart. I'm shocked to see she doesn't look that much different from that old picture I'd seen circa 1985, twenty-five years ago. The woman has to be in her early sixties, yet could easily pass for early forties. She has the same pale-blonde hair that is now styled in a sleek, shoulder-length bob, and her skin is creamy, nearly flawless except for tiny lines around her eyes and the corners of her mouth. Blue eyes stare at me in cool appraisal as she sits behind her desk, elbows resting on the arms of her chair and her hands steepled in front of her chin.

"Sit down, Leary," she says, her voice oddly warm in contrast to the aloofness of her body language, because she doesn't rise to greet me or offer me a hand to shake.

When I take one of the chairs opposite her desk, I look up at her with a nervous smile.

"Welcome," she says softly. "I've been looking forward to meeting you ever since your impressive interview."

Impressive interview? She wasn't even there.

"Thank you," I say, lamely squeaking out my words.

She chuckles and puts her hands down on the armrests, leaning back farther in her chair and kicking her feet up on her desk. She's casually dressed in a low-cut, purple cotton T-shirt and dark denim jeans. Her feet are encased in olive-green patent-leather pumps with a square toe that have to be at least five inches tall and make my feet hurt looking at them.

I take a quick peek around her office, surprised by how barren it is. No degrees on the walls, no photographs on her desk. Her bookshelves are stacked with law books and periodicals. Her desk is crammed with documents, manila files, and three-ring binders. She has three computer screens sitting on one corner of her desk and a large-screen TV mounted to the wall that is tuned to CNN with the volume muted. Soft tones of music play in the background, and when I listen closely, I'm surprised to hear Missy Elliott's "Pass That Dutch."

This woman is strange and utterly fascinating.

"I watched your interview on video," she says with amusement. "Overall, you weren't anything special . . . not compared to the other applicants."

My jaw drops and my face flushes red. What could I possibly say to that? She doesn't expect me to respond, so she continues. "However, you answered one question better than any of the other twenty-three applicants, and for that reason you got the job."

I wait for her to tell me what amazing piece of wisdom popped out of my mouth, but she doesn't enlighten me, and unfortunately, I'm so nervous I don't have the guts to question her.

"I expect great things from you," Midge says firmly.

Swallowing hard, I say, "I'll work very hard, Ms. Payne."

Her eyebrows furrow inward, and I can see she's displeased. "I'm sure Danny told you we go by first names here."

I nod. "I'm sorry. Just nervous."

Her gaze warms up a bit, and she swings her legs off the desk, surging out of her chair. She's tall . . . really tall, maybe five ten, five eleven, in those heels. Her presence is magnetic, and my eyes are pinned to her.

"I understand," she says as she walks around her desk to sit in the chair beside me. She stares at me thoughtfully, and I'm entranced. She reaches toward me, and I'm powerless to even flinch away from her.

Deft fingers go to the back of my head, where she pulls at the one pin holding up the severe bun in which I'd wrapped my long hair. When her hand clears, my hair falls down to the middle of my back in a cascade of chocolate. She takes one of my locks and rubs it between her fingers, staring at it thoughtfully. "You need to change, though."

I jerk minutely and she drops my hair, bringing her gaze to my confused eyes. "I don't understand."

"You will," she says confidently. "I have great plans for you. Your interview intrigued me, and I know you will be one of my top stars. But this meek trailer-trash image you're carting around has got to go."

Her words hypnotize me so much I'm not offended by her statement. Besides, it's true. I *was* raised in a trailer park, and my clothes are cheap, as are my perfume and discount-store makeup.

"You're a brilliant woman. Your law school grades and interview prove that. But you have other qualities that you need to play up."

"Other qualities?" I ask, dumbfounded. Because, past my intellect and work ethic, what more could she want?

Leaning forward, she rests her elbows on her knees and clasps her hands together. I couldn't look away if I wanted to.

"I'm talking about using *all* of your skills. You are a woman in a man's profession. You're on the bottom of the ladder, and it will be ten times harder for you to climb just one rung while a man skips up ten. Now . . . you're smart, but no smarter than any other man I've employed here. So you need more. You need to work your other talents."

"Talents?"

"You're a beautiful woman, Leary. You hide it, though, and I'm guessing it's because the last thing you want is to rely on your beauty for anything. I'm guessing there's a sordid little story there that makes it so . . . maybe coming straight from the dusty front yard of the little trailer you were raised in."

I cringe, because she's hit too close to home, and there's no way she could know about my past. I raise my chin, daring her to continue, yet am oddly fascinated with where she's going.

"You see, Leary, in order to succeed in this world, you need to work it . . . and work it hard. Your brain, your wit, your determination, your confidence, your sex appeal. Lose the baggy, cheap clothes and show off your body. Get a good haircut, leave your hair down, and get someone to teach you how to wear makeup properly. Make men notice you, and when you've fogged their senses with lust, slap them with your brains.

9

Make women want to be like you, but be so confident in your abilities that they will inevitably fall flat on their face. When you finish with your opponents, don't let them have a moment's doubt that they've met their match." She leans in closer. "I'm talking about winning at any cost. Doing whatever is necessary to get the victory, and as a woman, you need to use every weapon in your arsenal. It's how I succeeded, and it's how you will succeed, too."

I know I should be offended, maybe feel let down over this revelation that Midge Payne seems to be interested in my physical attributes as much as my mental, yet I'm not. I'm strangely titillated by it and feel a sense of power flushing through me. It's a power I imagine my mother employed on more than one occasion, and while I have the utmost love and respect for my momma, I never once wanted to use the same charms she had to use to make sure we survived in a harsh world.

But oddly, the way Midge is advising me to work my assets doesn't seem as seedy as when my momma lay on her back and spread her legs for money to put food on the table.

Midge stands up and walks back behind her desk. "Danny's waiting for you outside and will show you to your work area."

I stand up, smoothing down my polyester skirt and having an insane urge to run to the mall right now and spend my meager savings on a new wardrobe. "Thank you," I say, feeling a little bit lost.

"Great things," Midge reminds me with a hard look. "It's what I expect."

I stare at her a moment, not sure whether I can truly subscribe to her philosophy. Whether or not I can meet those expectations. She's asking me to completely change my way of thinking, and I need just a moment to see which direction my logic will tell me to take.

My logic doesn't wait around, apparently knowing what I need to do.

Steel courses up my spine, and determination and excitement fill me.

"It's what you'll get," I tell her as I turn away from her and walk out of her office.

CHAPTER 1
LEARY

An orgasm crashes through my body, causing my back to arch in my chair and my fingers to pull hard at the hair of the man who's working his tongue between my legs. A groan pours out of me, and he lashes his tongue against me harder yet.

"Enough," I command, because I don't beg well, and I push his head away. Ford sits back on his haunches, grinning up at me. He's in my office, kneeling before my chair, while my skirt is hiked up around my waist and my thong is pulled haphazardly to the side to give him access. My suede ankle-strap Alexander McQueen pumps are perched on the edge of my desk, and my knees are spread wide, baring myself to Ford's fantastically gorgeous face and his shiny, wet lips.

"Feel better?" he asks with a grin, because I was having a craptastic day, which he'd keenly picked up on. But then again, Ford knows all of my moods, and yes, I do feel better, so apparently he knows how to bring me out of a funk. A shattering orgasm does the trick.

"Much better," I say with a grin and pull my legs off my desk, setting my four-inch heels on the hardwood floor on either side of Ford's hips. I vaguely notice figures moving around out in the Pit, just outside my glass-paned office wall, which is now grayed out with smoke so no one can see the nasty things Ford and I are doing. My door is unlocked but I'm not worried. No one but Midge would dare walk in here without a knock, and Midge has never once stepped foot in my office since I moved in here almost two years ago when I made junior partner at Knight & Payne.

Wiping his mouth with the back of his hand, Ford asks, "Wanna feel even better?"

"You know I do," I say as I stare at the massive bulge behind the zipper of his Hugo Boss pants. Ford is as serious about fashion as I am, and we're well suited to each other in other respects, too. We're pretty much in line with our tastes and proclivities, and he's the closest friend I have in the world.

He reaches in his pocket and pulls out a condom, handing it to me. I tear it open with my teeth as he unzips his pants and pulls out eight gorgeous inches of "wanna feel even better." Leaning forward, I roll the condom over his straining erection, loving how after five years, he still groans when I touch him there. Placing my hands on his shoulders, I pull myself from my chair and squat down over him, bringing the tip of his cock in perfect alignment with me.

I sink down slowly onto him while his hands help to guide my hips. When I'm fully seated, we both give a moan of appreciation, and then I start to rock.

Using my hands on his shoulders for balance, I pull myself up . . . push back down. Over and over again, I fuck the man who used to be my boss when I first started here but is now my good friend, close legal confidant when I need to strategize on a case, and occasional lover when I've had a bad day.

Like today.

Because some asshole attorney thinks he can try to screw me over on one of my cases, but he has another thing coming. Right after I come again, and get Ford off as well, I'm going to come up with a stellar plan to mop the floor with this douche. I'll make him regret crossing me, that's for sure. Midge would be proud of my moxie.

"Where'd you go?" Ford pants as he nuzzles his face into my neck and tilts his hips upward as I push down.

"Nowhere," I assure him and pick up the pace.

He seems to accept my word, because he murmurs, "Feels good, baby."

It does . . . feel good.

Damn good, but then again, Ford has always been able to push all my buttons. Ever since my first day on the job here at Knight & Payne, when Danny took me from Midge's office back through the Pit to a desk outside a large office in which a man was talking on the phone.

The man was Ford Daniels, and he was to be my supervising attorney.

He glanced up and saw Danny standing there with me, then motioned for us to come in. His eyes ran down my body briefly, but he never gave any other indication of interest. I was fresh off my meeting with Midge, and my mind was buzzing. I immediately wondered if I should use these extra talents Midge seemed to think I possessed on my newest boss but then thought better of it. I wasn't cut out just then to be a sexy seductress. Oh, I intended to learn, but I knew I was an amateur, at best, at that point in my life.

I couldn't deny my attraction to Ford. At thirty-four, he was ten years older than I was. Light-brown hair, maybe dark blond in the right light, that was slightly wavy with natural curl. He had dark-brown eyes and a strong jawline, was tall, and wore his suit in a way that told me he was built underneath.

Ford was very professional those first weeks of our working relationship, and by professional I mean he never made an untoward move. He looked plenty, particularly when by the third day of employment I'd ditched my conservative polyester suits for a chic, casual office wardrobe, convincing myself it was a wise use of my money. I traded in Walmart for Burberry and Elie Tahari, making sure my clothes showed off my assets, as Midge had instructed me to do.

I cut three inches off my dark-brown hair to just below my shoulder blades and wore it long, loose, and layered with softly curled waves. I learned how to put on makeup to accentuate my golden-brown eyes and full lips, and I walked the Pit with confidence.

By my third week of employment, Ford and I were sleeping together, and I never had a moment's regret. I didn't have sex with him for any gain within the firm. I made it clear to him that sex had nothing to do with work. It did, however, have everything to do with the fact that I wanted to explore my sexuality, which was something I'd never had need of prior to my employment at Knight & Payne. I'd lost my virginity my senior year of high school, and I'd had sex with a few men since then, but I never viewed sex as all that important in my life. Maybe because it never rocked my world. Maybe because they never told us in law school that it could be a tool.

After Ford, I needed it. Not only did he teach me that sex felt damn good and was a great tension breaker but that I had power, and it had everything to do with the fact that I had boobs and a vagina. Ford taught me how to be sensual, which I used in small doses when the time called for it. My sensuality has served me well the last five years.

"I've lost you again," Ford growls before biting at my ear.

"Ouch," I whine as I jerk against him, which causes him to go in deeper and then fuels him to pump into me faster.

"Well, damn, Leary . . . you're not paying attention here," he complains, still heaving upward into my body.

And he's right.

My mind is wandering more and more lately, and I feel restless. While Ford tends to be a great diversion for me, he's just that . . . a diversion. He's my friend, occasional lover, and confidant. He knows me probably better than anyone at this point, and yet Ford will never be anything more than an occasional fuck, a great colleague and a guy I can pal around with sometimes. We just don't have that burning, deep connection that compels us to want to be around each other all the time. We use each other as a sounding board, as a cheerleader in our work lives, and to get our rocks off if the occasion calls for it.

My stomach bottoms out when Ford surges to his feet, his powerful legs easily pushing both of us up from the floor while his hands support me under my ass. He turns, dumps me on my desk, and with the stapler stuck in my lower back, starts to really pound me hard. He's doing this as a way of keeping my attention, and damn . . . it's working. From this angle and the way he's driving into me, I can't think about anything other than the way he feels and the second orgasm firing up low in my belly.

He senses my body getting ready to unleash and he picks up the pace.

Then I'm flying apart, and so is he. My day is definitely a little bit better than it was before.

Condom disposed of, my fringed Tory Burch skirt pulled back down, and Ford sitting across from my desk, you'd never know that we were both fucking like animals just five minutes ago. God, it was good. It had been a long time in coming, too—no pun intended—because Ford had been in a relationship with a physical therapist for several months, and one thing we didn't do was cheat if either of us tried to date someone else. In the past five years, neither one of us has had a relationship that stuck, so we always end up becoming fuck buddies in between our failed attempts to find love. Ford broke up with that woman last week, and I knew it was only a matter of time before we hooked up.

Today just happened to be that day. He poked his head in my office and said, "What's up?"

I growled at him because I was frustrated with this douche of an opposing attorney, and he knew exactly what I needed. He didn't even say a word. Stepped in, closed my door, hit the smoke button on my desk, and went down on me.

It was sublime.

"So what's wrong with you?" Ford grumbles as he watches me carefully from across the expanse of my desk.

Leaning back in my chair and fiddling with a paper clip, I shrug my shoulders. "Not sure what you mean."

Ford cocks an eyebrow at me, one of his patented moves that I adore and that always makes me smile because of his skepticism. "Cut the shit, Leary. You're edgy, tense. This case has you worked up, and it's not even that big of a deal."

I glare at Ford and stick out my lower lip. "It is too a big deal. I don't like this jackass nipping at my heels like a little Chihuahua who thinks he has balls the size of Texas."

Snickering at me, Ford casually crosses one leg over the other. "He's filed a motion to dismiss. Big deal. Happens all the time."

"Yeah, but not to me. Most attorneys know not to screw with me over something so trivial."

"He's new to the area. I'm sure he hasn't heard of your greatness," Ford says in a mocking tone.

"Don't be condescending," I chastise him. "Besides, this case is important to me. You know that."

He nods because he *does* know how important this case is. Other than Midge, he's the only one who knows about my past and why I have so much riding on this lawsuit. This case is a means to help absolve me of my own sins, and if I can't get salvation with it, I'm doomed to a life of guilt.

Midge.

I smile inside—sometimes on the outside, too—whenever I think of her. While I'm very close to Ford, Midge has always been there for me, too, although almost all of our communications are through e-mail or phone. But she had an influential hand in helping to shape me my first few years at Knight & Payne. She gave me advice and guidance on cases and taught me how, as a woman, I could be the best possible attorney.

Midge once confided in me, during one of those rare occurrences when we sat in her office, sipping on whiskey, "Leary, I want people who are risk takers. People like you, who are not afraid to push the envelope, stretch boundaries, get their hands a little dirty."

"Cheat?" I asked her with a smile.

"If necessary," she said without cracking one.

"Lie?"

"In the right circumstances," she confirmed.

"Use my womanly ways?" I asked with a grin.

"Always," she murmured, and we clinked our glasses together in celebration while we laughed.

Yes, Midge Payne shaped and molded me into a fearless attorney who acted like she had the biggest balls in the state. I took risks, I lied and cheated sometimes, and I used my female charms over and over again to daze and confuse my opponents. Her advice served me well, but most important, it served my clients well. I do work that has meaning. I represent people who have been beaten down. I offer protection and advice to those who would otherwise be taken advantage of by the system. I uphold the common man's constitutional rights. I do all of this because I know all too well what it's like to feel powerless. I have made a profound difference in other people's lives, and I'll never apologize for using every trick in my bag to get the job done.

Ford stands and leans over my desk. "Do you want any help brainstorming how you'll argue the motion tomorrow?"

Shaking my head, I say, "No. I've got it."

And I do. It's a simple motion that shouldn't take more than ten minutes, but it pisses me off I even have to argue it at all, that I'm being made to waste my time just so my opposing counsel can bill a few more hours to his client.

"Are you sure you're okay?" he asks, his eyes roaming over my face.

Smiling, I say, "I'm sure. More than okay after the way you just made me come."

Laughing, Ford turns his back on me and heads for my door. "My pleasure, babe. I'll catch you later."

And just like that, Ford is gone and I probably won't see him for several days because we're both so busy with our practices. However, if I ever needed the man, he would drop everything to be by my side.

As a friend, and only as a friend . . . sex benefits aside.

Sighing, I reach out and open the binder sitting on my desk with the words *LaPietra v. Summerland General Surgery*. It's the case for which I'll be arguing against a motion to dismiss tomorrow morning. Opening it up, I briefly scan the motion. The defendant's counsel is asking the court to dismiss my case because I've failed to state a claim upon which relief can be granted.

Which is total and utter bullshit.

The complaint I filed in superior court was cogent and clear, and left no doubt in anyone's mind that I'm suing the prick, Dr. Garry Summerland, and his medical practice for butchering my client in a breast-reduction surgery gone bad.

Jenna LaPietra came to me over a year ago, distraught over the fact that when Dr. Summerland got done with an operation to reduce her from a double D to a moderate C cup, she was left with boobs of two different sizes and one nipple pointed north and the other pointed southeast. It was a horrific result, and she's had three subsequent reconstructive surgeries to try to minimize the damage. Unfortunately, there's too much scar tissue to completely fix the deformities. Her nipples still point in different directions, and she has large, puckered sinkholes around the fleshy globes of her breasts.

Kind of a big deal to a twenty-four-year-old topless dancer without a high school education who strips to put food on the table to support her disabled son.

Acid burns in my veins as I think of all the ways that Jenna has struggled, trying to make ends meet since losing her job at Pure Fantasy. She went from bringing home two grand a week to living in the back of her car and stealing food from convenience stores to feed her kid. All of her money was paid under the table, so she can't claim unemployment. Her kid's father is a heroin junkie who hasn't been seen in two years and is presumably lying dead in a ditch somewhere. She has no family and no friends, and I put my law license at risk when I put Jenna up in a low-income apartment and provided a bank account in which I deposited money every two weeks so she could eat and pay rent. That was a huge no-no to the North Carolina State Bar, but fuck 'em. I'm not about to let that family live out of a car and off stolen food.

Pushing the binder aside, I know I'm better served to study my opponent than the law, because the law is clear and in my favor. Tomorrow's courtroom battle will be nothing more than my swatting away this annoying flea and making it clear he doesn't want to fuck with someone like me.

I pull up the law firm of Battle, Carnes, and Pearson on my computer. It's a powerhouse defense firm that's the polar opposite of Knight & Payne. Whereas we fight nobly to save the downtrodden, Battle Carnes sits in a gilded roost and only represents the nation's elite one percent.

I navigate their roster of attorneys and click on the link for Reeve Holloway. He's pretty damn good-looking. Dark, wavy hair that's cut short on the sides and back, with the top just slightly longer, and very JFK Jr. His eyes are light colored, but I can't tell if they're blue or green, and his lips are sensual. He's actually really hot. His online profile states he's been practicing for eight years, which puts him at about thirty-two, and he just started with the firm six months ago. Prior to Battle Carnes he was working in foreign acquisitions in New York City, which sounds slightly boring and nauseating to me.

The rest of his profile reveals the most important piece of information I can glean, though.

He's single, and while it truly doesn't matter if he's married or not, I can definitely work much more quickly against a single guy than someone who's bound by commitment.

An idea starts brewing in my head.

CHAPTER 2

REEVE

Glancing down at my watch, I see that I have plenty of time to make it to courtroom 21A on the twenty-first floor of the judicial building to argue my motion to dismiss. It's a bullshit motion.

I know it.

The judge knows it.

My opposing counsel, some guy named Leary Michaels, knows it.

Everyone who'll be standing in courtroom 21A knows this is a bullshit motion, and that after just a few minutes of argument, Judge Henry will deny me. The only reason I'm heading to court on this seasonably warm October day is because my new employer, Battle, Carnes, and Pearson, has an unspoken policy to bilk our corporate clients for as much money as possible. Seeing as how I bill $300 per hour, preparing for and arguing this unwinnable motion hearing will bring in about $1,200 to my esteemed employers. Doesn't matter that I'll lose—it will earn money for the firm, and our client is too rich and self-absorbed to question the billing or why I'm arguing a losing motion.

My phone buzzes from my jacket pocket, indicating a text. Pulling it out, I smile when I see it's from one of my buddies inviting me for a few beers tonight. As I walk toward the courthouse, I shoot a quick return text that I'll see him later.

Just as I hit Send, I slam into something extremely soft and very movable, and my hands come out to grasp at whatever I hit before it can get knocked over. I wince at the cracking sound my phone makes as it hits the sidewalk, and my fingers clasp toned arms encased in red silk.

I hold on firmly to what I now realize is a woman who I easily could have slammed to the ground because I wasn't watching where I was going. When my cognizance kicks in full force, I find myself looking into a pair of amber-colored eyes set into a stunningly beautiful face.

Flawless skin.

Full lips.

Perfectly arched eyebrows.

Dark hair pulled back into a sleek ponytail that rests at the back of her neck.

She exudes a chic, confident style in her power suit, with a tasteful but narrow pencil skirt in cherry red and a matching formfitting silk jacket with notched lapels. Her long legs are encased in sheer black stockings, with the fucking sexiest black pumps ever made to walk across a man's back.

Utter perfection.

"I'm so sorry," I tell her, refusing to let her go just yet.

She smiles at me with genuine warmth, and chuckles. "It's all good. I wasn't watching where I was going, either."

I stare at her, unsure of what to say next. It's a rarity that I'll lose my tongue around a woman, but damn if her voice isn't smoky rich, sexy beyond belief, and fuck . . . she even smells delicious from where I'm standing.

"I'm afraid you may have broken your phone, though," she says as she looks pointedly at the ground.

"Shit," I mutter as I release her and bend to pick it up, glaring at the shattered screen. Looks like I'll be making a trip to the store rather than the gym and drinks with the boys tonight.

Shoving the phone in my pocket, I grab the courthouse door and hold it open for her. Giving her a "no worries" smile, I motion for her to precede me in. She inclines her head in thanks and walks in, carrying an expensive-looking, black patent-leather purse over her shoulder.

I'm not a southern man, having been born and raised in the small but great state of Vermont, so it certainly wasn't due to ingrained manners that I opened the door for her. I merely wanted to get a gander of her ass in that narrow skirt.

Just kill me right now. I groan internally because her ass is slammin' and her sex appeal is ramped up by the fact that those sheer stockings have a thin black seam running up the back of each leg.

We reach the elevator at the same time, and she pulls out her own smartphone to study something. She hasn't given me a backward glance, so I use the opportunity to continue checking her out. This woman oozes sophistication; her eyes—from what little I was able to see—hold intellect and maybe even a bit of cunning.

I wonder what she's doing in the courthouse, because while her cherry-red suit is professional, it also shows a hint of cleavage and borders on just a tad too sexy for an attorney, and besides, she's not carrying the telltale briefcase that would give her away as one of my legal brethren.

When the elevator doors open, she doesn't even lift her eyes, but we both wait for it to empty. A young guy in a short-sleeved shirt and skinny tie, whom I peg as an overworked, underpaid clerk, joins us, and then all three of us enter for the ride upward. I immediately walk to the back of the car and lean my back against the wall, setting my briefcase on the floor.

The guy pushes the second-floor button, and I roll my eyes. *Lazy ass, can't walk up one flight of stairs?*

The woman in red pushes the button to the twentieth floor, and I say to her, maybe in a vain attempt to get her attention, "Number twenty-one, if you don't mind."

She cuts her eyes at me with a small smile and hits the button, then ignores me as she steps to the wall to my left and studies her phone.

The ride to the second floor shouldn't take any time at all, but these old elevators in the justice building seem like they're powered by hamsters or something. After several seconds of chugging upward, the car slowly stops and the dude exits. No one else joins us, which isn't surprising because it's late Friday afternoon and the courthouse is pretty much dead at this time. There are only a few judges milling around hearing stupid motions like mine, with the other courtrooms usually cleared of the dockets by Thursday.

As the elevator starts its slow ascent again, I can't help but notice movement from the vision in red. She glances down at the side of her leg and whispers, "Shoot."

My attention moves with laser focus, and I watch as she drops one hand down to the side of her right knee, fingering the material at the hem of her skirt. Against the dark shading of her stockings, it's not hard to see that she has a tiny tear in the silk, and I have to wonder if my briefcase snagged up against her when we ran into each other.

I expect her to just drop the hem of her skirt, but instead she raises it a few inches higher, tracing the path of the run that's creeping up her leg. My breath catches in my throat as she slides the edge of her skirt up an inch, two, three . . . right to midthigh, and yet the run seems to go higher than that.

I silently beg her to keep going, but she drops the skirt and looks up at me with a sheepish grin. "Well . . . that just won't do at all."

I open my mouth to say something that I'm sure will be full of wit and charm while trying to figure out how I can get her phone number, but she stuns me when she holds out her phone to me.

"Here . . . if you don't mind holding this."

I push off from the wall and accept her phone under no volition of my own. She smiles at me coyly and I return the smile with uncertainty.

She stuns me yet again when she puts all her weight on her left leg, balancing herself with one hand on the wall. Lifting her right foot up and back, she bends to the side and takes off her shoe, dropping it the floor.

Shocked is not the word I would use to describe my feeling when she shoots me a grin and then starts to lift the hem of her skirt back up with both hands. She slides the silk material up her thighs and I'm helpless to look away as it climbs higher and higher. Right to the fucking tops of her stockings, which are trimmed with black lace and tiny red bows and clipped into place with red garters.

Swallowing hard, my pulse hammering madly, I watch as she uses her perfectly manicured hands to pop the clips holding her stocking up.

I see the pale, smooth skin of her upper thigh, and if she'd move that fucking skirt up just another two inches, I'd get a peek of what I'm betting is matching black lace covering her pussy. But no such luck. She then deftly hooks her thumbs under the lace edges of the stocking and slides the offending ripped silk down her leg.

Vaguely, I hear the chiming of the elevator as it passes floor after floor. My heart is galloping over the thought that the car could stop at any moment to let another passenger on, but she doesn't seemed to be fazed in the slightest by undressing in a public place in front of a perfect stranger.

Right about the time the silk travels down over her knee, I start imagining what it would be like to have my tongue trace that same path, and I start to get hard.

When the silk finally clears her foot—which I might add is a fantastically sexy foot with cherry-red nail polish to match her suit—I finally remember to pull a breath into my starved lungs before I suffocate.

Standing back up straight, the woman reaches her hand out with the stocking in it and says, "If you don't mind holding this, please."

I wasn't going to say no, so I reach out and grab the delicate material from her, rubbing it in between my fingers as I bring my own hand back toward me. My cock is now pulsing in my pants, and pornographic images of me pushing her against the wall and hammering my way inside her flood my senses.

My eyes are burning as she reaches calmly into her purse and pulls out a spare stocking.

That's handy.

She efficiently, but in no less sexy a manner, bends over and slides her foot into the silk, pulling the edges up her calf, over her knee, up that smooth thigh, while pulling the skirt up along the way, and then she's clipping the lace with the garters again.

Fucking beautiful.

She makes a little bit of a show of smoothing the edges of the stocking against her skin, then she slowly lowers the material of her skirt. I take a quick glance and see we're almost to the twentieth floor, and a sense of urgency takes hold of me as I realize this sexy-as-hell woman will be walking away from me in just a few moments. I want to slam my palm against the Stop button and demand that she change her other stocking, but that would, of course, be ludicrous.

Because there's nothing strange about a woman stripping in front of me in the elevator, right?

She reaches down and picks up her shoe, puts it back on, and snaps her purse shut. Turning to me, she gives me another coy smile and says, "Can I have my phone back?"

I blink hard, just as the twentieth floor chimes and the car comes to a slow, grinding halt. I hold her phone out to her, and she takes it, scraping her pinkie nail across the back of my hand, which causes lust to bubble hot inside me and my dick to swell larger.

"Thanks," she murmurs, and steps toward the doors as they start to open.

"Wait," I call out, and she looks over her shoulder at me. Holding out her stocking that I'm now clutching quite tightly in my hand, I say, "Here."

I can't think of anything else to say, because most of my blood has congregated south of my waist.

She grins at me, gives me a quick wink, and says, "Keep it."

My hand drops down, my thumb and forefinger rubbing against the soft material that I'm betting smells fucking delicious.

Turning away, she starts to walk out of the elevator car.

"Wait," I call out again and slam my other hand against the button that keeps the doors open. She turns all the way around to me and tilts her head in curiosity. She's a fucking vision. "What's your name?"

Cocking an eyebrow at me briefly, she leans in slightly and whispers, "That's for me to know and you to find out."

She then walks away and doesn't look back. A quick glance at my watch shows me I have about two minutes to get to the courtroom for my motion hearing, which means no time to chase her.

"Then how do I find you?" I call out to her retreating figure as she makes her way down the hallway, her heels clicking against the tile.

She doesn't even turn around, but I distinctly hear her laugh and say, "Oh, I'm sure we'll meet again. Karma has a way."

I release the button to the doors, and they close slowly. I practically stagger backward against the back wall and involuntarily bring her stocking up to my nose. Hints of lavender and vanilla. Yup, fucking delicious. As soon as this motion hearing is over, I'm going back down to the twentieth floor and finding this woman. I'll get her number, and if there's a God, I'll talk her into going out with me tonight. And if miracles really do occur, I'll be fucking her, too.

Grinning stupidly, I shove her stocking into the side of my briefcase and try to banish my erection so it's not standing out when I walk into the courtroom.

I can't believe that just fucking happened to me.

Shit like that never happens to me.

Absolutely surreal.

It's now five minutes past the time my motion hearing should be starting. The courtroom is eerily silent. It's only me, the judge, and the bailiff, and we're patiently—okay, not so patiently—waiting for Leary Michaels to show up. The judge doesn't look too perturbed, but then again, Judge Henry has a reputation for being mellow and laid-back. He's got his reading glasses perched on the end of his nose, scanning something on the laptop that sits in front of him. The bailiff looks supremely bored, but that's par for the course. I can't imagine his job is very exciting.

I didn't think I had a snowball's chance in hell of winning this motion, but if opposing counsel doesn't show up, the judge will probably grant me the unexpected victory. Of course, the partners in my firm will go apeshit, because we'll lose out on the opportunity to bill thousands of dollars in future legal fees to our client on this case. Quick victories don't pay the bills.

I hear the door at the back of the courtroom open, and Judge Henry looks up with a slight smile on his face. "Ah, Miss Michaels. Glad you found some time in your hectic schedule to join us here today."

Miss? Well, I guess that question has been answered.

I turn slightly in my chair to take a quick peek at my opponent, and gravity pulls my lower jaw down hard as I see the woman in red sauntering up the aisle toward us like she was on the catwalk.

What. The. Fuck?

She doesn't even spare me a glance as she pushes herself through the low swinging door that separates the gallery from the area that houses the judge's bench, the counsel tables, and the jury box.

My eyes narrow as I watch her take the table to my right, saying in a crisp tone as she sits down, "My apologies, Your Honor. I think all of our time is going to be wasted today with this motion."

My head jerks back in surprise at her temerity, not only because she didn't sound at all apologetic for keeping a judge waiting but by the blatant venom of her tone. She's clearly not happy to be here.

Can't say I blame her, as this motion borders on a fraudulent use of the court's time, so I just shrug and lean back in my chair, letting my gaze rake over Miss Michaels. She's sitting up so straight, I'm sure a steel pole is fused to her spine. Her hands are clasped firmly on the table, and she stares straight at the judge.

"Mr. Holloway," Judge Henry says, and my eyes snap to his. "I believe this is your motion, if you'd like to start. I'm sure we all have better things to do with our Friday afternoon."

"Yes, Your Honor," I say as I stand up, even though my head is spinning. I still can't let go of the image of her taking off that silk stocking in the elevator. That flash of skin on her thigh, the promise of the sweetness that was just beyond.

I'm discombobulated at best when I make my argument, fumbling several times in the process. This, of course, is almost unheard of for me. I'm a fucking phenom in the courtroom, and the last time I was tongue-tied was when Mary-Beth Schubert stuck her hand down my pants in junior high when we were playing Seven Minutes in Heaven.

Fifteen minutes later, having made the lamest and most excruciatingly unmeritorious argument in the history of law-dom, I sit back down and wait to see what Miss Michaels will do. She really shouldn't do much more than stand up, sneer in my direction, look back at the judge with arms outstretched, and go, "You're seriously going to listen to this dipshit, Your Honor?"

That's what I'd do . . . if I didn't think it would land me in jail.

Miss Michaels stands with the cool sophistication she's exhibited from the moment I barreled into her. It's quite hard for me to remember that just twenty minutes ago, she was giving me quite a striptease, and I have no clue why that even occurred. My cock still twitches when I think about it, so I hastily try to focus on her argument, just in case I need to react.

"Your Honor, I'm not even sure I should waste my breath responding to Mr. Holloway's small-minded and timid arguments. The standard is that the allegations in Plaintiff's complaint should be deemed admitted for the purposes of this motion, and outside of Mr. Holloway showing some evidence of fraud, we really shouldn't even be here. Not only did he fail to make a showing of such, but clearly he needs to wipe the cobwebs out from what I would loosely call a brain to even think such a motion would pass muster under your keen gaze."

Fuck, she's ballsy and completely going out on a limb. Her tactic isn't to attack my argument but to attack me, as evidenced by the fact she slammed my intellect in front of Judge Henry by actually raising her hands and making air quotes when she referenced my brain. The woman is vicious and she hasn't even yet addressed the merits, or lack thereof, of my motion.

"But let me make clear to this esteemed court," she continues in a haughty tone. "Jenna LaPietra went to Mr. Holloway's client, Dr. Summerland. She paid him good money to have breast-reduction surgery, and in return, he left her maimed. Now, Mr. Holloway might not be a breast man, and in fact, based on what little dealings I've recently had with him, I'm not sure he'd know how to find one with a GPS, but I can assure you, Miss LaPietra's disfigured body has left her life in a shambles, with catastrophic medical bills and no means to earn a living."

My man card in crucial need of saving, I surge out of my chair. "Objection, Your Honor. I am indeed a breast man and know my way around them with my eyes closed—but legs tend to be more my thing," I say with a lascivious smile aimed toward my opponent.

"Couldn't prove it by me," Leary Michaels sneers back at me.

"Well, it takes a real woman—" I start to say, but I'm cut off.

"Children . . . I mean, counsel," Judge Henry says in a tired voice. "Let's use our inside voices when making snide comments that have nothing to do with the merits of this case."

"Totally agree, Your Honor," Leary says in a placating voice. "Mr. Holloway is being completely inappropriate."

"I'm being inappropriate?" I snarl as I stand up. "Your Honor, despite the fact Miss Michaels purports to hold a law degree, she's yet to argue one iota of law. I have to wonder who has cobwebs in that hollow space of a skull that's supposed to hold *her* brain."

Did I just say that out loud?

Judge Henry picks up his gavel and bangs it on his desk, but it's not loud enough to cover up the snarl emitting from those beautiful lips that would look amazing wrapped around my cock.

"Enough," Judge Henry barks at us. "God, they don't pay me enough to listen to this crap. Mr. Holloway, your motion is denied. There is no basis for it, and the one thing that Miss Michaels did say that is utterly accurate is that this is a waste of the court's time. Now, is there anything further you two brats want to discuss with me today?"

"No, Your Honor," the witch in red says sweetly. "As always, you make a well-reasoned decision."

"No, Your Honor," I grumble. "I apologize for wasting the court's time."

"So be it," Judge Henry says as he raps his gavel once more. "Court's in recess."

I close the file on my desk as Judge Henry steps off the dais and heads through the door to his chambers. When I turn, I see that my opponent is already walking down the aisle, her black purse slung over her shoulder. It's then that I realize she didn't even bring a file to court with her, she was so assured that she was going to win.

"Hey," I call out to her as I scramble through the swinging door, wincing as I bang my knee against it.

She doesn't slow down, so I quicken my pace, grabbing her elbow just as she clears the back door.

"Want to tell me what that little show was in the elevator?" I ask her as I turn her to me. "You knew who I was, didn't you?"

"Of course I did," she says as she leans in toward me with a husky voice that hints at sex and dirty words. "And let's just say your reaction, or lack thereof, told me all I needed to know about you."

Dropping her elbow, I rake my hand through my hair. "Oh, yeah? And what's that?"

Leaning in closer, she puts her lips near my ear, and I almost shudder from the nearness as she whispers, "You're all talk and no action. A docile baby, really. It's going to be so easy to kick your ass in this case."

I jerk back, my man card now having been fully stomped upon. "You're fucking kidding me?"

Reaching up, she pats me on the cheek with her hand and laughs. "I never kid about stuff like that, Mr. Holloway."

She starts to walk away, but there is no way I'm letting that happen without redeeming myself and my poor, busted ego. Quick as a striking snake, my hand shoots out and grabs hold of her wrist.

In one fluid motion, I spin her around and pull her toward me. I reach out with my other hand and lay it in the center of her chest, pushing gently and walking her backward into the wall. When she's pinned flat against it, I step in close to her . . . really close.

Leary's eyes flare briefly, then narrow with anger. "What the hell are you doing?"

Keeping my hand on her chest, I drop my other to the hem of her skirt and start dragging it up her leg. For a moment, she does nothing, then one of her hands grabs my wrist, attempting to stop my progress. "Are you crazy?" she hisses at me.

Her strength is no match for me, and I keep my hand moving upward. When her skirt gets to the top of the lace on her stockings, I bend my body to the side so I can see what I'm revealing. "I want to see if your panties match your stockings and garters."

"We are in fucking public," she practically wheezes, and her head flips to the right to make sure no one's coming down the hall. I can feel her heartbeat ratchet up a beat, thumping madly under my palm that's still resting on her chest.

Shrugging and with my eyes pinned to the black lace and creamy flesh exposed just above it, I tell her, "Oh, well. Besides, didn't seem to bother you when you put on that little striptease in the elevator. So quit being a *baby* and let me see."

I dare a glance up, and her eyes are no longer heated through with offense. Instead, I see challenge staring back at me, and I'm thinking she didn't like being called a baby. Her hand goes lax against my wrist, and I push the material of her skirt past her hip.

"Just as I thought." I breathe out softly when I get a look at her lingerie. "Black lace panties . . . goddamn perfect."

For a brief moment I'm overwhelmed with the urge to slide my hand between her legs and cup her lush heat. But I'm all about proving a point.

I let my thumb graze along the elastic edge that sits in that sexy crease just between her pussy and her upper thigh. She gives the tiniest gasp and my eyes seek hers again, which have a slightly fevered look to them.

"Oh, Miss Michaels, what I wouldn't give to run my tongue right along this edge," I tell her as my thumb sweeps back and forth against it.

Leary swallows hard and her bubblegum-pink tongue slips out and swipes at her lower lip. I nearly groan but tamp it down hard. I'm the one in control now.

Staring at her for a moment more, I whisper, "Maybe another time."

Dropping her skirt and stepping away, I shoot her a charming smile. "Can't wait to see you again . . . in or out of the courtroom."

Her mouth hangs open slightly when I turn to walk away.

CHAPTER 3

LEARY

I'm a pretty smart cookie. Graduated first in my class in high school and went on to do my undergrad at Duke and then law school at Stanford. While I didn't graduate at the exact top of those two schools, I was in the top ten percent of both. I was also on law review at Stanford, as well as a member of their trial advocacy team that placed third in the nation during my third year.

Again . . . smart cookie.

But even the brainiest of people have their weaknesses, and unfortunately, mine happens to be legal research. I have a trial starting next week, and there's going to be a huge argument over a statement I'd like to introduce into evidence that the other side is claiming as hearsay. I know there's an exception to the hearsay rule that applies to this exact situation . . . at least, I seem to remember reading something along those lines in another case, but fuck if I can find it now.

I normally assign this shit to my paralegal, but she's on maternity leave, and the temp I have working in her place doesn't know how to do legal research. So, here I am . . . slogging through the overwhelming

LexisNexis database to find this obscure case that expounds on the exception I might have read about but am not really sure if I did. It could just be that I want that exception to exist, so maybe I created it in my mind.

Pushing back from my computer, I glare at my monitor.

Give me the answer! I shout at it telepathically.

My cursor just blinks in monotonous fashion, mocking me.

Knock, knock, knock.

Looking up, I see Ford standing at my door. I wave him in and peer back at the computer, hoping something will leap out at me.

"What are you doing?" Ford asks as he takes a seat on the other side of my desk.

I don't even spare him a glance. "Legal research."

"You? Doing legal research? Are we on the cusp of Armageddon or something?" he teases me.

"Stuff it, Ford," I say while reading a court-of-appeals case summary on my screen. "My paralegal's out so I had to break down and do it myself."

"Want some help?" he asks amiably.

"No, thanks. I can figure it out on my own."

"Such stubborn pride," he muses, and I finally slide my eyes to his. He's smirking at me.

"What's that look for?" I ask as I push back from my desk a little.

"Nothing. It's just . . . you've been wound up pretty tight since your motion hearing last week. You won, right? What's the deal?"

"I'm not wound up," I mutter, but God, I'm so wound up. I'm no longer pissed that Reeve Holloway would waste my time with that motion. It's done. I won. Anger gone.

But jeez . . . what he did to me after the hearing was over?

In the freakin' hallway, just outside the courtroom. Where anyone could have walked up on us. He shocked me and then—I admit, with no small amount of shame—turned me on more than I've ever been in my life.

I thought the guy was a pushover. The way he just silently watched me in the elevator as I took my stocking off clued me in to all I thought I needed to know about him. He didn't have any game. He had no confidence, no gumption. He would be easy pickings.

Then he turned it all around and practically had me begging for him to touch me more when he pulled my skirt up and looked at my lace panties.

I didn't miss the hard-on he was sporting, either. He was as turned on as I was, and there's no denying he is sex on a stick. He was handsome in his profile picture on his firm's website, but he was even better looking in person. When I saw him outside the courthouse with his head down as he looked at his phone, I couldn't help but stare. He's tall with broad shoulders and a narrow waist, and with each stride, his well-muscled thighs pulled at the charcoal gray of his dress pants.

When we "accidentally" ran into each other and he first raised his gaze to me, my girlie parts nearly rolled over and sighed at the light green of his eyes staring at me in apology. Framed by the thickest, darkest lashes, they finished off his sex appeal with a flourish.

"You need an orgasm . . . maybe two."

"What?" I exclaim, wondering if Ford can read my thoughts about Reeve.

His palms are resting calmly on the armrests of the leather chair, and he has one leg crossed casually over the other as he smiles at me. "You need an orgasm or two. I can tell by the pinched look on your face, which isn't very attractive, by the way."

I immediately lessen my frown, roll my eyes at him, and turn back to my screen. "No, I don't."

"Yes, you do. Let's go. I'll take you out to dinner, and then we'll go to your place. I'll have a smile on your face in no time. Then you can return the favor."

"Not tonight," I say absently as I stare at the computer and try to refocus on the research.

"Okay, who is he?" Ford asks curiously.

My eyes fly back to his, and I try for my most innocent look. "What do you mean?"

"Whoever has you in a knot," he says with a knowing look. "You've never turned me down before unless you were involved with someone. That's the only thing that would have you turning your nose up at the magic my lips can work on you."

Sighing, I push back from my desk again and rub the bridge of my nose. Not only does Ford know me well, he's also my closest friend. While we might indulge in pleasure with each other, there's also a mutual care and trust that's been fortified over the years. Besides that, neither one of us has a jealous bone in our bodies, and we've always stepped out of the picture if one of us wants to pursue someone else.

"It's that attorney I had the motion against," I admit.

One of Ford's eyebrows arches high with skepticism. "You won the motion. How can that still be bothering you? Your temper doesn't work that way. Once it blows and you purge it, you're cool as a cucumber again."

Yup . . . see . . . Ford knows me as well as I know myself.

"It's not the motion. It's what happened before and after."

Leaning forward in his chair to rest his elbows on his knees, his eyes light up with curiosity. "Oh, do tell."

"Well . . . I timed my arrival to the courthouse at the same time as him, and when we were alone in the elevator, I got this wild idea. So I sort of performed a tiny striptease in front of him."

"You did what?" Ford asks as he rears back in his chair.

"Relax," I tell him with a laugh. "I just changed one of my stockings that had a run in it. He didn't get much more than a flash of lace."

Ford stares at me, mouth slightly agape. His eyes have a slight look of censure.

"Stop looking at me that way," I chide him. "I wanted to see how he'd react. Get a read on what type of man he was."

"And exactly what did you learn?" he asks, his tone now intrigued.

"He didn't do anything. Just watched me. Although he finally found his voice when I got out on a different floor. Asked for my name, but I didn't give it to him. He had no clue who I was, and I wanted him to be shocked when I walked into the courtroom."

Ford shakes his head back and forth as he leans back in his chair again. "What did he do when you walked into the courtroom?"

"No clue," I tell him honestly. "I didn't make eye contact. I wanted him to know that he wasn't worth my time."

"But that's not all that happened?" Ford guesses.

Standing up from my desk, I walk around it and take the chair that sits next to Ford. Turning slightly so I'm facing him, I cross one leg over the other, gently swinging my foot. Leaning toward him conspiratorially, I tell him, "We had a moment in the hallway . . . after the hearing."

"A moment?"

"A moment. I goaded him, pretty much called him a pansy ass for the way he did nothing in the elevator, and I guess he didn't take kindly to it. He pushed me up against the wall and told me he wanted to see if my panties matched my silk stockings and garters."

"Are you fucking serious? He attacked you?" Ford growls.

"No, it wasn't like that. It was all sexy slow. Seductive. He was proving to me that he could do something about it if he wanted."

Ford stares at me quietly and his face is impassive. Finally he asks, "Did you ask him to stop?"

Odd, that tone of voice he's using on me. I would expect him to be a little protective, but it smacks of jealousy.

"No, I didn't ask him to stop. I wanted to see how far he'd take it. I wanted to know exactly what type of opponent I'm dealing with."

"Bullshit, Leary," Ford says in a rush. "You liked it, plain and simple. You like him."

"I absolutely do not like him," I argue, but then because I'm always honest with Ford, I tell him, "but I did like what he did. I liked that confidence, that ego. But that's all there was to it. Even if I wanted to check this guy out some more, it's impossible. We're on opposing sides of the case. It's unethical."

Sighing heavily, Ford looks at me a moment more, then smiles softly. "So, I'm definitely not going to be giving you an orgasm tonight?"

Ordinarily, that would be lovely. A quiet dinner with Ford where he'd make me laugh, and then his mouth on me all night. But for some reason, I'm not into it. At least not tonight.

"Rain check? Okay? I have a lot of work to do tonight, and I'm looking forward to a quiet night alone after that."

Slapping his palms on his thighs, Ford gives me an understanding smile and then stands up. "Sure. I'll catch you later."

I watch as he leaves, and wait for something to flash through me where I change my mind and tell him that I want to see him tonight.

But it never comes.

Fortifying myself with determination, I make my way back to my computer and the legal research that's not going to do itself.

"Miss Michaels?" I hear hesitantly from my office doorway.

I glance up from the deposition transcript I'm reviewing and see one of our runners, a young girl who just started college and is working for our firm for the fall semester. She wants to go to law school eventually and—like a lot of the young people who work here—has grand aspirations of joining the team of Knight & Payne one day. Until that day, they start at the bottom, running errands back and forth between the lawyers and the courthouse.

"Hi, Keri. What's up?"

"You had a hand-delivered package up at the front desk," she says as she steps into my office, "and they asked me to bring it back to you. It says, 'personal and confidential,' so it didn't go through the mail room."

"Thanks," I say as I take the box from her and set it on the middle of my desk.

"No problem. Have a great evening," she says before leaving.

"You, too," I murmur, but I don't look back at her. I'm staring at the box and the big white label that shows a return address of Battle, Carnes, and Pearson.

Reeve's firm.

My skin tingles with awareness and my heart beats faster. What in the hell could that firm have sent me that's personal and confidential?

No, not "that firm."

Reeve Holloway.

No doubt in my mind that this is from him.

Pulling a pair of scissors out of my drawer, I cut along the securely taped seams. The box isn't very big, maybe only a foot by a foot and about six inches deep. My curiosity is on overdrive.

When I finally cut my way through the tape and pull the flaps back, I immediately see a cover letter on top of a stack of documents—the Battle Carnes logo prominent, top and center. Beneath the stack of documents is a small white envelope that looks like it holds a card, as well as a smaller box wrapped in glossy white paper.

I remove all of the contents, pushing the small envelope and white-wrapped box aside, and look at the legal documents first, starting with the cover letter.

After the requisite formalities of my name, address, and the case reference, Reeve writes as follows:

Dear Leary:
His informal use of my first name is not lost on me.

Enclosed please find Defendants' First Set of Interrogatories, Requests for Production of Documents and Requests for Admissions. As you know, you have thirty days to answer these, but I'll be happy to grant an informal extension of time if you need it.

Sincerely,

BATTLE, CARNES, AND PEARSON

Reeve Holloway

He signs it "Reeve," and I'm lost as to why this was a personal or confidential matter. These documents were expected. I plan on sending my own interrogatories and requests out to him late next week after I finish my other trial.

I start flipping through the pleadings, scanning the interrogatories, which are nothing more than questions that my client is bound to answer, in writing and under oath. They look pretty standard to me. Same for the requests for production of documents . . . all standard stuff, requesting my client's medical records, both as a result of her surgery and those ten years prior, lost wage documentation, photographs, yada, yada, yada.

Finally, I pull out the requests for admissions. This is a method of discovery that a party can use to narrow down the issues by having the opposing party admit or deny certain statements. Normally you don't see them used by the defendants in a case, so I'm slightly surprised to have them in my hand, but again . . . not by any means something that would be personal or confidential.

I scan through the requests for admissions addressed to my client, Jenna LaPietra. They're ordinary . . . no surprises.

Admit your name is Jenna LaPietra.

Admit your age is twenty-three.

Admit you sought out Dr. Summerland for a breast-
reduction surgery.
Admit you worked at Pure Fantasy as a topless
dancer.

Yup . . . all benign, ordinary requests.
My eyes scan farther, seeing nothing that jumps out at me.
Until I get to request number eighteen.

18. Admit or deny that at the time of your employment
as a dancer at Pure Fantasy, your job duties included
taking off your clothing in exchange for payment of
money.

Okay, that's a bit inflammatory, but still within the bounds of a
reasonable request, because we certainly aren't hiding what she did for
a living. It might not be considered the most respectable of professions,
but damn it, she worked a steady job to provide for her family. No
shame there.
I read the next one.

19. Admit or deny that at the time of your employment as a dancer at Pure Fantasy, you solicited and
performed sexual acts on the customers in exchange
for money.

What. The. Fuck?
I read the request one more time, and yup . . . they're basically ask-
ing Jenna if she was prostituting herself.
My blood pressure rises and my head feels like it's going to explode.
I read through the rest of the requests, and there are no other questions
that are inappropriate. Just this one.

I push the documents aside and turn to my computer, intent to pull up the contact information for Reeve Holloway so I can call him and give him a piece of my mind. But before my fingers can even touch the keyboard, a thought crosses my mind.

This was not a long list of inappropriate questions. All of the questions seemed well within the normal boundaries of what I'd expect. All except request number nineteen.

Which makes the hairs rise up on the back of my head.

If Reeve was trying to goad me, he would have sent me a slew of crazy questions. Instead, he only asked one, and he placed it in a chronologically appropriate place with the other requests asking about her work at Pure Fantasy.

Which means that he must have some type of information to lead him to believe that Jenna was selling herself in addition to just dancing topless.

Fuck!

I quickly dial Jenna's number, needing to put this issue to rest as quickly as possible. I pray to God she tells me that it's not true, because if it is, that's going to throw a big fucking monkey wrench into her case.

She doesn't answer and I leave her a voice mail, asking her to call me immediately.

Drumming my fingers on my desk, my mind starts working on overdrive. *How will I handle this if it's true? Can I do a pretrial motion to keep the information out? Is it even relevant?* That will definitely call for more legal research.

My eyes drift over my desk, lost in thought over this conundrum, and come to rest on the white envelope and smaller box I'd pushed aside.

Reaching out, I decide to open the box first, because I love to get to the surprise. I peel the paper back efficiently and lift the top off a small black box.

Inside, nestled in deep-purple tissue paper, is a pair of black silk stockings. Picking them up, I see that they're almost identical to the ones I had on last week when I chose to show Reeve my partial goods. Sheerest of silk with a two-inch band of black lace around the tops. The only difference is that these don't have little red bows on them. My finger and thumb rub the soft material for a moment, then I set them down.

Picking up the white envelope, I break the seal and pull out a note card with blue-ink handwriting on one side. The message is simple:

Leary,

Stockings to replace the ones you ruined last week and to take the sting out of request number nineteen. It's a legitimate question... check it out.

Reeve

P.S. Are you wearing black lace right now?

I read the note one more time, not sure how to feel. Reeve couldn't have been clearer. He believes Jenna might have been involved in some criminal activity as part of her job at Pure Fantasy. He's warning me loud and clear.

The silk lingerie is a different matter. He sent those stockings to remind me that there's a sexual tension now existing between us. And his postscript? He's telling me that he wants to continue our sexual byplay.

Everything about this note and gift is wrong, according to normal standards. He's crossing personal boundaries and his gift is completely unethical. His postscript highly unprofessional.

But I'm not normal, and fuck . . . it turns me on.

CHAPTER 4

REEVE

The phone on my desk rings and I hit the speaker button. "Talk to me."

"Mr. Holloway, you have a visitor down here in the lobby," our receptionist says in a low tone. "She's not on your appointment calendar."

I glance down at my watch. The package was delivered to Leary about an hour ago, so she's right on time.

I can't help the grin that forms on my face.

"Let me guess," I say casually. "Leary Michaels from Knight & Payne."

"Yes, sir," she says smoothly.

"Sign her in and send her to my office."

Disconnecting the call, I lean back in my chair and take a deep breath, my eyes pinned on my door. Leary will be walking through it any moment, and I suspect she will be either very pissed off or very turned on—perhaps both.

Even with what little I know about her, I'm going to guess both.

That, of course, is an easy guess. I've already proven that I have an uncanny ability to piss her off. And our little interlude in the courthouse hallway? Yeah . . . she was fucking turned on when I slid my finger along the edges of her panties.

I know that I'm playing with fire. Any sane, rational female attorney would have taken the stockings and note card and made a direct complaint to the North Carolina State Bar about my behavior.

I'm taking a bit of a gamble with Leary. I don't figure her for the type to cry to the teacher when her pigtails get pulled at recess. No, I expect she's the type who'd throw a right hook back, and the mere fact that she's here—in person at my office—well, that leads me to believe I've got her pegged.

She's not going to report me.

Leary doesn't even bother to knock on my closed office door. She merely opens it and strides right in as if she owns the place, not even bothering to shut it behind her.

Looking magnificent in a formfitting black shirtdress with black tights, knee-high tan boots, and a scarf around her neck in taupe, orange, and black, she comes off with polished sophistication. Her hair is loose, cut in long layers of chocolate silk that frame her shoulders and pour down her back.

And those soft brown eyes, looking almost bronze from the afternoon sun pouring in from my office window.

I'm a sucker for eyes.

"This is a pleasant surprise," I say cordially and motion with my hand for her to take a seat.

She smiles at me nicely enough but ignores my invitation, instead walking beside my desk right up to my office window. It's floor-to-ceiling tinted glass that overlooks the capitol building. If I lean all the way back and to the right in my chair, I can see the top of the Watts Building, where she works just a few blocks over.

Crossing her arms over her chest, she gazes out with an almost serene look on her face. I swivel my chair forty-five degrees so I face her, but I don't say a word, waiting for her to make the first move in this metaphorical chess game we seem to be playing with each other.

"Jenna wasn't prostituting herself at Pure Fantasy," she says in an even voice.

"So just deny the request," I reply matter-of-factly.

"I will," she says, uncrossing her arms and flicking an impatient hand at me as she turns her body toward mine. "But I want to know why you asked. That wasn't a shot in the dark. You had some reason to ask it."

We lock eyes for a moment, then I let my gaze casually travel down her body. She's built like a damn swimsuit model, dressed in expensive designer clothing, but I can tell she'd look fantastic in burlap.

Or just those silk stockings I bought her.

"You know I can't divulge that," I tell her. "It's attorney work product."

"Cut the shit, Holloway," she snaps as she narrows her eyes at me. "You know I can find out with a few craftily questioned interrogatories of my own. Why not throw me some professional courtesy and tell me?"

My eyebrows raise at her, because I hear more than just irritation in her voice. I hear something close to sadness. Something about this case, maybe this question in particular, is very personal to her. I find this intriguing, and I also know that I can potentially use this as a weapon at some point down the road.

Resting my elbows on my armrests, I steeple my fingers in front of my face and give her a calculating look. "I'll tell you for an exchange of information. Tell me why this particular question has you wigged out so much. You could easily deny it, and if your client truly hasn't committed any crime, you have nothing to worry about. So tell me what *I* want to know, and I'll tell you what *you* want to know."

The corner of Leary's lip turns up in what I'm thinking might be a sneer, but before she fully engages, she turns away from the window and heads toward the door. "Sorry . . . I don't negotiate."

Whoa, what the fuck?

I lunge from my chair and snag her wrist, stopping her before she can even make it past the edge of my desk. Her skin is soft under my hand, and she smells fucking fantastic. If it weren't for the glare that she's shooting me right now, I'd consider kissing the answer out of her.

Instead, I surprise myself by giving her exactly what she wants without the expectation of anything in return. "I ran a criminal background check on the owner of the club. He's been busted twice before for whoring his girls out. This was during the time your client worked there."

"That doesn't mean she was prostituting herself," Leary asserts.

"No, it doesn't," I acquiesce, stroking the inside of her wrist with my thumb. Leary still wears irritation all over her face, but her body relaxes slightly. "But based on what I found, you know that it was a legitimate question."

"It was dirty," she seethes.

"Probing," I counter.

"Slick."

"Wait a minute, are we still talking about the question or something else here?" I murmur, tugging on her wrist and pulling her in just a tad closer to me.

I'm stunned when Leary's cheeks turn pink and she lowers her eyes coyly. I didn't think this woman had a shy bone in her body, but I'm enjoying the power I'm obviously wielding over her.

"I can't believe a little double entendre has you blushing," I taunt, rubbing my finger over her wrist. A tiny gasp escapes her lips, and her eyes raise up to mine filled with confusion and desire.

I find it incredibly difficult to get one up on this woman, and just moments ago, she had me rolling over and spilling my guts to her. This moment now . . . where I have her flustered?

Feels fucking awesome and causes my cock to harden.

Leary takes in a stuttering breath, nibbles on her lower lip.

My cock goes harder yet.

"I can't tell if you're baiting me or you're truly attracted to me. I find it confusing," she whispers, and for a moment, I'm confused myself. This hesitant, almost shy side to Leary is at odds with the woman who stripped in front of me in the elevator.

I'm not sure I like it.

"But," she says with more confidence in her voice, stepping in closer to me until mere inches separate our bodies, "there's only one sure way to find out."

Then she drops her free hand down and cups me between my legs. Her fingers immediately grasp and curl around my erection, squeezing me tight and even giving a firm stroke up my shaft. My eyes close, my head tilts back, and I can't stop the groan that comes out of my mouth.

Just like that, she's back in control.

Just like that, I realize her shyness was nothing but a fucking act.

"Mmm," Leary purrs. "Very nice. I'd have to say you're definitely attracted to me."

A brief thought runs through my head: my office door is open, and anyone could walk by and see what we're doing. But for the life of me, I can't seem to care enough to stop whatever this is.

Instead, I cover her hand with my own and urge her fingers to grip me harder as I push my hips forward to create more friction. If her hand feels this good, I can't imagine what her mouth would feel like.

"I can't believe you'd even have any doubt I was attracted to you," I tell her gruffly.

She laughs, deep and husky, and no doubt she feels me swell even larger in her hand. "I never doubted it. I just wanted an excuse to see what you were packing down below."

Pressing up on her tiptoes, she leans toward me and nips my chin with her teeth. Then she's pulling away from me, those sweet fingers letting my dick go, and I almost grab her back to me.

"Well, this has been enlightening," she says as she turns away and walks toward the door. When she gets to it, she turns to me as an afterthought. "And thank you for the stockings. They're lovely."

"And might I be seeing them on you sometime?" I ask as I reach down and adjust myself.

Her eyes follow my hand and she smirks. "Now that would just be a bit unethical, don't you think?"

"You just had your hand on my dick," I point out courteously. "I think we crossed that line already."

Shooting me a grin, she doesn't respond but turns back toward the door.

"Wait," I call out, and she turns once again, an amused look on her face. "Let me take you out to dinner tonight."

"Can't," she says simply. "I have plans."

"A date?"

"Possibly," she says with an impish grin. "But not really any of your business."

In three long strides, I'm across my office floor and my hand is circling the front of her neck. I grip her hard enough to get her attention and reel her in closer to me. I can tell she's been enjoying our banter, and I can also tell she enjoys when my alpha tendencies take over, as evidenced by the way her eyes flare hot.

Leaning in, I place my lips along her jaw, skim them lightly to her ear. "It's irrelevant to me if you have a date tonight. I'm only interested if when you go to bed, you'll be thinking of your date or my cock. Maybe you'll call me tomorrow and tell me."

I release my hold on Leary, relishing the uncertainty in her eyes. If she expected me to get jealous over a potential date, she can put that right out of her beautiful head. It's not that I don't have the power to get jealous, it's that I don't like being goaded into it.

Confident I've had the last word and this conversation is ending with me having the upper hand, I turn from Leary and head back toward my desk.

"Is there anything else we need to discuss about this case?" I ask as I grasp the back of my chair and swivel it around to me.

I'm met with silence, and when I look back toward the door, she's gone.

Pulling out my phone, I send a quick text to my buddy Ford. Heading out early. Want to get a beer?

We met last year playing in a rugby league together and since then have become pretty tight. He works at Knight & Payne as well . . . is a partner, actually, so maybe I can get some personal scoop on the beautiful Miss Leary Michaels. Their firm is gigantic, so he might not even know her all that well, but I figure it doesn't hurt to ask. Maybe he'll help me get a better grip on what I'm dealing with.

I drain the rest of my beer, pushing the empty glass toward the edge of the bar just as I see Ford walk into Carter's, a local hangout just across the street from the courthouse, where most of the litigation attorneys hang out.

After stopping for handshakes, back slaps, and one woman who caresses Ford's chest when he leans over to kiss her cheek, he finally makes his way over to me. After he's perched on the stool next to me, he waves at the bartender and points to my glass, then holds up two fingers, effectively ordering the next round.

"So what's up, man?" he asks casually. "I think sign-ups for the rugby league are starting next week. You in?"

"Definitely in," I tell him. "Nothing like getting your ass pounded into the ground to make you appreciate the day job, right?"

Ford laughs and reaches for the beer the bartender just set down in front of us.

"Put it on my tab," I tell the bartender, who nods and saunters off.

"Working on any good cases?" I ask Ford as I snag a few peanuts from the bowl before me.

"Same old shit, different day," he says unenthusiastically. I've noticed a certain lack of excitement over his career lately, and I wonder if he's getting burned out. He's been practicing for fifteen years, and litigation is a tough business. The stress factor is extremely high.

"What about you?" he asks.

"Actually, I wanted to get some scoop from you on one of your associate attorneys. I have a case against her, and she's been a little difficult to deal with so far."

"I don't know all the associates, but I'll try," he says, grabbing some peanuts for himself.

"Her name is Leary Michaels. It's a medical malpractice case we have together that we just started."

"Fuck," Ford groans and then leans forward to bang his head lightly against the wooden bar. "Fuck, fuck, fuck."

"What?" When Ford sits back up straight, he pins me with a death glare.

"You're defending the *LaPietra* case?" he practically snarls.

"Yeah," I say with some hesitation. "And I'm sensing this pisses you off for some reason, but fuck if I know why."

Leaning toward me, he growls, "Maybe because you had your hand up Leary's skirt at the courthouse the other day."

I rear back, completely astounded that Ford knows this.

And then it immediately stands to reason in my mind that he knows this because Leary told him.

This naturally leads me to conclude that they are very close, otherwise she would never have casually mentioned something like that.

"Are you fucking her?" I grit out, completely annoyed over the surge of jealousy that just flowed through me.

Ford is now the one who rears back from me, surprise in his eyes. "No, I'm not fucking her. What kind of question is that?"

His voice sounds firm and confident in his denial, but there's something in his eyes that seems a bit secretive. I ignore his question, instead pushing him on his relationship with Leary. "What exactly is your relationship, then? Why would she ever tell you what happened at the courthouse?"

"Because we're friends," Ford says defensively. "Very good friends. I was her supervising attorney when she first started at the firm, and she's a partner, by the way, not an associate attorney."

"She's a partner?" I ask, astounded. "She can't be more than twenty-eight."

"She's twenty-nine, and she earned it. She's got a hundred percent win record, which I don't have to tell you is almost impossible to achieve."

I whistle through my teeth, considering that and feeling for the first time in my legal career perhaps a bit intimidated. Not only is Leary the most confident and sexiest woman I've ever met but she uses her confidence and sex appeal like a weapon, which coupled with her apparent legal prowess means I need to bring my A game to this war.

"Look, man," Ford says, sounding a bit more conciliatory, "not cool what you did."

I snort and then take a sip of beer. I give Ford the stink eye. "She started it."

"Seriously?" he asks with his jaw dropping. "You're going with 'she started it'?"

"Well, she did, and let me tell you . . . she has some metaphorical balls forged of steel and lined with platinum. I'm assuming she told you what she did to me in the elevator?"

"Yeah, she did, but—"

"And did she tell you she also completely assassinated my character in front of the judge and trampled all over my man card in open court?"

"No, she didn't say that, but—"

"For fuck's sake, Ford." I turn on my stool to look at him. "She practically fucking dared me to do that to her. And just so you don't have any doubts, she liked it."

"How could you even know she liked—"

"And before you even think about keeping that perch on your high horse, you should know she was in my office this afternoon flashing her metaphorical platinum-and-steel balls around, with her hand wrapped around my cock. Now, I can tell you I most certainly liked that, but I'm betting you already know by the look on your face . . . so did she."

Ford's jaw tightens, and for a moment I think he might hit me. But then I see something close to sadness filtering into his eyes, followed maybe by regret. He blows out a frustrated breath and turns away to take a swallow of beer.

Treading carefully, unsure of what this is, I ask, "Are you sure you don't have something going on with Leary?"

Staring at his glass, he shakes his head. "No, man. We're just really good friends. I care about her, but nothing past that."

"Ford," I say insistently, making it clear I don't want him fucking around with me. "Truth time."

Swiveling his head toward me, he finally admits, "Yeah, in the past we fucked around. But never anything serious."

"Christ," I mutter, picking my own beer up and taking a healthy swallow. This presents a major problem. Regardless of what I learned from Ford, my intention was to pursue Leary Michaels outside the courtroom. All afternoon I kept thinking of her hand on my dick, and I knew that I couldn't just let this attraction go.

But now things have changed. Ford clearly has feelings, and shit . . . he's admitted to fucking her, which I do not like one bit. Not because I'm proprietary. We don't have any type of relationship to be proprietary about.

It changes things because Ford is a friend, and that tiny bit of sadness in his eyes has me feeling like I need to back completely the fuck up and walk away.

"Listen, man," I start, trying to make myself as clear as possible, "I don't want to step in between you and Leary. You're my friend first. I promise, from now on, nothing but aboveboard professionalism from me."

Ford doesn't say anything for a moment, and then he gives me a wry smile. "She likes you."

"Pardon me?"

"She likes you," he says with a wave of his hand. "Likes your ego, your confidence. Likes your cunning. She's intrigued by you."

"How do you know this?" I ask skeptically.

"Because she's talked about you. I didn't know it was you she was talking about, but she told me enough."

"Doesn't matter," I say, but he cuts me off.

"There is nothing between me and Leary. Just a close friendship. You two are free to . . . well, whatever it is you're doing."

I don't know what to say. The friend in me wants to argue with him and insist I'll stay away, but the vast majority of me is celebrating a victory I didn't even know I was in the running for.

Ford drains the rest of his beer, pushes the glass away, and stands up. "I gotta get going. Thanks for the beer."

"Yeah, sure," I say distractedly, not quite sure where we stand with each other.

Ford starts to walk away but then turns back. "Don't hurt her, Reeve. You two are walking a fine ethical line by fucking around with each other. I get you needing to defend your case, but you need to know that this case has personal merit to Leary. Don't use this personal shit to fuck her over. I will not be happy."

"I would never do that," I assert, because I wouldn't. I have absolutely no doubt that if anything is to transpire sexually between the two of us, it can be done outside the bounds of this case.

Besides, it's just a fuck . . . or two, or maybe even three.

Regardless, it's not like we want to date each other.

It's just a fuck, I tell myself firmly.

CHAPTER 5

LEARY

Ford is unusually silent as he drives us to a charity event hosted by our regional trial lawyers' association. It's the one time of the year that plaintiff's and defense lawyers put down their gloves and come together to raise money for a selected charity, this year for Alzheimer's.

Ford and I made plans a few months ago to go to this thing together. It's not a black-tie affair, but it's dressy enough that I have on an above-the-knee cocktail dress in sapphire blue, and Ford is looking handsome in a dark-gray suit and a cobalt-blue tie with thin gray ribbons of color dissecting it on the diagonal.

"Cat got your tongue?" I ask him cheekily.

He turns to look at me, and even though it's dark outside, the neon-blue lights from the interior electronics cast the angles of his face handsomely. He gives me a tiny smirk, then reaches his hand out to my bare knee for a squeeze.

It's friendly enough, but it feels odd to me for some reason. I suspect it might have something to do with the fact I can't seem to get Reeve Holloway out of my mind. Since our moment in his office four days ago, he seems to be spending obsessive amounts of time in my mind.

He hasn't contacted me and I sure as hell haven't contacted him. I thought a time or two about sending a business-related e-mail, but then immediately put it out of my mind. I plan to leave the ball in his court for now and concentrate on the merits of the case—not on how unbelievably big his dick is.

"I met a good friend for a beer a few nights ago," Ford says, cutting into my thoughts. His hand inches its way up my thigh.

"Oh, yeah?" I ask cordially while my heart starts beating quickly. Not because what Ford is doing to me is necessarily arousing, but because I'm actually considering telling him to stop, and I'm not sure how.

"Yeah, I think you know him," he says mysteriously.

"Who?" I ask.

Ford squeezes my thigh, his fingers pressing deep into my muscles, and then he pulls his hand away. His voice is a little tight when he says, "Reeve Holloway."

"What?" I exclaim, turning in the seat toward him. "You know Reeve?"

Ford nods. "Met last year playing rugby. He talked about you the other night. Imagine my surprise when I found out the pain-in-your-ass defense attorney you've been complaining about is my friend."

"What exactly did he say?" I ask hesitantly.

"Hmm," he says while rubbing a forefinger thoughtfully over his chin. "He wanted to know if you and I are fucking."

My jaw drops, because why in the world would Reeve ever think to ask Ford that?

"And," Ford continues, "he said you went to his office, taunted him, and then wrapped your hand around his cock."

I groan and fling myself back in my seat, crossing my arms over my chest. "I can't believe he told you that."

"Well, in fairness, I sort of berated it out of him," Ford concedes. "It's not like he was kissing and telling."

I chew on my bottom lip, trying to imagine that conversation. While Ford and I are close, and we've been fuck buddies who've stepped away from each other when we were interested in someone else, we've never shared details of our other sexual relationships with each other. It just seemed . . . poor form or something.

Ford starts slowing down so he can turn in to the parking lot of the Marriott Hotel where the charity silent auction will be held.

Turning my head so I can gauge his honest reaction, I ask him, "Are you okay with this?"

Ford snickers. "We're not exclusive, Leary. If you're interested in him, I back away. You know that."

"I'm not interested in him," I mutter. "I was trying to intimidate him. Test him. Get the upper hand. Throw him off his game."

"Fine, then," he says as he pulls into a parking space and puts the car in park. Taking off his seat belt, he leans across the seat toward me, slips his hand back on my thigh, and murmurs, "Let's blow this party and go back to my place."

"What? No," I say quickly, pushing at his hand with no success. "I want to go to this charity event."

Releasing his grip from my leg, he reaches up and tweaks me on the nose. He grins and says, "You're cute when you lie, you know that?"

"Whatever," I say as I turn to open the car door.

"He's going to be here," Ford says, and I instantly go still, my hand hesitating on the handle. It crossed my mind, and the thought was making my heart thump and my girlie parts tingle. "Tell me to back away, Leary. You've done it before when you wanted to pursue someone."

My shoulders sag as I sigh and pull on the door handle. It opens and I step out, taking a moment to smooth down my dress. Leaning back down, I look inside the car, Ford's face now completely awash in light. "I want you to back away," I tell him quietly.

He nods at me with a smile, and I close the door.

I didn't tell Ford to back away because I'm interested in a relationship with Reeve. There's no way that could happen, not with us on opposite sides of an emotionally explosive case.

But I am intrigued by him, and I can't say I'm hating our sexual flirtations. So I can't in good conscience continue something with Ford. I might be liberal and open-minded when it comes to my sexuality, but I don't mess around with two men at the same time.

I'm also not averse to no-strings, hot and steamy sex. Maybe I'll cross that line with Reeve and maybe I won't, but I know I needed Ford to back away, leaving me to continue this war I have going on with Reeve.

Ford is off talking to some peers about boring shit like golf. I've already put in my bids on a few items for the silent auction, but I hate this networking shit, so now I sit at the bar just off the lobby entrance wanting a little time away from the music, dancers, and egotistical attorneys swarming the ballroom.

The bar is a massive, square-shaped unit that can seat probably ten people on each side. Maybe because it's a Tuesday night and not much is happening during the week, or maybe because everyone is in the ballroom for the charity event, the bar is completely devoid of people except for me and the young bartender who's been shooting me flirty looks since I arrived.

My back is to the windows that overlook the Raleigh skyline, and I have an open view of the hotel lobby so I can catch Ford if he's looking for me. Otherwise, I'm completely happy here in my little bubble, being left alone so I can ruminate about Jenna's case and the problematic defense attorney with whom I have to deal.

I sip my martini and then swirl the skewered olives around in the glass. I've been here for forty minutes and no sign of Reeve. I'm thinking of catching a cab home, not wanting to impose on Ford for a ride since it looks like he's having a good time.

A warm hand presses to my lower back, and hot breath spreads over my bared shoulder. Lips to my ear, someone presses in close, and I recognize Reeve by the sexual confidence oozing off him. I have no clue how he sneaked by my watch. Probably while I was staring at my olives.

"Don't you look lonely sitting here all by yourself," he breathes into my ear. I can't control the shiver that runs up my spine.

I slowly look at him, making a point to uncross my legs and recross them, knowing it pulls my cocktail dress a little higher up my leg. Another inch and he'll be able to see the black lace of the stockings he bought me.

Not missing a thing, that man, his gaze goes down to my legs. He fingers the edge of my dress casually, slipping just the tip of his finger under it. Raising his eyes to mine, he asks, "Are those my stockings?"

"*My* stockings," I correct him with a smile. "But yes . . . they're the ones you bought."

"Am I going to get to see them tonight?" he asks with a boyish grin, tugging on the end of my skirt.

"You've already seen them. You bought them, after all," I quip.

"Tease," he murmurs with an amused smile, and his hand falls away from my leg. I find it amusing myself that I'm disappointed by the loss of his touch.

Reeve orders Woodford Reserve neat. I fiddle with my olives while his drink is made. After the glass is set down in front of him and he pays, he turns his attention back to me by propping his right arm up on the bar, his left casually resting on the back of my chair.

"So, I'm curious," he begins as I take another sip of my martini. "All this stripping and cock grabbing . . . is that what I can continue to expect as we proceed through this case?"

"Why? Don't you like it?" I purr in a sympathetic tone.

Reeve chuckles and his left hand reaches out to caress my shoulder briefly before returning to the back of my chair. "On the contrary, I like it very much. It's just that I've never met someone who uses so much more than just regular legal tactics to win a case. It means I have to change *my* tactics."

"Well, don't expect me to divulge all my battle plans to you. I don't want you prepared for what I'm going to throw your way."

Mischief fills Reeve's eyes and he gives me a wide grin. "Looking forward to it. But I'm also curious—do you fight like this with every other male defense attorney you come up against?"

I hear a bit of censure in his voice, maybe jealousy. I bat my eyelashes at him. "Only if the case is important enough."

Reeve actually grimaces slightly and his voice is slightly strained. "Have you ever had a case this important before?"

"No," I tell him softly. Because it's true. I haven't.

I might have had cases that were bigger and worth more money, but never one as personally important before.

"What makes this case so special?" he asks, his head tilted in curiosity.

"That is none of your business," I say firmly, hardening my gaze against his inquisitiveness. There's no way I would ever tell Reeve about my motivations. Only Midge and Ford are privy to that information, and I only told them so they understand that there aren't many lines I won't cross in the pursuit of victory for Jenna.

Reeve stares at me, then gives a slight nod of acceptance. He swivels his head to look around, and I notice that the bartender has his back to us, watching a baseball game on one of the TVs mounted on the wall. Satisfied with the small measure of privacy we have at this moment, Reeve looks back at me. "Now let me see a little bit of those stockings."

My breath hitches as his gaze drags down to my lap and his left arm leaves the back of my chair. He turns his body to shield me from the bartender and takes the edge of my skirt in between his index finger and thumb. He drags it up slowly—just a few inches are all that's really needed before the lace edges are revealed. Reeve turns his hand and runs his knuckles over my skin that's peeping out.

"Spread your legs," he murmurs, giving my thigh a nudge.

I tilt to the side again, confirming that the bartender has his back to us. No one else is in the bar, although I can see several people walking in and out of the lobby not thirty feet away. Still, Reeve has me blocked from anyone's view.

My legs slowly uncross, but they're not spread enough for Reeve's liking. He sticks his hand in between my thighs and gives another nudge. "Farther."

I comply, thrilled and frightened at the same time that we could be caught. My heartbeat is hammering and prickles of excitement race across my skin.

Reeve angles his head to the right slightly so he can get a better view, using his hand to inch my skirt up a little higher. He smiles approvingly then lifts his gaze to mine. "Black lace panties sort of your thing?"

"I have other colors," I say tartly.

"I like the black lace," he says offhandedly, then immediately inches his finger underneath the elastic at my hip.

"Reeve," I say in a whispered gasp. "Don't."

He ignores me, running his finger over me and inching farther down to where I know he's going to find me starting to get soaked.

My hand flies to his wrist in a feeble attempt to halt his progress, but he's too strong, and really, I don't want him to stop.

"We'll get caught," I say.

"So what?" he murmurs, the tip of his finger now running up and down my folds. His gaze is pinned to his hand between my legs, lustful fascination filling his eyes.

The fact he doesn't care if we get caught is a turn-on, and even though I'm afraid we'll get busted at any moment, my legs spread even wider.

Reeve gives a barely audible groan and then easily slides his index finger inside me. My lips part, my eyes close, and I let my breath out in a shaky stutter, trying to control my reaction. It most certainly would not be good to let out the deep moan that's swirling inside my chest.

"Fuck, this is hot," Reeve whispers, curling his finger inside me before relaxing it to slide out. Leaving me partially unshielded, Reeve removes his right arm from the bar. Before I can protest, he uses both hands to roughly pull my panties to the side, completely baring my pussy to him. Then his right arm goes back up on the wooden surface, his body turns again to hide me, and I have to wonder if the bartender is still watching the TV or us.

Reeve drops his left hand back down between my legs and runs his knuckles over my mound. "I could feel you were bare," he mutters with a smile, "but seeing it is even better. Wish I could bend you over right here and run my tongue over you."

"Oh God," I moan as my head tilts back. Reeve uses my distraction to push two fingers in me, and I can't help but jerk in pure pleasurable torture.

"Shh," he soothes me. A quick look back over his shoulder seems to satisfy Reeve. He turns back with a big grin. "Don't want the bartender to know what we're doing, do we?"

"This is insane," I gasp as he slowly pumps his fingers. "We need to stop."

"Tell you what," he says thoughtfully, his eyes pinning me with challenge. "I'll give you a choice. You continue to let me finger-fuck you until you come, right here, or you go with me to the bathroom where we'll have a bit more privacy."

"Bathroom," I gasp as his fingers pull out of me and brush against my clit, causing my hips to rocket off the chair.

"Good choice," he growls, pulling his hand away. My own hands go to the edges of my dress, pulling it down.

Reeve turns, takes his drink, and downs it in one gulp, hissing through his teeth over the burn. I stand from the chair, grab my purse, and ignore my martini.

I don't even look backward at the bartender as Reeve takes my hand and leads me into the lobby. I have no clue where the bathrooms are, but apparently Reeve does, because he moves with purpose. He nods his head at a few people who appear to be leaving, but doesn't stop to chat. No, this man is on a mission to finish me off.

Leading me back past the elevators, he turns right down a short hall, and I see a recessed alcove that houses men's and women's restrooms.

Reeve walks straight to the men's room, pulling me along. He pushes the swinging door open and sticks his head in, listening carefully. Satisfied it's empty, he walks in and I have no choice but to follow.

It's the first time I've ever been in a men's bathroom, and I look around curiously—marble double sink, dark navy-blue walls with copper sconces, and two urinals on the wall.

"Bingo," Reeve says, and my attention turns to the three stalls on the back wall. They're encased floor to ceiling in dark stained-wood carpentry, the front doors inset with thick louvers that are angled so you can't see in but most assuredly can see out. They afford the person—or persons, as may be the case—inside complete privacy from prying eyes.

Prying ears, probably not so much, but it's a risk that Reeve is apparently willing to take as he pulls me toward the stalls. He gives a brief rap of his knuckles on each door, and when no one answers, he chooses the stall on the end, farthest away from the sink and urinals.

Before I know it, he has me pushed inside, the door slammed shut behind us and locked, and his hands on my face to pull me in for a brutal kiss. I sink into it immediately, my own hands grasping his wrists for support, tasting the mellowness of Kentucky bourbon on his lips. Our tongues duel as he pushes me up against the side wall. He nudges one strong thigh in between my legs and then leans into me so hard I can barely breathe.

I've always felt oxygen was overrated, though, so I continue to kiss him with a rising fever within me.

Abruptly, Reeve pulls away from me, and I actually moan at the loss of his mouth on mine. I reach for him, but he bats my hands away, his breathing harsh and strained. He drops to his knees, his ass bumping into the opposite border of the stall as his hands dive under my skirt.

In one fluid motion, he hooks his fingers into the waistband of my panties and drags them down my legs. He's efficient, grasping an ankle to pull the panties free; then his hands go back between my thighs to push my legs apart.

"What are you doing?" I gasp, because all of this happened in about five seconds flat, and my lips are still tingling just from our kiss.

"Gotta taste you," he says in a guttural voice I recognize as fueled by lust.

"Oh God," I moan as his hands peel me apart and his mouth closes over me. His chest rumbles in appreciation over my taste. He runs his tongue up my center, puts his lips around my clit, and nips me with his teeth. My hips shoot off the back wall, straight into his face, and he groans in approval. He dips his chin, shoves his tongue inside me, and pumps it in and out.

And never have I ever felt something like this before. So primal, hard-edged, completely wild, and uninhibited, with no thoughts to consequences or regrets. I've never had a man move his mouth over me like this, as if his very life depended on possessing this part of me.

My head falls back, cracks loudly on the wall, and I bite my tongue to stop from screaming in pleasure.

CHAPTER 6
REEVE

Holy fucking Christ, she tastes good.

Her soft, bare pussy presses against my face, and her inner muscles contract around my tongue. Her hips gyrate, urging me on.

I feel like my lungs are constricted from the pleasure of this hard-core mouth fucking I'm giving Leary, and I'm possessed with the need to make her come harder than she ever has in her life.

I need to do that to show her that I'm in charge of her.

At least for the moment, until she manages to one-up me again.

Leary's hands come to my head, her fingers sliding through my hair and then gripping it hard. She pulls against me, shoving my face deeper into her. I pull my tongue back, lick upward slowly, and then concentrate on that clit of hers. It's swollen, stiff, and in much need of release.

I swirl my tongue around it, sometimes stiffening it to push hard, other times lapping at her gently. It's at the gentle times when she jerks my hair to silently demand I go harder. I'm so fucking turned on right now by her reaction to me, and I can't help dropping one hand to rub myself through my pants.

Fuck, I need to come.

Leary's movements against me get more insistent, and she sucks in a deep breath, her legs stiffening. She's close to blowing and I'm not ready for that to happen just yet.

Reluctantly pulling my mouth away from her, I stand up and start working my belt open.

"Why'd you stop?" Leary says with need.

I risk a glance at her and my heart slams hard against my chest over the blazing-hot lust in her eyes. Her cheeks are pink, her forehead shiny with sweat, her breasts heaving with strained breath.

I pause in my quest to free my cock just long enough to tell her, "I'm going to fuck you now. Want to be inside you when you come."

If I thought Leary's eyes were hot before, they go absolutely molten from my declaration. She stares at me just a moment; then her hands shoot out to my pants, knocking my own out of the way to work at my button and zipper.

I use the opportunity to grab my wallet out of my back pocket, and although I'm smoothly able to grab the condom I tucked in there earlier today—because I was hoping this might happen—my urgent need to fuck Leary causes me to bobble my wallet. It falls from my hands, almost lands in the toilet, but luckily bounces off to the floor. I'll worry about it later.

Leary's hands push at my pants and boxers until they move past my hips, and my cock springs free. One hand goes to the base of my erection, where she squeezes me roughly as she urges, "Hurry."

I rip open the condom and grab the tip, and while Leary holds me, I roll it on. I lean in briefly to give her a hot, deep kiss and then pull away so I can concentrate on getting inside her.

Bending down, I hoist her up under her ass, her arms immediately going to my shoulders for leverage. I push her back into the wall, reach down with one hand, and guide the head of my shaft into her slick folds. I rub it back and forth, spreading her moisture, thumping it a few times against her clit, all of which causes Leary to squirm in my arms.

With a slow circle of her hips and more guidance from my hand, the end of my cock nudges into her just a fraction of an inch. I glance down and, fuck . . . that's hot . . . me getting ready to impale her.

I look back up to Leary, and while holding her up with my forearm wedged under her ass and the support of the wall, I let go of myself and clamp my other hand firmly over her mouth. Her eyes go wide in confusion.

"This is going to make you scream, baby," I warn her before slamming my hips forward. My cock sinks deeply into her until my pelvis is pressed tightly against hers. Just as I suspected, Leary lets a cry of pleasure loose, but my hand muffles it. I have to bite the inside of my cheek hard to suppress the animalistic sounds that want to break free.

"Shh," I whisper. "Still need to be quiet. Someone could come in."

She nods and I remove my hand from her mouth. I readjust her weight in my arms, now using both hands to spread her wide and hold her back against the wall.

Then I start moving within her. I don't bother with a slow buildup, because this is about us both getting off as quickly as we can to avoid detection, and besides, I don't want to waste that delicious orgasm that had started to break free from her before I stopped eating her pussy.

I tunnel into Leary, forcefully ramming myself into her. She closes her eyes and her lips curl upward in dreamy pleasure. Her arms tighten around my neck as I rest my forehead against hers. We both valiantly suppress the noise level we want to unleash, but there's no stopping the heavy breathing or the slapping of my skin against hers.

The debauchery of it all, the frantic fucking, the risk of getting caught—it's all almost too much to bear, and I can't hold back the orgasm that starts building inside me. I decide to let it go, hoping to God that Leary will be with me but intent on getting her off with my mouth afterward if I blow before her.

Game plan in effect for a massive fucking nut bust, I start thrusting into her faster.

That's when the bathroom door opens, and I hear two men talking to each other as they walk in.

My hips slow down, but there's no way I can stop moving. It's physically impossible for me to stop fucking Leary.

Pulling my forehead away from hers, I take a cautious look to see how she's doing, still pumping in and out of her at a much slower pace. Her eyes are filled with flaming lust and just a tiny bit of fear as she stares at me. The men continue to talk, and then I hear them both pissing in the urinals.

She mouths at me, "Don't stop."

I give Leary a mischievous grin and pick the pace of my thrusts back up. Not hard enough to create the skin-slapping sound, but deep enough to cause her breathing to start hitching again. When I hear the flush, I use the opportunity to mask the sound and slam into her hard, grinding my pelvis against hers.

Leary can't help it and lets out a tiny moan that shouldn't be heard over the flushing and the men talking, but they abruptly go silent. They move from full-blown piss chatter to utter quiet, and I know, without a doubt, that they know there are two people in the stall fucking.

This should give me pause, make me stop my movements, but God help me, it only turns me on more. Knowing there are two people out there listening to us fuck.

I raise my eyebrows at Leary to see what she wants me to do. She bites her lower lip as if in consideration while I move my cock against her shallowly. The men still don't talk, and I imagine they're probably grinning at each other, heads cocked to the side to see if they can hear anything else.

The men apparently decide to get busy with washing their hands, because the sinks turn on at the same time Leary tightens her arms around me, grinding her hips around my cock.

Breath hisses out from between my teeth, and I start to increase the depth of my thrusts once more. I keep the pace slower so as to minimize the noise of our skin slapping, but that doesn't stop me from still fucking her hard.

The sinks turn off and the men seem to be taking their time drying their hands. I smile at Leary and she smiles back at me while I continue plowing her.

I can only hope that the men leave before we reach our conclusion, because I think it's going to be a futile attempt to stay quiet, but they don't seem to be moving. I don't know how much longer I can hold back, but I'm sure as hell not going to stop, either.

The decision on when to come, though, is completely taken out of my hands when Leary reaches between our bodies and starts rubbing her clit. She gives a tiny hum when her fingers make contact, and fuck, that right there is sexy—knowing that she's desperately wanting to get off.

I can't help it. I start thrusting faster while Leary plays with herself. Blood roars in my head, so loud that I have no clue if the men have left or not, but I couldn't fucking care less. Now I'm in a desperate race to come right alongside Leary, and I start pounding her into the wall, not giving a shit who's standing out there.

Leary's the first to go. Her hand stills on her body, her eyes squeeze shut. I have to give her credit . . . she suppresses every bit of sound as her pussy clamps down hard on my dick and her body starts to shake in my arms. She comes quietly and very beautifully, and it's my undoing.

I push into her one more time, feel the fire boiling upside of my balls and shooting straight out the end of my dick. My cock spasms hard inside her, pulse after pulse of orgasmic release as I empty into her without making a fucking peep.

The roaring in my ears starts to quiet, my forehead now back against Leary's as we both try to catch our breath. My legs are so weak from that orgasm that I have to lock them so I don't drop to the floor with her in my arms.

Lifting my head, I give Leary a silent but deep kiss of satisfaction. When I pull away, she's smiling at me.

"Nice," we both hear from outside the stall.

And then another voice. "Fucking hot."

Leary snickers and then we're rewarded with the sound of the door opening and footsteps receding.

"I think you broke me," I mutter. "I have to put you down before I fall down."

Leary loosens her legs and I slip out of her, still quite hard, actually, even though I think I just emptied about a gallon into the condom. I lower her and when her feet hit the floor, I pull the condom off and throw it in the toilet.

We're both silent while we get dressed, rearrange our clothes, and take a few deep breaths to even ourselves out. I grab my wallet from the floor and carefully open the door to peek out, ensuring no one else is in the bathroom.

Motioning for Leary to wait a moment, I open the main door and take a quick look around. No one is in the immediate area, so I wave my hand at her, and she walks casually out of the men's bathroom, right past me and down the hall.

I catch up to her, grabbing on to her elbow. "Want to have another drink with me?"

"Can't," she says crisply. "Have a huge day tomorrow and I need to get some sleep."

She pulls against me and tries to turn away, but I don't let her go. Instead, I reel her back to me, grabbing on to her hips with both hands. Leaning in close to her, I ask, "So, are we just going to pretend this didn't happen?"

"Of course not," she says, but her voice still remains aloof. "But tonight, we're done."

I stare at her, intrigued by her cool demeanor when just moments ago she was writhing for release. She's utterly fascinating, completely intoxicating.

Rubbing my thumbs against her hip bones, I lean in a bit closer. "You know, you started something in that elevator. Your intention then might not have been for what just happened, but you did intend to arouse my sexual interest. And you, Leary Michaels, have no idea the beast you've awoken with your antics. You've invited me to come out and play, and now I'm *ready* to play."

"We just played," she murmurs, and I'm happy to see the aloof reserve has lifted from her gaze.

"And we'll play again, no doubt," I tell her with a smile. "I just don't want you to think that this is over."

Leary raises a hand, lays it over my chest, and gives me a humoring pat. "This is just sex."

"Damn right it is," I tell her gruffly, pulling her hips into mine. "But it's not just onetime sex."

"But it's not a relationship, either," she clarifies, dropping her hand from my chest. "No strings. It's just physical."

"That's fine by me," I tell her, because I'm always down with the pleasures of fucking and the avoidance of commitment.

"And this cannot interfere with the case," she says sternly.

I make an X pattern over my chest. "Cross my heart. No case pillow talk."

"Then fine," she says in agreement. "We'll be fuck buddies."

I throw my head back and laugh, level it back to her when I hear her own chuckles. "Fuck buddies? I've never had one before."

"Well, I have," she says tartly. "So remember . . . it's just sex."

"Was Ford a fuck buddy?" I ask suddenly, with no clue why I've opened myself up to a truth I might not want to hear.

"Yes," she says simply, holding her gaze level with mine.

"Is he still a fuck buddy?" I ask carefully, holding my breath for the answer, because I honestly don't think I can share.

"No, he's not. We're just friends."

And one last question so I can breathe easier. "And might you have other fuck buddies?"

She gives me a wry smile. "Um . . . no. I don't have time to juggle men."

This makes me very happy for some reason and smacks of my need to avoid jealousy, which doesn't sound very no-strings to me, but I mentally shrug that thought away.

"I don't care if you have other fuck buddies, though," Leary says as an afterthought. "Just keep it wrapped . . . you know . . . for your own safety."

I stare at her, trying to figure out if she's joking or not. She doesn't smile and there's no mischief in her eyes. So that means she's dead fucking serious.

She absolutely does not care if I fuck other women.

This is intriguing to me as well as a bit appalling. I've never come up against a woman who is so sure of her own sexual identity and what she wants. It should feel liberating, but it makes me feel slightly displaced.

Reaching a hand up, I grip her by the back of her neck and pull her to my lips. My mouth closes over hers and I give her a slow kiss of understanding. When I release her, I say, "I think you might be all the woman I can handle for right now, but I appreciate your flexibility."

Leary gives me a nod of her head and then pulls away from me. "Good, we've just entered fuck buddy–dom. May the odds be ever in our favor."

"What the hell does that mean?"

"Nothing," she says with a snicker. "I'll see you next week for Jenna's deposition."

I watch her ass a moment as she walks away from me before I call out, "So I won't see you before then?"

"Nope," she says as she turns around but keeps walking backward so we can maintain eye contact. "Too busy."

Fuck, I think to myself as she walks out of my line of sight.

I don't think I can go a week without seeing her.

I thought the whole point of being fuck buddies was to actually do some fucking.

CHAPTER 7

LEARY

I should have given in to Reeve's demands over the last week. Instead, I ignored call after call in which he all but commanded me to get together with him. The more I ignored him, the more insistent he became.

Except for the last two days. I haven't heard a peep out of him, and I'm wondering if he's no longer interested.

I hope that's not the case, because I didn't ignore him because I wasn't interested. I ignored him because I was *too* interested.

All week, my thoughts have been almost obsessively consumed with Reeve. I keep replaying every single interaction we've had over and over, ultimately realizing it was a slow, sensual buildup to an explosive outcome.

What we did in that bathroom was beyond explosive, actually. I've never in my entire life given in to abandon that way. I gave up absolute control to him and the surrounding environment. I gave not one whit about my career if I were to get caught. I didn't give a shit that two strangers listened to us.

I cared about none of it because for the first time in my life, when a man was lodged deep inside me, I was absolutely consumed by him. There was simply no room for anything else.

And that bothered me.

Bothered me to the extent that I practically rushed out of the Marriott after hastily agreeing to be his fuck buddy.

Fuck buddy?

Who in the hell says they have a fuck buddy? Maybe a college freshman, but not a twenty-nine-year-old professional woman who's a partner in a prestigious law firm.

At any rate, when these obsessive thoughts didn't wane, but instead increased, I felt the need to try to put some distance between Reeve and me. Thus, I ignored his calls, hoping this insatiable desire for him would just go away.

Fat freaking chance.

And now he sits across from me in one of the smaller conference rooms at Knight & Payne, looking completely relaxed and in charge of this deposition. And there's something about Reeve Holloway in a custom-tailored suit in a navy so dark it could be black, perfectly cut white dress shirt, and silver-gray tie with black crosshatching detail, with messily styled hair that's just a little too long on top to be considered stuffy and stubble because he just apparently didn't feel like shaving this morning . . . well, just . . . damn. How in the hell am I supposed to concentrate?

The room is only large enough for a small rectangular table that seats two each on the long sides and one each on the short ends. Reeve and the adjuster from Dr. Summerland's insurance company, a young man about my age named Thomas Collier, sit opposite Jenna and me. The court reporter sits on the end to my right. She'll be dictating into a soundproof mask everything that is said in this room, word for word, so a transcript can be typed up later.

We're here because Reeve followed standard protocol and formally requested that my client Jenna LaPietra attend this deposition. Before the trial, this is Reeve's one and only chance to talk to my client, who will be placed under oath with the expectation of telling the truth. Contrary to the way many legal formalities are portrayed on TV, depositions are not generally a place where the parties get combative. It's usually fairly laid-back, and it's nothing more than an opportunity for Reeve to learn as much about my client as he can, with the ultimate hope he'll discover something that benefits his case and can later be used against Jenna.

Reeve drones on and on, calmly asking question after question about Jenna's prior medical history. He spent very little time getting into her personal life, instead seeming to want to concentrate on the medical aspects, since at the crux this is a medical malpractice claim.

He looks entirely too gorgeous sitting directly across from me, and more than once my mind drifts to the way he pounded in between my legs last week. I have to wonder if he still thinks about it the way I do, but I can't gauge, because he's barely said two words to me since the deposition started.

"If you'll give me just a moment, Jenna, so I can go over my notes," Reeve says after she finishes answering one of his questions.

He began this deposition immediately calling my client by her first name, a solid tactic to help develop some level of trust. I, of course, prepared Jenna for almost an entire day yesterday, and she wasn't going to lower her defenses. I told her to keep her answers simple and answer only the question, without expounding. So far, she's been doing an admirable job.

Reeve's head is bent over his notes, his brown hair falling over his forehead so I can't see his face. It irks me the way he's ignored me the last two days, and I'm not one for being ignored. I should be the ignorer, not the ignoree.

I uncross my legs under the table, and when I cross them again, I make sure to kick my leg out just a tad farther so the tip of my Stuart Weitzman pump brushes against Reeve's calf. He jerks at the contact and his head snaps up.

"Oops," I say with an apologetic grin. "Not much room under this table, I'm afraid."

And there it is . . . what I've been hoping for. An absolute genuine smile, and because I'm the only one in this room who knows the size of Reeve's dick and what it can do to a woman, I also recognize a sizzle of lust in his gaze.

My leg immediately extends back out, and I graze my foot up his calf, across the inside of his knee, and nudge gently at his inner thigh. I notice the barely perceptible tightening of Reeve's jaw as he bows his head back down to his notes and starts to ignore me again.

That won't do.

I pull back, roll my foot so my pump slips off, and raise my leg again. This time I stick my foot right in between his thighs and, as I thank God for my longer-than-average legs, my toe gently probes against his cock.

Reeve's thighs slam together, trapping my foot as his head slowly raises up, and he pins me with a death glare. I try to look at him as innocently as possible.

"Can we go off the record?" Reeve says tightly to the court reporter, without taking his eyes off me.

The court reporter lowers the mask away from her face in capitulation.

"In going through my notes, I find that I'm getting ready to delve into some things that might be a bit sensitive to Jenna," Reeve says as he looks at me with a bland face. "If you don't mind, Miss Michaels, I'd like to take a short break and discuss these issues with you in private. You can perhaps guide me if there's anything that might be too upsetting to Jenna."

I blink at him in surprise and pull my leg back slowly when his thighs loosen their grip. This isn't normally done, but then again . . . who's to say what's normal? I just accosted defense counsel under the table.

"If you think that's necessary," I say with an incline of my head. Turning to Jenna, I say, "We'll break for a bit if you want to step out and smoke. I'll come get you when we're done."

Jenna nods at me gratefully. Reeve has been questioning her for two hours now, so the break comes at a good time.

Everyone stands up from the table except for the court reporter. Jenna scurries out, already reaching in her purse for her cigarettes. I've tried gently to get her to quit during this last year I've been handling her case, but she swears she needs to have at least one vice. I accept this because I know all too well that women in her predicament often turn to much stronger addictions to help cope with their situations.

Reeve puts a hand on the insurance adjuster's shoulder, giving him a slight push downward. "You stay here, Tom. Something that I'm noticing in my notes actually applies to another case that I have against Miss Michaels. It could be a problem. I'm not sure, but those talks would be confidential on the other case."

I again blink in surprise, because Reeve and I don't have any other cases together, but then it's clear. He wants to speak to me privately, probably to rail against me for playing footsie under the table.

Lowering my face to hide my smirk, I exit the conference room with Reeve hot on my heels. He doesn't say a word to me but silently follows me across the Pit, right into my office. He shuts the door and immediately stalks over to my desk, hitting the smoke button. He's never been in my office before, but he saw me do the same trick with the button on the conference room table before the deposition started. The glass immediately turns dark gray, and we're alone.

His back is still to me when I say, "Apparently you're done ignoring me."

Reeve spins on me fast, his face a mask of fury. In two strides, he has me by the shoulders and pulls me to him so he can slam his mouth down on mine. His teeth scrape brutally against my lips, but then his tongue is plunging inside me and the bite of pain is forgotten. His kiss is punishing and needful all at once, and I can feel anger vibrating off him.

I melt.

It's a complete turn-on knowing he's pissed at me yet still wants me beyond measure. When he pulls his mouth away, he grabs one of my hands and presses it to his crotch, pushing his hips forward so I can feel his erection burn against my palm. My fingers curl and clutch at his shaft even as he pulls his mouth from mine.

"You think you can ignore my calls for five days, put your foot against my cock, and not get a reaction out of me?" he growls menacingly.

I know I should be scared by the tone of his voice, but I'm not. I'm consumed with lust now and at a complete loss as to how to handle this enraged bull with a bull-size dick in my hand.

Reeve doesn't give me a chance to make amends, though. His hand shoots up, grabs a handful of hair at the back of my head, and gives me a tiny shake before pulling back so my face tilts up toward his. Leaning in so his lips almost touch mine, he growls, "You need to fix this, Leary."

Fix this? What?

Reeve's hand slides up to the top of my head, and the next thing I know, he's pushing me down. I brace against him, just for a moment, but then he barks, "Fix it," and my knees immediately buckle, so I sink down to the carpeting.

When my face is in front of his straining, cloth-covered erection, his hand goes back to grasping my hair again. He gives me another gentle shake and repeats in a much quieter but no less threatening tone, "Fix it, Leary."

God, I want to fix it. I want to take him in my mouth, suck him hard until he's begging me to stop. But I'm also enjoying this display of alpha power he's unleashing. I want to see how far I can push him.

I don't move. Just stare up at him as he glares down at me.

"Fuck this shit," Reeve snarls as he releases my hair and his hands work his belt in a frenzy. He unbuckles it quickly, slamming his zipper down and pulling his cock out of his pants.

It's beautiful. Thick and hard . . . an angry blush to it and a drizzle of pre-cum leaking from the tip. I lick my lower lip in anticipation, but Reeve doesn't notice. Instead, he gives a few pumps of his hand over his dick before grabbing my jaw. Pressing his fingers in firmly at the joints, he forces my mouth open, which doesn't take much effort, because I really, really want him in my mouth.

"Take it, Leary," he orders while he guides the tip toward me with his other hand.

I try to turn my head away, a vain attempt to show resistance, because I'm not going to fight him much longer. I want to blow him too badly.

Reeve's hand holds my jaw tighter, forcing my mouth wide-open. "Suck it," he hisses at me and sticks the tip in my mouth.

He's staring in fascination at his huge dick in my mouth but then slowly moves his eyes toward my own. "Fix this, Leary," he says hoarsely—almost pleading—and my panties immediately get soaked with need.

My hands shoot out and grab him by his hips, pulling on him hard so his cock slides all the way into my mouth, bumping against the back of my throat.

"Yes," Reeve moans, both of his hands now coming to hold on to the sides of my head.

I hum in pleasure at the feel and taste of him in my mouth. I move my tongue as best I can, but there's not much room to maneuver because his size is so invading. I slide my hands around to his ass and press my fingers in, urging him to move.

Reeve doesn't need any further encouragement. He starts pumping his hips, fucking my mouth as I suck gently, alternating with laving strokes of my tongue along the underside of his cock. He groans, grunts, growls as he thrusts back and forth.

His pants aren't pulled down enough, so I can only settle for fondling his balls through the material of his pants, careful not to press the zipper into his flesh.

"Fuck, that's good, baby," Reeve whispers as he pushes in and out of me.

Yes, it is. Great, even.

It's funny—I can brush my teeth and have the bristles hit the back of the tongue, causing me to retch and gag, but for some reason, a cock hitting the back of my throat has never bothered me. Maybe it's the silky texture of skin, or the sinful nature of the act, but for whatever reason, my body does not rebel against a deep blow job.

And in this instance with Reeve Holloway sliding in and out of my mouth, I find I want him deeper still. His movements are measured, so I take matters into my own hands, pushing my face against him hard, taking him partway down my throat so my nose is pressed against his pelvis.

"Holy shit," Reeve mutters with a hard jerk, and when he pulls back slightly, I feel the warm, salty gush of him start to fill my mouth.

This has never been my favorite part of a blow job, but for some reason, Reeve's taste is compelling. Rather than wanting him to finish in a hurry, I keep sucking at him, hoping he gives me more.

"Oh, baby," he groans as he fists my hair and his cock leaps again in my mouth. "Fuck, fuck, fuck."

I keep at him . . . sucking, gently licking his flesh, scraping my teeth against him, until he finally has to push me away. Licking my lips, I raise my eyes to his and am momentarily stunned to see the tender look on his face. He releases my hair, sliding both hands to my face, stroking his thumbs over my cheekbones.

"You are magnificent," he murmurs.

Reeve pulls me up, and I rise on shaky legs. He keeps tugging until my face comes level with his, and he kisses me deeply, surely tasting his orgasm on my tongue.

"I don't have many more questions for Jenna," Reeve says quietly when he releases me from the kiss.

I nod, completely sated and fulfilled. Triumphant, even.

"You're coming to my house after we're done. Take the rest of the day off," he commands.

My first instinct is to rebel and say no, but I can't. I want him too much, and I want him to return the favor with his mouth between my legs. Then I want him to fuck me with that big dick and make me come again.

"Okay," I breathe out, wondering how in the hell I'm going to concentrate on this deposition when I know that he just fucked my mouth so exquisitely.

CHAPTER 8
REEVE

I'm calm and relaxed.

How could I not be with what just happened in Leary's office?

That teasing minx. I can't believe she was trying to give me a foot job right in the middle of a deposition. At her first touch, all of the repressed sexual energy I'd been battling this past week came surging to the forefront. I knew there was no way I could continue with one more question to Jenna LaPietra until I made Leary suck me off.

Oh, she tried to act like she didn't want it at first, but I'm not stupid. She not only wanted it but loved my domineering nature. For all of Leary's sexual confidence and uninhibited attitude, I just learned that she very much likes being controlled in her fucking. I tuck this information away to experiment with later tonight.

"Let's go back on the record," I say to the court reporter. When the mask covers her face and she gives me a nod that she's ready, I turn back to Jenna.

"Thank you for your patience so far, Jenna. I don't have many more questions left," I say with a warm smile.

While I'm fighting tooth and nail against Jenna and her case, I've found throughout this deposition that she's actually a very intelligent woman. She's soft-spoken, and no doubt intimidated by this entire process, but still has enough confidence to give me clear answers that might have been slightly coached by Leary. Needless to say, I'm impressed with Jenna LaPietra, and that will definitely be considered if we offer any money on this case. Of course, that all depends on Tom Collier. He controls the purse strings, and my opinion on settlement won't matter too much.

"I want to talk for a moment about your decision to have this surgery, okay?"

She nods at me.

"Good. Now, was this breast reduction medically necessary?" I ask.

"Objection," Leary says calmly. "You're asking for a medical opinion. Save it for the experts."

"Let me ask this way," I say without giving Leary a glance. "Did any doctor tell you that this surgery was medically necessary?"

Jenna shakes her head. "No, but I was having a lot of back pain because of the size of my breasts. That's why I decided to have it done."

"So it was purely voluntary?" I prod at her.

"Yes."

"Other than some back pain, you had no medical need to get the reduction?"

"No."

"I'm curious, Jenna, and pardon me for asking this, but as a topless dancer, isn't it more lucrative for you to have larger breasts? I mean, wouldn't men generally tip you better having double Ds versus a C cup?"

"Not necessarily," she says carefully and turns to look at Leary. Leary, however, is staring at me, shooting daggers out of her eyes over this line of questioning.

She finally looks over to Jenna and nods her head, telling her it's okay to expound.

Jenna continues. "I mean, sure, there are plenty of men that like bigger breasts, but plenty of men don't. And it's actually easier to work on the pole with smaller breasts."

"Excuse me?" I ask. I think I know what she means, but I need to make sure.

"The extra weight and movement of the double Ds, not to mention the back pain, made pole dancing difficult, so much so that I had to cut it out of my routine. Men tip better when you dance on the pole, so it seemed the smart decision to make."

I nod in understanding. "Just so I'm clear then . . . is it safe to say you had the breast reduction done so you could increase the money you would make by being able to strip on the pole again?"

"Yes," Jenna says quietly, her face flaming red.

I dare a glance at Leary, and she is livid over these questions, but she also knows they're legitimate. She can't stop me from asking them, and I can't worry that it's pissing her off. I hope to God she remembers her own words—that we don't let our sexual relationship affect this case and vice versa. She might be pissed at me after this is over, but her ass is still coming home with me this afternoon, and I'm not letting her out of bed until the morning.

I flip through my notes, ask a few more questions dealing with Jenna's job. I don't ask about the prostitution allegations I found through the criminal background check of the club's owner, because I haven't been able to verify that Jenna was involved. I have an investigator interviewing past employees, so maybe something will turn up I can use. Until then, I stay away from that, because I know in a million years, Jenna would never admit it.

After Jenna walks me through how she was paid, I prod her a bit on whether or not she paid taxes on her income. Leary jumps in with a well-placed Fifth Amendment objection and instructs her client not to answer. This is a bone that I can pick if I want—the law isn't clear, and it's possible we could get a judge on the phone to let us argue whether or not she has to answer.

But I let it go.

I don't have the inclination to extend this deposition longer than necessary because I'm impatient to get Leary back to my house. I mentally wince over that thought, because contrary to what we agreed upon, I just let our sexual relationship interfere with this case.

Oh, well. The information isn't crucial and I can get it by other means.

I set my pen down and smile at Jenna. "That's all the questions I have. Thank you for your time today, Jenna."

Jenna smiles at me and the court reporter lowers her mask.

"I actually have a few questions," Leary says.

The court reporter raises her mask again as I blink at Leary in surprise. Although she's certainly allowed to ask questions, it's normally not done. My goal during this deposition is to gather as much information as I can while Leary hopes I don't find everything, hopes I stay in the dark. Thus, her asking questions only increases the risk that more information will be revealed that might lead me to learn something dangerous to her case.

I pick my pen up and flip to a blank page on my legal pad and push back from the table a bit. After crossing one leg over the other, I lay my pad on my lap so no one can see what I'm doing. I write the words *Leary Cross-Exam* across the top and underline them twice. Then I doodle a little picture of a cock with two balls and an open mouth beside it. Clearly, I'd rather be thinking about that blow job than sitting here in this deposition.

"Jenna," Leary says gently, "Mr. Holloway asked you several questions about the reason you had this surgery."

Jenna nods in agreement.

"You admitted that you would make more money stripping if you had the surgery done."

"Yes," Jenna says quietly.

"Why is making more money important to you?" Leary asks in a soothing tone.

"Because my son is severely autistic," Jenna says sadly, and my head jerks up from my doodling. "He has state-assisted insurance, but it doesn't pay for much of his therapy, plus I need qualified sitters to watch him when I'm working. I have to pay for that out of my own pocket."

"Are you married?" Leary asks, and it's with shame that I realize I have no clue whether or not Jenna is married. It didn't seem important to me.

"No."

"Does your son's father help to contribute to the child?" Leary pushes.

"No."

"So you are the sole means of support for your family?"

"Yes."

"What's your education level?" Leary gently pries.

"I graduated high school."

"Do you have any other job skills?"

"No."

"Have you tried to apply to other jobs?"

"Yes. Many times. It's hard to get hired with no work experience, but even if I did I doubt I could leave stripping. The money is too good. It's really the only way I can pay for Damien's treatment and other expenses."

I swallow hard, for the first time understanding how devastating it was for this woman to lose her job.

And that was directly related to the results of the surgery my client performed.

I shoot Leary a glance, hoping to convey to her that I understand what she's doing. That I don't need her to go any further, but she refuses to look at me.

"Why did you lose your job at Pure Fantasy?" Leary asks Jenna, this time not so gently and with a little anger in her voice.

"My breasts were too deformed to dance," Jenna says as her voice breaks.

I stare at Jenna, unable to look away from this woman to whom life has not been kind. I have a job to do. It's my job to prove that she wasn't injured due to my client's negligence. It's a tough pill to swallow sometimes, but it doesn't mean I can't commiserate.

I do.

Truly.

"Stand up," Leary says, laying her hand gently on Jenna's back.

Jenna stands up from the table, and I sit up a little straighter, not sure what Leary's getting ready to do. Tom is sitting next to me, slouched down in his seat, and in my peripheral vision, I can see he is surfing on his iPhone. He's not moved in the slightest by Jenna's tale.

"Take off your shirt," Leary orders her softly, and Tom actually jerks to attention, his face now rising toward Jenna.

I don't know if Jenna knew this was coming so she could prepare for it, but she doesn't hesitate, swiftly unbuttoning the navy-blue blouse she paired with a matching skirt.

"Leary . . . that's not necessary," I say softly, and I see Jenna's hands still against the buttons.

"Oh, I think it is," she snaps at me and then points to Tom, who goes deathly still now that Leary is focusing on him. "Mr. Collier hasn't paid a damn bit of attention during this deposition, as he's clearly more interested in playing Angry Birds."

"We need to go off the record," I say to the court reporter.

"Don't you dare put that mask down," Leary growls at the court reporter, who slaps it back to her face in fear.

Turning back to Jenna, Leary pats her on the arm. "It's okay. Take your shirt off and show them what Dr. Summerland did to you."

"I'll lodge an objection for the record. It's not been proven that Dr. Summerland committed negligence," I say quickly.

Leary glares at me, and I'm seeing my chances of getting laid tonight dwindling.

Jenna finishes unbuttoning her shirt, and Leary helps her to slide it from her shoulders.

"Your bra, too, Jenna," she says.

Jenna reaches to a clasp in the front and releases it, pulling the cups back wide. I don't look at her breasts at first, instead keeping my eyes on Jenna's face. I wait for her to raise her head, then she pins me with a direct stare, lifting her chin up in defiance.

Finally, I lower my gaze, and I've never struggled with anything more in my life than I do to not let a look of disgust cross my features.

Jenna's chest is truly mangled.

I've seen photos of the results, but they don't do justice to the damage done. I let my eyes rove over the C-cup globes, still beautiful in their shape and roundness. But that beauty is completely marred by the left nipple, which is pulled grotesquely to the side by contracted scar tissue around her areola. There's a large dimpled crater on her right breast, just below and to the right of her areola, two more smaller craters to the left, and worst of all, the tissue at the bottom of her areola is contracted and puckered so hard that it causes a small flap of skin to hang down in a V where the nipple hangs off the end.

It's hideous, and my stomach churns for this poor woman, although I'm not admitting this has anything to do with negligence at this point, as Dr. Summerland and our expert witnesses agree he did nothing wrong in the surgery, and that this is just a normal risk of the procedure that can happen with scar tissue.

"Oh no, you don't," I hear Leary hiss, and my eyes leave Jenna's mangled breasts. Leary is glaring at Tom. "Don't you dare avert your eyes. You had the balls to deny this claim, landing us in this very room. You can at least have the balls to look upon this woman, who's putting all of her pride aside to show you the horror of her life."

"Leary," I warn, knowing she's crossed over a line now that's not going to be acceptable to any judge. The last thing she needs is for Tom to report her behavior, which has gone from crusading to downright unprofessionally obnoxious.

She doesn't even look at me but continues to pin Tom with her stare, daring him to look at Jenna's breasts.

He refuses.

"I'm done here," Tom mutters, pushing up from his chair. "I'll call you tomorrow, Reeve, and we can discuss filing a motion for sanctions."

I let out a sigh of frustration and run my hand through my hair as Tom storms from the room. Gravity seems to pull me down into a dejected slouch in my chair.

"You can get dressed, honey," Leary says gently, and I don't raise my face, allowing Jenna the privacy to put her clothes back on. The court reporter quickly packs up her equipment and leaves, promising to have the transcript ready in two weeks and sliding the bill for her services across the table to me. I take it, jam it into my briefcase, and then watch as Leary walks Jenna to the conference room door.

"You did great, Jenna," Leary says softly, and then much to my surprise, she pulls Jenna into a hard hug. Leary holds on to her for a while, and I see Jenna's fingers clutching Leary's suit jacket almost in a desperate fashion. When they part, Leary squeezes Jenna's shoulders and murmurs, "I'll call you tomorrow. Get some sleep and kiss Damien for me."

My eyebrows rise over this display of care and affection Leary has toward her client and her child. It's not natural, not in the normal course of business, but then again, Ford told me that the personal nature of this case to Leary goes far deeper than I could ever imagine.

When Jenna clears the door, Leary closes it and, with a tired sigh, makes her way back to the other side of the table to collect her belongings.

"What the hell has gotten into you?" I ask, not in a threatening manner, but genuinely confused by her bizarre behavior.

She shrugs as she starts laying documents on top of one another into one pile. "No idea what you mean."

"Come on, Leary," I say as I stand up and grab my briefcase. "You don't have clients strip in depositions. There was no purpose, and it was nothing more than a stunt. It wasn't even on video for the jury to see. You did it to embarrass Tom, and I want to know why."

"You know why," she snaps at me, eyes blazing. "He's a prick. He denied the claim and then couldn't even be bothered to look Jenna in the eye when she was answering your questions."

"You went too far," I admonish, not to make her feel bad, but to make sure she doesn't do something like that again. "I'm going to have to talk Tom down off the ledge, but I think I can get him to let go of this stupid idea of sanctions."

"I don't need you defending me," Leary says quietly, and I'm taken aback by the soft conviction in her voice. "I handle my own battles, and I pulled that little 'stunt,' as you called it, knowing damn good and well I could be sanctioned. I did it not caring if I get sanctioned. It was worth it to me to see that look on Tom's face when I called him on the carpet about it."

"What did you think about the look on *my* face?" I ask quietly.

Leary's gaze lowers down to the table. She straightens the papers as she says, "You were empathetic to Jenna. It was subtle, but you were horrified by what you saw."

"That I was," I say tiredly, still sick at heart for what this woman endured and now perturbed that I'm worried about Leary getting sanctioned for her behavior. "Let's get your things packed up and head out."

"You still want me to come to your house?" Leary asks in surprise as her head snaps up.

"Well, yeah . . . I thought we discussed this."

"But that was before I just pissed you off with my stunt," she points out.

"You pissed me off earlier playing footsie with my cock, and that didn't stop me from fucking your mouth, did it?"

Her lips turn upward and her eyes shine with amusement. "I suppose not."

"Then rest assured, your little stunt isn't going to stop me from fucking your pussy with my tongue and then my dick when we get to my place."

I take immense pleasure in seeing Leary suppress a physical shudder that ripples through her body as her eyes grow hot.

"Then what are we waiting for?" she asks impishly.

I motion with my hand for her to precede me to the door. Just as she reaches it, I ask her something that is frankly driving me nuts. "What's your relationship with Jenna?"

Leary doesn't even stop to look at me. She pulls the door open. "She's my client."

"She's more than that," I assert as I follow her out.

"Yes, she is," Leary says softly.

"Are you going to tell me?" I ask again.

"No, Reeve. I'm not," she says with a firm tone that effectively shuts me down. And because we agreed that this is just physical, no-strings sex without the complications of commitment and all the other fuzzy things that might go with actually dating someone, I let it drop.

CHAPTER 9

LEARY

"Um . . . I need to warn you about Mr. Chico Taco before we go in," Reeve says as we walk up the sidewalk to his front door. We'd taken separate cars—at my insistence—so I won't be stranded if I want to leave. I've seen enough of Reeve's domineering ways to know that if he doesn't want me to leave, he'll just refuse to take me home.

"Mr. Chico Taco?"

"My dog," he says as he searches for his key ring to unlock the door. "He's a little, um . . . exuberant."

As Reeve slides the key home, I start to ask what type of dog, but the big, booming bark that comes from the other side of the door stops me in my tracks. I'm pretty sure it's not a dog, but a T. rex on the other side.

Looking over his shoulder at me with his eyes shining bright, he says, "He's really nice, but he gets excited when I come home."

And then a strange and slightly unwelcome thought comes into my head. If I was with Reeve, in a relationship, I would probably be just as excited for him to come home to me. I'm pretty sure he could make me bark like a dog.

Reeve pushes the door open but we can't move inside because a huge, massive beast with shiny gray fur and a head the size of a basketball jumps up on him. Laughing, Reeve actually hugs the dog as he puts his gigantic paws the size of salad plates on his shoulders and starts whining in pleasure to see his master. His head hangs over Reeve's shoulder, and light-blue eyes stare at me with a happy grin on his face that causes his tongue to loll out of his head.

"All right, buddy," Reeve says and, with a big heave, pushes the dog off him. With a gentle but firm command, Reeve says, "Sit."

The dog, which I recognize as a Great Dane, flops his butt to the floor, his eyes pinned to Reeve in adoration. "Come say hello to Mr. Chico Taco."

I step forward hesitantly. "Do I have to address him by his formal name?"

"Nah," Reeve says with a laugh. "Chico is fine."

"He should be called Brutus," I mutter as Mr. Chico Taco cocks his head at me in curiosity. "He *looks* more like a Brutus."

"Now that's just mean. He takes offense to that," Reeve chides.

I reach my hand out and bring it to the big dog's head. "Hi, Chico. I'm Leary."

I scratch him a few times, but when I try to withdraw my hand, his head bumps against it, urging it back up to pet him. I laugh and scratch him again. "You're just a big baby, aren't you?"

"Now that *I* take offense to," Reeve says over his shoulder as he walks into his living room, pulls off his suit jacket, and tosses it onto the back of a dark-blue suede couch. He pulls at his tie and loosens it enough so he can pull it over his head.

Throwing the tie on top of his suit jacket, Reeve turns to wink at me. "I might tie you up with that later."

God, I hope so.

Reeve continues to walk through the living room, so I follow him. Mr. Chico Taco walks at my side, continuing to bump my hand with his head for attention. Turning left, Reeve is momentarily gone from sight, but when I round the corner, I find him in his kitchen, rooting around in the refrigerator.

His kitchen is gorgeous, all stainless steel and granite with dark-cherry cabinetry. "What are you doing?" I ask uncertainly, because the way things went back at the office, I was pretty certain that Reeve brought me to his house so we could have sex.

"Going to make us an early dinner. I'm thinking lemon pasta with blackened chicken."

"You're going to cook?"

Reeve stands up, pulling a pack of chicken and three lemons from his fridge. He gives me a knowing look with a touch of sympathy. "Yes, I'm going to cook."

"I don't understand," I say as I cock my eyebrow at him, and Chico nudges me again. I absently pet the dog's head.

"I'm going to cook," he says again with an annoying smirk.

"You're going to cook?"

Throwing the chicken and lemons on the counter, Reeve walks up to me. His hands rest lightly on my waist. Bending down so his nose almost touches mine, he says, "This conversation is a little redundant, so let me clarify for you. I'm going to cook us an early dinner. I'm loading us up on protein and carbs, because after said meal, I intend to take you back to my bedroom, and then I'm not letting you out of said bedroom until morning. With me so far?"

I can't help the tiny smile that pops forth, and I give him an understanding nod.

"Good," he continues. "When we get into that bedroom, there's going to be very little rest. I'm a fast recharger, so there's no telling how many times I'm going to fuck you tonight. Plus, I have toys. Lots of toys that I want to play with. Thus, we need fuel before we fuck. Clear?"

"Clear," I whisper, now so completely turned on that I want to beg him to take me right here in the kitchen.

But he releases me and points to a stool that sits on the opposite side of his massive kitchen island. "Now sit. I'll pour us a glass of wine and we can relax for a bit."

I do as he commands, not because I'm obedient, but because now I'm very curious as to what in the hell he thinks he's doing. Cooking us a meal, sipping wine? That's not in the general order of fuck buddy–dom.

At least I don't think it is.

Reeve pulls a bottle of red wine from the back kitchen counter. "Do you like Cab?"

"Sure," I say as I prop one elbow up on the counter and stick my chin in the palm of my hand so I can watch him. He moves about with surety and casual grace. Only I know the raw and dirty power he has hidden underneath this elegant persona.

Reeve pours two glasses then hands one to me. He holds his glass out and I tap mine to his. "To fuck buddies," he says with a grin.

"Fuck buddies," I echo and take a tiny sip of my wine.

There's a quick knock on Reeve's front door, and then the door swings open, and I hear a woman's voice. "Reeve, it's just me."

"In the kitchen," he calls back, and I hear the padding of feet coming through the living room.

My eyebrows rise when a beautiful young woman of about twenty or so walks into Reeve's kitchen. Her golden-blonde hair is long, her makeup flawless. She has exquisite features with high cheekbones and a straight nose. Her blue eyes are bright, wide, and focused on Reeve in what I immediately recognize as lustful adoration.

This pisses me off.

Chico spins away from where he'd been sitting by my stool and bounds over to the woman. She bends over, slaps at her thighs, and says, "Hey, big boy. Come here."

Chico launches his frame at her, putting his front legs on her shoulders—he towers over her by a good five or so inches. I glance back at Reeve, and he's watching the pair with an amused smile.

This also pisses me off.

Reeve's dog clearly knows and likes this woman.

It also pisses me off that Reeve is amused by the relationship this woman has with his dog.

"Everything okay?" Reeve asks her.

"Yeah," she says pertly. Her gaze—which is no less adoring or hopeful looking—cuts from Chico over to him. "Just wanted to let you know that Chico had a good day today. We walked about two miles."

"That's great," Reeve says as he starts opening the pack of chicken, intent on his work.

"Who's this?" the woman says as she slides her gaze over to me.

Reeve's head snaps up, and an almost guilty look flashes over his face. "Oh, shit . . . sorry. This is a friend of mine, Leary Michaels. Leary, this is Vanessa. She lives next door with her parents and walks Chico every morning for me."

"Hi," I say with a smile that I hope comes off as friendly and genuine.

"Hi," she says, in a flat tone that does not come off as friendly and genuine. Her message is clear—she has her sights on Reeve and does not like me sitting here. I have to wonder if he's fucking her, but sadly, I can't be mad about that. I told him last week I didn't care if he saw other women.

Stupid, stupid, stupid.

Vanessa turns her attention back to Reeve and walks up to the counter, resting her arms on the edge next to me. "So what are you making?"

"Lemon pasta and blackened chicken," he says as he pulls out a cutting board and knife. I take another sip—well, gulp—of my wine.

"Sounds fantastic. I'm starved," she says and actually sits her ass on the edge of the stool next to me.

My jaw drops open slightly because I'm wondering if we now have a dinner guest. This also pisses me off, and all of my fantasies of Reeve being completely immersed in me go crashing down into dejected disappointment. I actually start to push up off the stool, intent on walking out the front door, when Reeve looks up to Vanessa.

"I'm sorry, Vanessa," he says in a sympathetic but firm tone. "I'm actually on a date with Leary. Wouldn't be quite as romantic with you joining us, now would it?"

I know we only agreed to be fuck buddies, but damn . . . it feels nice having him validate me to this stunning and youthful beauty.

Vanessa's face flames, her eyes going round with surprise. "A date?"

"A date," Reeve affirms and then shoots me a quick smile. I smile back—big—and take a delicate sip of my wine, now enjoying the show.

"But you don't date," she says in confusion, and I have to wonder how close she is to him to know that.

"I do now," he says with a grin, and then he points to me. "I mean, look at her. How could I not date that?"

My chest actually puffs out a little.

Vanessa's face flames redder, and I think it's from anger, not embarrassment. Reeve just stares at her, waiting for her to take the hint to leave. She stares back at him, and I might just have to take matters into my own hands and throw her out.

Finally, her shoulders sag and she says, "Okay. I guess I'll get going. Enjoy your dinner."

"'Bye," Reeve says, and Vanessa doesn't bother looking at me as she walks out of the kitchen. A moment later I hear his door open and close.

Reeve starts cutting the chicken up, a knowing smile on his face. I'm desperate for him to tell me about her, but he's clearly not going to do so willingly.

Finally, I prompt, "So . . . she seems nice."

"She is," he agrees.

"Beautiful, too."

"Yeah, sure . . . I guess."

"Young," I prod.

"I think she's twenty."

I have to bite down on my tongue not to gnash my teeth in frustration. "Big, big boobs," I goad him.

"I guess. Didn't really pay attention."

Aha! He didn't look at her boobs. Vindication.

No, wait. All men look at boobs.

"Oh, give me a fucking break," I snap at Reeve, and his eyes slide to mine with a mischievous grin. "All men look at boobs. So tell me the deal . . . is she a fuck buddy, too?"

Reeve sets the knife down, calmly steps over to the sink, and washes his hands. He takes a towel and dries them, then says to me in a slightly taunting voice, "Well, well, well. Who would have thought it? My little fuck buddy, Leary Michaels, is jealous."

"Am not," I deny.

"Are, too," he says in a silky voice as he sets the towel down and starts rounding the kitchen island.

"You're demented," I sneer at him, but my heart rate accelerates as he clears the corner and steps up to me.

"Hmm," is all he says as he turns the stool I'm sitting on toward him. His hands go to my knees, and he pries my legs apart so he can step in closer. "I'm finding I like this jealousy."

"I'm not jealous," I snap at him. "Just curious."

"This jealousy sort of turns me on," he murmurs, completely ignoring my denials. He bends down to nip at my lower lip, and I can't help the tiny moan that escapes. My hands come up to grab his shoulders.

"I. Am. Not. Jealous."

"So jealous," he says with a grin; then his hands come to my hips, and he lifts me up and deposits me on the counter. "Lie down."

"What?" He places his hand on my chest and pushes me backward on the island.

When my back hits the cold granite, his hands are already working at my clothes. My pumps hit the floor, and I send a brief prayer up that Mr. Chico Taco doesn't eat my Stuart Weitzmans. I stare at his recessed lighting as I feel my garters unsnapped and my stockings pulled off. Then he's bunching up my skirt and pulling my panties down.

"Black lace," he murmurs, but I don't even bother looking up. I know what he's going to do, and I'm going to just lie back and enjoy it. "Did you wear that for me?"

"No," I deny, but he just laughs softly.

"Liar."

I smile to myself and my eyes flutter shut when I feel his hands spreading my legs wider. His fingertips probe at my pussy, and I feel hot breath on me, then a tiny flutter on my clit from his tongue.

"Ooh," I murmur and then sigh contentedly.

"I wanted to do this in my bedroom," Reeve says, then gives me a long swipe of his tongue, causing my hips to buck. "I wanted to use a G-spot stimulator on you while I ate you out."

"Oh God," I moan at the thought of him and his toys.

"Guess I'll just have to use my fingers. The old-fashioned way," he says before plunging his tongue inside me. He pumps and swivels and swirls it, his nose pressed up against my clit. His face is buried in deep, and my hands automatically come to his head.

Reeve pulls back, takes a deep breath, and then pushes two fingers inside me. He curls them, hits the right spot, and a bolt of pleasure spears through me. He starts massaging me from the inside with his fingers while his mouth comes down to cover my clit.

Then in a series of circles, flutters, and lashings, he starts to work me over hard. My hips gyrate on their own, completely ruled and possessed by the lust he's stirring up and the insanely terrible need I now have to come.

I grip his head hard and mutter, "Too bad Vanessa didn't walk in on this."

Reeve laughs against my pussy, and even the vibrations of his humor are fueling me higher. His mouth pulls away from me, and I give a soft whine of disappointment.

"Hey," Reeve says softly, his fingers still deep inside me.

My eyes pop open and I lift my head from the counter. He's peering up at me in between my legs.

"She's not a fuck buddy," he says. "Never has been and never will be."

Warmth spreads through my chest, and I'm oddly touched that he would take the time to ease my worry. I smile at him, hoping he sees my gratitude and that he understands that maybe his answer is more important to me than even I give it credit for.

He smiles back.

"Thank you," I tell him softly.

"Anytime," he murmurs.

I squeeze my fingers on his skull and lay my head back down, closing my eyes. "Now finish me off, baby."

"With pleasure," he says, and then his mouth is back on me.

He doesn't fuck around, either. He goes right in for the kill, doing something with his tongue that batters at me, causes my orgasm to furl inward for a brief moment, then pulse outward until my entire back arches off the counter and I'm coming, coming, coming.

"So damn beautiful," Reeve mutters as my body shakes and spasms, and his fingers pump inside me a few more times.

Then he's gone and I hear the rustle of his pants, the clink of his belt buckle, and the sound of foil being ripped.

My eyes open just as Reeve's hands are back at my hips, pulling me off the counter. I'm loose and weak as a baby after that orgasm, so I just let Reeve do all the work as he turns me away from him and bends me over one of the kitchen stools.

He props my ass up, tilts it, and pulls back on my hips. I feel his cock rubbing between my legs from behind, and a low growl coming out of his chest.

"Your ass is so beautiful, Leary," he whispers as one hand comes up to caress my skin. He pushes the head of his cock into me at the same time he turns his hand, dragging an index finger down between my ass cheeks. His finger lightly touches and prods at my opening, and my breath catches.

"Ever had your ass fucked, Leary?"

I shake my head violently back and forth, not because the idea is abhorrent to me but because, God help me, his finger there is entirely too sinful and erotic, and I yearn for him to push me.

"Maybe I will one day," he murmurs, stroking his finger lightly over me. I push back a little and he gives a hoarse chuckle. "Yeah, I think you'll like it, but we'll start with some toys first."

The idea frightens yet titillates me, so I won't rule it out.

His hand moves away, back to grasp my hips, and he pushes into me in a slow, fluid stroke, straight to the hilt.

"Ah," I moan as his fingers dig into my flesh.

He holds himself within me just a moment, and I wait for him to start pounding away. His thumbs move softly over my lower back, and I can feel the pulse of his cock thumping lightly inside me.

"I'm confused," Reeve says, grinding into me just a bit.

"Why?" I gasp and push back against him.

"I don't understand how one woman can feel this good," he says with naked honesty.

His words strike at me deep. He's voicing the same thoughts I've had all week.

How can one man be so vastly different from the others I've had? How can he bring me so quickly to dizzying heights? How can he fully entertain and annoy me at the same time? And how can I actually be starting to have feelings for a man who should be my sworn enemy?

I don't respond, although I feel like he's waiting for me to validate what he just said. I can't. My emotions are too clogged up right now to sort them out and voice them correctly. Instead, I grind back against him, pull forward so he slips out of me a bit, then slam back again.

His fingers dig in again and then it's on.

He starts thrusting into me deep and fast. I slam back against his forward motion.

It's brutal, the type of fucking that's going to leave bruises, and it feels so amazing, I think I'm going to blow quickly again.

I listen to Reeve's harsh pants coming faster, almost wheezing. My heartbeat is thundering so hard, I feel light-headed. With every knock against my deepest wall with the end of his cock, my orgasm starts to gather tightly.

"I can't hold it, Leary," Reeve gasps as he lurches against me frantically. "Going to come."

Not without me, you're not.

My hand goes between my legs, and with the slightest touch of my fingertips to my clit, the dam of pleasure bursts wide-open and I start to moan with the release.

"Oh God, baby," Reeve pants in between hard pumps of his hips. "I can feel you coming all around me."

His words alone spark me again, and tears spring to my eyes from the overwhelming pleasure I'm experiencing.

Reeve slams into me so hard my chest goes to the stool seat, and the crack of his flesh against mine rebounds through the kitchen. He goes utterly still and then a long groan pours out of him. His cock leaps inside me a few times, and I know that every movement corresponds to a jet of release pouring out of him.

"Holy shit," Reeve wheezes as his chest drops to my back. "Holy fucking shit."

I giggle, but that's all I can do, as I'm having a hard enough time sucking in oxygen.

"So good," Reeve mutters, and I nod my head. His arms come around my waist, and he squeezes me tight. "So damn good."

CHAPTER 10

REEVE

My client is a schmuck. Dr. Garry Summerland is the sole owner of Summerland General Surgery. He's been practicing medicine for twenty-seven years now, having first cut his teeth in various ER trauma wards, and later opening up his private practice in Raleigh, just shy of twenty years ago. He employs fourteen general surgeons to perform a variety of surgeries, with most of their expertise focused on abdominal and gastrointestinal procedures.

About ten years ago, Summerland got into the gastric-bypass business because it was big bucks and could be considered a medically necessary procedure, which equated to big payouts from private and state insurance as well as Medicare.

This should have been enough to satisfy Summerland, but it wasn't, which meant that he would still take any type of surgical case that walked through his doors. Jenna LaPietra was the unfortunate soul who walked through those doors.

She originally saw him for an emergency appendectomy, for which he happened to be on call at the hospital. During her postsurgery follow-up appointment with him, she mentioned the back pain she was experiencing from her large breasts. That conversation perked Summerland's ears. He smelled money and suggested a reduction.

Now most of the medical experts will agree that a general surgeon is qualified to perform certain breast surgeries. Usually that means lumpectomies and mastectomies for breast-cancer patients. I believe Summerland's line of thinking was, *I've lopped off many a woman's boobs, thus I'm qualified to handle Jenna's breast-reduction surgery.*

The absolute fight in this case boils down to whether or not Summerland should have performed this surgery. Leary has three medical experts who will testify on Jenna's behalf. They're good.

Damn good.

Two are from Duke—a general surgeon and a plastic surgeon—and the other is a general surgeon from the University of North Carolina. Leary's experts will testify that although it's within the standard of care for general surgeons to perform breast surgeries, including mastectomies, it is generally not within their field of expertise to perform cosmetic breast reductions.

Leary's doctors will testify that plastic surgeons have much more certification and training in the complexities and delicate nature of such a surgery, and a breast reduction is not a mastectomy. A mastectomy without reconstruction is done for full breast removal without any thought to the way it looks after. A breast reduction is a delicate procedure to remove a defined portion of breast material that involves shaping and contouring, something a general surgeon is not qualified to do. If a breast-cancer patient wants a mastectomy with reconstruction, then a plastic surgeon is called in to handle that type of surgery.

Thus, Leary's theory of negligence is very simple.

Dr. Summerland was only qualified to perform a breast surgery that would require full removal of the breast without any expectation of nondeformed results.

My client is a schmuck because he sees it differently.

Garry Summerland sees it differently because he has a God complex. He's one of those doctors who believes he can do anything, and he's cocky and egocentric enough not to let little things like advanced training get in the way of his desire to make money.

Today is the last of three straight days that Leary and I have been in depositions. I've deposed her expert witnesses, asking painstakingly crafted questions to delve into and reveal every potential piece of evidence and testimony that they may give on Jenna's behalf. I'll use these transcripts to compare to the medical research I've done, as well as my own experts' opinions, and hopefully discredit these witnesses on the stand during my cross-examination during trial.

These last three days Leary has also deposed my experts, who I admit are not as good as hers. Two of my experts went to medical school with my client and one is a golfing buddy, so there's bias there. My other expert is from Oregon, and it's hard to match up an out-of-state doctor with her experts from Duke and Carolina.

If this case boils down to a battle of the experts, Leary will most likely win, and the odd thing about that is I don't care if she wins. I mean, I want to win because I'm competitive, but when all things are considered, I have to admit to myself I believe in Leary's case more than my own.

Some would think this would create an ethical dilemma, but it doesn't. I don't have to believe in my cases. I only have to use the evidence I have and do my best to present and argue them to convince a jury to see my way of thinking. I get paid a good salary to do this, and I have no qualms about keeping my emotions and personal feelings out of it, because ultimately I wasn't hired to protect Dr. Summerland. My actual client is his insurance company, TransBenefit Insurance, which makes billions of dollars every year and hires people like me to fight against claims like this so they can preserve their billions of dollars.

Leary and the type of law she practices are a bit different. She represents people, not corporations. She not only invests her time and effort into the actual evidence, but she has an emotional connection to the people she represents. Put money aside, and the stakes are higher for her than for me.

Now, back to Summerland being a schmuck.

Leary saved his deposition for last. After three solid days of being immersed in complex medical testimony, we're both exhausted. My brain is fuzzy, and luckily all I have to do this afternoon is listen to Leary's questions and object if necessary.

Summerland walked into the conference room, chest puffed out, chin raised, and condescension in his eyes. I prepared him last night via phone and highly encouraged him to come in humble, but I could tell right away that was a concept so foreign to him that he'd never be able to pull it off.

The first thing he did was refuse to shake Leary's hand when she stood up from the table to welcome him. The next thing he did was run his gaze up and down her body a few times, and even lick his bottom lip.

I get it. I really do. Leary is a phenomenal beauty and sexy as hell. What man wouldn't do that?

I wanted to punch the motherfucker.

Leary handled it like a pro. She grilled him for three hours straight, refusing to take a break when he asked to go to the bathroom. Every answer he gave her was short and clipped, and she had to fight with him the entire time to get him to answer her questions in a straightforward manner. She did it with an absolutely professional demeanor.

Total fucking schmuck, and I'm glad this deposition is almost over. I can tell when Leary starts winding down.

"Just a few more questions, Dr. Summerland," she says, flipping through her notes. "I want to talk to you about the finances of your practice, Summerland General Surgery."

"I don't think that's relevant," he sneers. "What I make has nothing to do with this case."

"Maybe, maybe not," she says calmly. "But I'm allowed to ask any questions that *may* lead to the discovery of admissible evidence. So I'm going to ask them, you're going to answer them, and it's up to your attorney—Mr. Holloway there—to keep anything inappropriate out of evidence. Okay?"

He just glares at Leary and that's enough for her. She presses on.

"Now, Dr. Summerland, I understand the majority of your practice relates to abdominal and gastrointestinal surgeries, is that correct?"

"Yes," he says.

"But you do other types of surgeries?"

"Yes." Glare.

"Minor surgeries like hernia repairs and appendectomies?"

"Yes." Eyes flick to her breasts.

"Surgical oncology, removal of tumors?"

"Yes." Eyes stay pinned on her breasts. My fists clench.

"And if I'm correct, the majority of your income earned comes from weight-loss surgeries like gastric bypass, right?"

"Yes." Lick of his lips. My nails dig into my palms.

"What percentage of your overall income is from the weight-loss surgeries?"

Summerland's eyes now snap up to Leary's. His lip curls up in a sneer. "I'm not answering that. It's none of your business."

"I have to wonder what you're so afraid of, Dr. Summerland. What could you possibly be trying to hide from the jury?" Leary says with wide-eyed innocence.

Summerland's face flames red and he stutters, realizing this will make him look like a fool to the trial jury. He is well aware of the camera Leary has rolling to later play to the jury—she's probably zoomed in now on his face. "I am not hiding anything. It's just that without my financial records in front of me, I can't honestly answer that question."

"And I assume you didn't bring those records with you today?" she asks politely.

"No, I didn't," he says confidently, giving her a smarmy smile, and his gaze goes back to her breasts.

"And may I also assume that if you did have those records here with you, you'd gladly disclose that information to the jury, who will later see this video?"

He gives a magnanimous incline of his head to her and says, "Of course I would."

"Then I'd like to go ahead and hand this to you," she says as she pulls a white form out from underneath her notepad.

Dr. Summerland blinks in surprise and reaches a tentative hand out to accept the document. She's been handing him various medical records all afternoon and going through his notes with painstaking detail, so he thinks nothing of taking this document from her now.

His gaze goes down to skim the paper in his hand and then jolts back to hers. I have no clue what she just handed him, and ordinarily I'd ask to see it, but damn . . . I'm kind of enjoying watching her hand him his ass.

"That's a subpoena, Dr. Summerland, demanding you turn over your tax returns for the last five years, as well as your accounting books, specifically asking your income to be broken down by the various types of surgeries you conduct each year."

Summerland starts to shake and I see him getting ready to explode. I want to cover my face with my hand to laugh at him. I want to shoot a smirk and a wink across the table to Leary, never having enjoyed one of my clients getting sandbagged before.

Instead, I remember my duty and say quickly, "Let's go off the record."

I half expect Leary to refuse, just like she did in Jenna's deposition a few weeks ago. Instead, she gives me an accommodating smile and says, "Sure."

"We're off the record," the court reporter says, and the assistant working the camera turns it off.

"This is fucking preposterous," Summerland bellows as he throws the subpoena back at Leary. It veers sharply and then floats harmlessly to the floor beside her chair.

"Dr. Summerland," I chastise firmly, "you need to calm down."

Leary simply leans over in her chair, giving me a quick peek at her luscious ass that I'm hoping to tap one day, and picks the paper back up. She does nothing more than hand it across the table to me.

"I'm sure you'll agree, Mr. Holloway, that your client was duly served with this subpoena."

I nod at her because she's right. As an officer of the court, she had him properly served the minute she handed the document to him.

"I'm not doing it," Dr. Summerland barks as he pushes back from the table and stands up. "I'm not turning over my financial records to some ambulance chaser who represents a whore trying to scam the system."

My jaw drops open at his crudity, and I immediately stand up to usher him out of the conference room. I want to kick this shit out of this asshole, but more important, I need to get him calmed down so he can finish the deposition.

"Let's go outside, Dr. Summerland," I say calmly. "We need to talk."

"I'm done, Holloway. Deposition is over," he says, and I'm surprised he doesn't stomp his foot. Now that he knows the camera is off, he's going into full-fledged tantrum mode.

"Damn," Leary mutters. "Should have kept the camera rolling."

Dr. Summerland shoots her a nasty glare and points his finger at her. "I'm reporting you to your bar association. Your behavior is unacceptable toward a member of the medical community."

Leary shrugs her shoulders, completely unruffled. "First, it's not the bar association. It's the North Carolina State Bar. Their phone number is 919-555-3955. Second, make sure to give them my bar number to make the process go easier. It's 4850A-45."

For a moment I think Dr. Summerland might stroke out. His face turns red, then a frightening shade of purple. I swear I can see steam coming out of his ears.

A quick glance at Leary shows her staring impassively at Dr. Summerland.

At this moment, I don't know that I've ever respected another attorney more than I respect her. She's brilliant, fiendishly clever, completely unshakable, and more mature than this douche who is twenty-plus years her senior.

God, I want to fuck her bad right now.

Leary turns her gaze to me and politely says, "I'm finished with my questions of Dr. Summerland, Mr. Holloway. For now, anyway."

I open my mouth to suggest to Dr. Summerland we leave, but he simply barrels past me and storms out of the conference room, slamming the door so hard behind him the prints on the wall rattle.

I can't fucking help myself. I turn to Leary, completely uncaring that the court reporter and cameraman are still in the room. I shoot her a grin and say, "I've never seen anything quite like that before."

The cameraman snickers, but I don't take my eyes off Leary. She shrugs and starts packing up her materials. "Your client is a prick, Mr. Holloway."

"Not going to argue there," I mutter, stuffing my own belongings into my briefcase.

"You have a few minutes to talk?" Leary asks me casually. "To discuss the case."

I look up at Leary and she's staring at me with a look that almost makes my knees buckle. It's one of starving need.

"Sure," I say, hoping my voice doesn't give way to the matching lust I'm feeling right now.

"I think we should have a legal rule that says we end all depositions this way," Leary pants in my ear.

She's lying on her back on the carpet of her office, her skirt bunched up around her hips and her panties dangling from one ankle. My pants and underwear have only come to midthigh, and my tie is tossed over my shoulder so it doesn't obstruct my view when I look down to see my cock pounding away between her legs.

"Fucking awesome rule," I groan as I push and grind in and against her.

"Shit . . . I'm going to come," she moans.

"Give it to me, baby," I encourage her with a particularly brutal thrust.

And she does . . .

And it's spectacular.

I follow right along behind, my mind going blissfully blank as I start to unload inside her, concentrating on nothing but the feeling of her wrapped around me, milking me dry.

When every last spasm has quieted in my body, I roll off Leary and lie beside her on the carpet. Our panting fills the air, but I can hear the noise of the Pit just outside her door.

I can't believe we just fucked on her office floor with dozens of people right outside. For Christ's sake, the door isn't even locked. I followed her into her office, thinking maybe we might make out. She'd no sooner shut the door than she was pulling me to the ground. She was instantly wet for me, and of course I was brutally hard for her.

And one hard and fast fucking later, I am completely at peace with my world.

I slide my hand over to hers and grasp it. She squeezes me and I can actually feel a satisfied smile in her touch.

"You tore my doctor up," I say offhandedly.

"He deserved it."

"Again, not going to argue," I say with a laugh. "It was kind of hot . . . watching you walk all over him."

"You were kind of hot just sitting there watching me walk all over him," she says with a chuckle. "I'd actually planned on torturing him a bit more, but then I made the mistake of looking over at you, and I was just done. Had to get you here in my office."

A languid smile comes over my face, but she can't see it because we're both still staring up at the ceiling, holding hands and waiting for our heartbeats to go back to normal.

Normal, I think with an inner smile to match my exterior one.

I don't think anything is going to be normal for me ever again. At least not where Leary's concerned.

CHAPTER 11
LEARY

Blinking my eyes, I give them a quick rub and then peer back at my computer monitor. I'm trying to read our bar association's weekly periodical that provides digest opinions on all recently decided appellate and supreme court cases. While this isn't actual legal research, it does qualify as highly boring.

I've always been the attorney who shunned relying on the actual particulars of the law, instead trying to argue my way through to victory using cunning and emotion. It's served me well so far, but I've also become dependent on my ability to talk my way out of just about any situation. It's made me weak on the actual law itself, so I sit down every Wednesday afternoon and read the digest, hoping that maybe if just one-tenth of what I read soaks in, I will be a better attorney for it.

Glancing at my watch, I see I've been struggling with this asinine idea for the last hour, and I'm not making any headway. I decide on a break and do a quick scan of my e-mail.

My lips pull into a smile when I see an e-mail from Reeve. He's been gone the last two days on out-of-state depositions, and I hate to admit it, but I miss him. He sent me a short message to let me know he'll be flying back into Raleigh tomorrow morning, and wants to know if we can do dinner.

I invite him to my house. While I won't have time to cook something on a work night, I'll make sure to pick up something good from the local market we can heat up.

My next e-mail is from a reporter from the Raleigh *Times*, wanting an interview about the *LaPietra* case. This pleases me immensely because it's always good to get public opinion behind you if possible. The bad news is that I suck at the PR stuff. The good news is that Midge does not and prefers to handle it anyway, so I forward the e-mail to her and ask if she can call the reporter.

Then I see an e-mail from Ford. It's short—not that I'd been expecting an essay. I invited him to lunch today, but his quick reply is that he already has plans.

My eyebrows scrunch up in skepticism as I read it. He's been avoiding me like the plague the last few weeks, since I started seeing Reeve, claiming that he's been too busy to get together. This could be true, because Ford is a busy man and we've gone long periods in the past when we couldn't hang. But usually he compensates by at least calling me to check in or stopping by my office to discuss a case.

Since the charity event at the Marriott, he's been completely absent from my life. This bothers me, because while I don't miss the sexual intimacy we've shared from time to time, I miss his friendship and wisdom.

Resolved to put this out on the table with Ford, I start to pick up my phone to buzz his office when Midge responds to my e-mail.

> Be glad to handle reporter. Come talk to me first,
> though. Bring me up to speed on the case. I feel
> like drinking a whiskey and I don't like drinking
> alone.

My heart starts racing.

I've been summoned. I'm being granted entrance into the reclusive Midge Payne's inner domain. I hate whiskey, but I'll gladly drink one with her just to spend some time in her presence.

I snicker to myself over the dramatics of my thoughts. It's true, I don't see Midge a lot, as she truly does hole herself up in her office. But we have sat down for some meetings on occasion over the years. But just because I don't have many face-to-faces with her doesn't mean we don't communicate. I talk to her several times a week through e-mail or on the phone, and over the years we've developed an easy personal and professional relationship.

My call to Ford forgotten, I shoot Midge back a quick e-mail that I'm on my way. Because I immediately get up from my desk and start across the Pit toward her office, I'm betting that I might actually beat my e-mail there.

Her secretary looks up as I approach, giving me a warm smile. "You can go right in, Leary. She's expecting you."

"Thank you, Danielle," I say while smoothing down my dress and straightening the scarf around my neck.

Deep breath in, slow breath out, and I open the door to Midge's office.

"Leary," she says as I walk in. "You're looking stunning as ever."

I appreciate that sentiment from Midge, but she's the one who looks stunning. Her hair is sleek and shiny, her makeup flawless, and she's rocking a pair of tan skinny jeans, over-the-knee black boots with four-inch heels, and an off-the-shoulder black sweater.

Midge is standing at the minibar that is recessed into her bookshelves. When she turns my way, she has two tumblers of neat whiskey in her hand. I have no clue what the brand is—never asked the one other time I drank one with her, when I got my partnership. She keeps her liquors in beautiful Waterford decanters, and only *she* is privy to what's actually in those bottles. Knowing Midge, it's expensive stuff.

"Let's sit on the couch," Midge says as she hands me the heavy highball glass. The cuts in the crystal make the dark-amber liquid inside shimmer.

Midge sits on one end of a plush cream-colored couch, and I sit on the other. I lean on my hip and cross my legs. Midge merely pulls one of her legs up under her and slings her free hand over the back of the couch.

"So, how have you been doing, kiddo?" she asks.

This is what I love about Midge. I hardly ever see her, but it's like that doesn't matter. When she talks to me, it's with absolute interest and obvious concern. She might not socialize with her minions, but I know without a doubt she cares deeply for all of us.

"I'm good," I tell her truthfully. "Jenna's case is coming along well. Our experts are going to shred theirs, and Dr. Summerland is a douche. The jury's going to hate him."

She nods and takes a sip of her drink. "Send me over a very short summary of our theory of negligence and the opinions that bolster it. Then I'll call that reporter back."

"I'll send it before I leave for the day."

"Now, what about Jenna? How is she going to do on the stand?" Midge asks.

"She's nervous but she'll be fine. I think the jury is going to empathize with her."

"Will they forgive her for being a dancer?" Midge asks wisely.

"Yeah, she's got good reason to do it. Her kid and all. She's clean, no drugs or alcohol. No criminal record. Just a hardworking mom who took an unconventional job to support an autistic child."

Midge nods and rubs her thumb over the edge of her glass. "Any potential problems?"

"Not so far," I tell her. "The insurance adjuster is a jackass. Doubt they'll offer anything at mediation, so this is probably going to go all the way."

Leaning over, Midge gives me a pat on my knee. When she sits back, she shoots me a confident smile. "I'm not worried. You have this one in the bag."

God, I hope so.

I haven't been able to even think about the possibility of losing. The actual thought of letting Jenna down is too terrifying to give credence.

"Now that business is out of the way, tell me, how are you doing personally?" Midge asks.

Taking a sip of my whiskey, valiantly able to not grimace, I give her a smile. "I'm good."

"Got a man in your life?" she asks me point-blank, and I have to contain the surprise on my face. Midge has never shown any interest in my personal life before. Does she know about Reeve?

"Why do you ask?" I say carefully, then take another sip of the whiskey for fortification.

"Why do you ask why I ask?" she asks with a mischievous grin. She scoots a little closer to me on the couch and gives me a hopeful look. "What are you hiding from me, Leary Michaels?"

What the hell is going on here? She has to know about Reeve to be pushing me like this.

I decide to show the moxie that Midge insisted I find within myself all those years ago. Narrowing my eyes at her, I ask pointedly, "Okay, what's going on here? Why the interest in my love life?"

Midge blinks at me in surprise, and then her face bursts into a smile. She scoots closer to me on the couch and slaps at my arm. "Okay, fine. You got me. I'm dying to know about you and Ford."

"Me and Ford?" I ask stupidly.

"Yes. There's something between you two. I've known it for years. I mean, hell, why do you think I assigned him as your mentor? I knew he'd teach you to be a brilliant litigator and an even better seductress."

Sometimes this woman is too frightening in her foresight.

I go ahead and decide to be honest, since there's no reason to lie. "He's done both well, Midge. But there's nothing between us other than friendship."

The smile drops from her face, and her brow furrows in confusion as her gaze drops to her lap. "I don't understand. I talked to Ford the other day, and I just thought . . ."

"What did Ford say to make you think something was there?" I ask carefully, because I can't imagine him ever saying something to Midge about our relationship—or lack thereof right now.

"Nothing, really. Maybe I misunderstood," she says distractedly.

"Misunderstood what?" I prompt.

"It's just, we were talking the other day on the phone, and I asked him about the charity event, and he said he went with you. I've known Ford a lot longer than you and had no qualms asking him if there was something going on. He quickly denied it. So quickly, in fact, I was sure he was hiding something. I just assumed, but I guess I was wrong."

"You're wrong," I assure her. "Ford and I have had . . . um . . . relations in the past, but it was a no-strings involvement. It's truly a good friendship."

At least I hope it's still a friendship. I have no clue, because he won't sit down two minutes with me so I can find out.

"Oh, well," she says with another bright smile. "You're still too young and ambitious to get tied down, anyway."

Normally, I would agree with that statement from Midge, but for the first time in my adult life, I actually long to be tied to someone like Reeve. We're so perfectly matched in so many ways that I find myself yearning for his company, both in and out of the bedroom. This is a complete about-face in my philosophy on life and love.

Sadly, I don't have anyone to discuss these feelings with. Ford is definitely out, and he's the only person I would consider asking to talk this through with me.

Except maybe . . .

"There is someone, actually," I blurt out.

"Oh, do tell," Midge says excitedly, and now I understand. Midge has no girlfriends, either. She spends her time locked in her office, crusading for people's rights, and she's made it so much of her life that she's never left room for anything else.

Because I know her to be a very private person, and because I also know that she'll find no fault in the way I first got involved with Reeve, I decide to lay it all out for her.

And I don't pull any punches.

"I'm involved with the defense attorney in the *LaPietra* case. We've been sleeping together for a few weeks now."

Midge's eyes flare with shock but absolutely no censure. In fact, she's smiling deviously when she says, "You're kidding me."

"Not kidding." I tell her about my striptease in the elevator. She cackles gleefully. I tell her about him pulling my skirt up in the hallway, and she dramatically fans herself. I don't tell her the details of our sexual relationship, but I tell her that the night of the charity event was when I gave in and that we've been going at it pretty strong since then.

When I finish, Midge just shakes her head with a smirk. "My dear, dear Leary. You're turning out better than I ever hoped for. You remind me of . . . well, me."

"I take that as a compliment," I say with a grin. And then, because my taste buds are starting to go numb, I take another delicate sip of the whiskey.

Midge leans back into the couch and looks at me appraisingly. "So, is it just sex? Or is there something more?"

I shrug and lower my gaze to the glass. Running my finger down the diamond cuts on the bottom of the glass, I say, "I don't know. I wanted it to just be sex, but I think we're surpassing that."

"A love story brewing," Midge says and almost bounces on the cushion with excitement.

I cock an eyebrow at her.

"What?" she exclaims and then downs the rest of her whiskey. Standing up from the couch, she walks to her minibar, speaking at me over her shoulder. "I'm a romantic, believe it or not."

"It's hard to believe," I say truthfully. "You aren't involved in a relationship."

"No," she says sadly, "I'm not. I lost my one true love when Grant died, and I've never found anyone since. Of course, I don't expect to find love boning twenty-something-year-old law clerks, but it works for me for now."

I snicker, and I need to remember to tell Ford that this particular rumor—of the millions swirling around about dear, reclusive Midge—is true.

After pouring another drink, she comes back to sit on the couch. "The point is, please don't let any of the things I've taught you, any of the things I expect out of you, dissuade you from a relationship. When I tell you to use your female powers of persuasion to get ahead in the legal game, it doesn't mean I want you to sleep with every Tom, Dick, and Harry out there. It merely means you should be cognizant of all of your gifts and use them as you can."

"Well, I appreciate the sentiment, but I can assure you the only opponent I've ever slept with has been Reeve."

"And that right there should tell you something," Midge points out. "This is definitely more than just sex."

"Maybe," I hedge, but I don't allow myself to fully give in to that possibility. Reeve and I still have a very volatile case to get through. "We'll see. I need to just make it through Jenna's case before I can really explore what we have."

"Want my advice?" she asks, a twinkle in her eye, and I have to laugh because she's clearly enjoying this.

"Sure."

"Don't wait to explore those feelings. Fuck the case. That has nothing to do with you and Reeve. Open up and take a chance."

"But what if things get nasty? So far, we've worked well in opposition. Well, at least after that first motion. But still . . . this has all been the beginnings of the case. It won't be so nice during the trial—not when I have to get rough with his client and the experts."

"He's a big boy. He can handle it," Midge says with confidence.

"And what makes you so sure of that?"

"Because look what happened when you tore his client up in the deposition. He respected you for it. He's going to be able to do his job without taking advantage of the personal relationship, and you'll do the same, I'm sure."

Of course I'll do the same. I have no desire to use my sexual sway with Reeve to get me further in this case. I don't need it. But I am concerned that I might not be able to keep my personal feelings out of the way when things start to get nasty.

And they *will* get nasty. Medical malpractice trials are brutal, with both sides bare-knuckle brawling. There's too much money at risk not to go all-in. It will be Reeve's job to attack Jenna. It will be my job to attack Dr. Summerland.

Will we be able to open ourselves up to sex, emotion, and genuine affection after a hard day of trying to tear each other down?

It seems impossible to me, but not enough of a mountain that I'm not willing to try to climb it.

And yeah . . . I still want to climb Reeve Holloway.

CHAPTER 12
REEVE

Chad Pounds, the managing partner of Battle Carnes, drones on and on, reporting on the final numbers for the previous quarter. He makes all of the partners and associate attorneys jam into a conference room three times too small to hold all of us at the table and insists on disclosing the income that each person brought into the firm's coffers.

This serves two functions. First, it praises and hopefully encourages those top earners to work harder, causing their already inflated egos to swell and puff some more. Big egos and overinflated senses of self are what drive money.

Or so the partners seem to think.

The second thing it accomplishes is to shame and humiliate the lower earners. Having their huge egos dinged and battered is a surefire way to get them motivated so they'll earn more.

Or so the partners seem to think.

I think it's all horseshit, so I tend to tune Chad out when he gets on his high horse. My earnings fall near the top, but that's because, based on my experience, I tend to get the larger cases that earn more money. Simple mathematics, really, so I keep my ego—which is healthy enough—firmly encased and untouched.

While Chad focuses his gaze on one of the associates, Teddy Baker, who immediately shrinks because he didn't have that great a quarter, my mind turns to more pleasant things.

Mainly Leary Michaels.

And fucking Leary.

And holding her at night.

And laughing with her.

And cooking her dinner and feeding it to her in bed.

And playing with her and my toys.

Okay, need to think of something else or I'll be sporting an embarrassing boner in front of my peers.

But damn, she's the perfect woman. It's as if God created her just for me. So perfect, in fact, for the first time in my adult life I feel like getting religious and praying to the Big Guy in gratitude.

I've seen Leary every night for the past two weeks, with the exception of one night when she had to work late to prepare for a deposition. I tried to talk her into coming over to my house to work there, but she was having none of it. In fact, her exact words were, "Seriously, Reeve. Do you honestly think I'd get any work done with you in the same room with me?"

Christ, I loved hearing that.

Loved hearing how much she enjoyed me and my company and my dick.

Early on in our relationship, we easily gave in to the realization that being fuck buddies would best be served by fucking on a daily basis when possible. But thereafter, our relationship sort of morphed and settled into something more.

We went out to dinner. She helped me give Mr. Chico Taco a bath, and we laughed ourselves silly when he bounded out of the tub and ran crazy through the house, throwing soap everywhere. We call each other during the day just to chat, and once she breathily told me that she couldn't wait to see me that night, and there was such feeling in it, my heart squeezed. I texted her a dirty joke, and she texted me back a picture of her boobs beautifully squeezed into a black lace bra with one hand pinching a nipple through the material.

I had to lock my office door and jack off to the picture, I was so aroused.

Yes, there's no doubt. We're not just fuck buddies. We're in a relationship. It's not something we've admitted to each other, and Leary still teases me about Vanessa and that she could be my fuck buddy, too, if I wanted. I didn't like hearing that, so I tied her facedown on my bed and spanked the shit out of her, then I fucked her hard. That didn't dissuade Leary from making that comment again, and in hindsight, I now realize that she enjoyed getting spanked so much that she brings Vanessa up quite a bit on purpose.

The one thing I haven't been able to do is get close to Leary. She knows quite a bit about me, as we've spent long nights talking while we lie exhausted in bed after some amazing sex. She knows about my childhood in Vermont, my crazy days of undergrad at Penn State, and my slightly less crazy days at Harvard Law School. She knows about my law school mate and best friend, Cal Carson, who practices in New York, and she knows my parents are still happily married and living in an old farmhouse in the valley of the Green Mountains. I've told her my dreams and aspirations as an attorney, and I even almost grew a vagina by telling her that I adopted Mr. Chico Taco because I was lonely and it seemed easier than having a girlfriend.

Leary knows a lot about me, and yes, I've come to know a little about her. While I paint vivid details of my life, I tend to get fade-to-black images from her. I know she grew up poor and put herself through college and law school. Her mom lives in eastern North Carolina, but she doesn't get to see her often because of her crazy work schedule. I asked about her father once, and she simply said she never knew him and then the conversation was closed.

Leary definitely keeps her private life private, and while I think we're developing a deeper relationship, the one thing I don't know is if Leary feels the same shift of the tides. It's not something we've discussed, but I do intend to bring it up at some point.

The main problem in our relationship is the *LaPietra* case. True to our word, we leave the case out of the bedroom. I've never brought up her relationship with Jenna again, and she's never spoken a word to me about it. I'm dying to know more, though, because when it boils right down to it, Leary has her heart invested in this case, and I am bound and determined to steal victory from her. This, in my opinion, spells disaster for us down the road—a thought that has me slightly nauseated at times.

The trial date is less than a month away, and as it looms closer, I feel like there's a giant bomb ticking down, moving us closer and closer to what I'm thinking could be the end of us.

And that is not something I want.

My thoughts are interrupted when Chad announces the meeting is over and the attorneys start pouring out of the stuffy conference room. When I move to the door, Chad calls out, "Reeve . . . stay a minute. We want to talk to you about the *LaPietra* case."

I nod and take one of the vacated chairs at the end of the table and wait for the room to clear.

When everyone is gone, Chad moves down closer to me, and the three litigation partners, Harry Bent, Lacy Carnes, and Gill Kratzenburg, do the same.

"The *LaPietra* trial is set for next month and we wanted to get an update on it, see how you think it's going," Chad says.

"And do you think it will settle?" Gill asks. "Obviously you know it will be better for us if it doesn't settle but goes all the way."

Of course I know that, I think drily. An early settlement means no more billable hours from this case. Pushing toward a full-blown trial means more riches for Battle Carnes's coffers. I have to suppress the urge to roll my eyes. It's the one thing that bothers me about this law firm—the quest for justice often falls prey to greed, but there's not a damn thing I can do about it. I'm a paid employee and I do what I'm told.

"We have mediation set next week," I tell the partners. "I think Summerland should put an offer on the table. The plaintiff, Jenna LaPietra, makes a sympathetic witness, and Dr. Summerland comes off too arrogant."

Lacy Carnes snorts. "She's a stripper, for God's sake. How sympathetic can she be? No jury is going to award her money."

"She's a mother with a severely autistic child who strips to earn money to care for him, and now can't do that because her breasts are horrifically mangled," I say calmly. "I think that's pretty sympathetic."

Lacy harrumphs but Gill backs me . . . somewhat. "Stripping is legal, Lacy. I don't see that having enough power to turn the jury against her."

"Has the investigator found anything else we can use?" Lacy asks, and my heart drops and thuds in my stomach.

I'd been dreading this question, and dreading even more the answer I have to give, as the investigator we hired has indeed found something that he sent me just yesterday. I waited to share it with TransBenefit because I was hoping I could find some legal research that would prevent the evidence from coming in.

And with professional guilt, I realize I was doing that because I knew this was going to hurt Jenna LaPietra's case, and in turn, I knew it was going to really hurt Leary.

"I just got his report yesterday," I say after clearing my throat. "There is something we can use."

All four partners lean forward with evil gleams in their eyes, and in that moment, I already start to mourn the loss of Leary. Because with this information, there's no doubt I'm probably going to lose her.

"The investigator found three former employees who knew of the prostitution that was going on inside the club. They quit because they didn't want any part of it. They'll all testify that Jenna LaPietra sold her body for money."

"Do they have actual knowledge?" Chad asks quickly.

"Her admission," I say with another drop in my stomach.

"Excellent," Lacy says with a lecherous grin. "Admission of a party opponent gets it past hearsay. I'd say that was money well spent on the investigator."

Yes, this is the really bad news. Overhearing someone say something does not mean it can come into evidence. It's generally prohibited as hearsay. However, there's an exception to that rule if an opponent in a case makes a statement that can be used as evidence against them.

These witnesses' testimonies are coming into evidence.

"Use it," Gill commands.

I nod in acquiescence because I can't say no. I can't say no because not only is my boss giving me a direct order, but my oath as an attorney demands that I represent my clients to the best of my ability, which means using all available weapons in my arsenal.

"I'll amend our discovery answers to provide the witnesses to opposing counsel," I say, and then hold my breath to see what they'll do.

This is a bad legal tactic, but one I'm hoping I can get away with. At the very least, I can give Leary a heads-up, and perhaps she can find something on these witnesses to discredit them. In revealing this, I'm doing something highly unethical. I've got the ability to destroy Leary's case, and maybe *her* in the process, but I just can't find it within me to care that I might be crossing a line. I'm determined to help her in any way I can, although she'll probably never know of my efforts.

"No." Harry Bent finally pipes into the conversation. He's the most brilliant of the partners sitting around this table, and I'm not surprised that he's the one who's going to ruin my plans of helping Leary. "Don't disclose the witnesses. Call them as surprise witnesses after Jenna LaPietra testifies."

This sucks and is what I was afraid was going to happen.

Ordinarily, I'm required to identify all my potential witnesses to Leary. The exception is a witness who's called in to rebut the other side's evidence. This can be sprung as a surprise.

Harry is commanding me to ask Jenna point-blank on the stand if she engaged in illegal acts of prostitution. She, of course, will deny it. Then I will parade these three witnesses in front of her and Leary, who will watch while they sit on the stand and call Jenna a whore. The judge is going to let me do it, too.

I feel sick to my stomach, but I nod in agreement. "Sounds good," I mutter.

"This is fantastic," Lacy chortles over the possibility of humiliating a nice woman. "And this is so good, you need to recommend to the insurance carrier that they don't offer a fucking dime to that woman. This needs to go all the way."

She's right, of course, because honestly, this evidence is so good they shouldn't offer money. This evidence is so good that it could completely prejudice the jury.

I have no clue if Jenna LaPietra prostituted herself, but frankly, I don't give a shit. Personally, I think it's irrelevant, and I can see how a desperate mother would do something like that. Unfortunately, though, my feelings don't seem to matter, and I've been given a direct order to exploit this evidence to our favor.

I want to vomit.

"I think I'll sit second chair on this case with you, Reeve," Gill says, almost cackling in glee. "A case this big should have two attorneys on it, and that way we can bill double."

Asshole. Greedy fucking asshole.

A weariness overtakes me. For the first time since meeting Leary, I actually regret said meeting. I regret getting involved with someone that was supposed to only be a casual fuck, and because she's so amazing, I now have feelings involved. I regret being the biggest idiot on the face of the earth for not recognizing that it's impossible to be in bed with your enemy and not understand that someone is going to get hurt.

Unfortunately, Leary is under my skin now. She's in my blood. While the appropriate thing would be to cut things off with her, I find myself too selfish to do so. Nope. I'm going to ride the Leary train all the way into the station, until I call those witnesses into court and destroy everything we're starting to build.

"Let me get this straight—you're fucking your opposing counsel?" Cal asks.

I have no clue why he's stunned. He knows I'm no angel. He knows that would never stop me.

"Yes," I grit out.

"And you have feelings for her?" he asks, stunned again.

I understand the disbelief. I've made it this far without a single long-term relationship. The fact I've been seeing Leary for three weeks has him perplexed.

"Yes," I say in a softer tone, because I most definitely have feelings for this woman.

"You are fucked," Cal says sympathetically.

I told him the entire sordid story, starting with meeting Leary in the elevator. I had to wait while Cal laughed hysterically, proclaiming that Leary might be his favorite person ever, even though he'd never met her.

When he finally stopped laughing, I told him the rest. I told him every bit of it and how in just the last several weeks, I've gone from fuck buddy to having feelings.

This he did not laugh about, because he knows this is serious stuff. The reason I called Cal is not just because he's my best friend, but because he's a true monogamous romantic at heart. He's the type of guy who always dreamed of a fifty-year marriage with adoring children and grandchildren. While I've seen him have his share of flings and one-night stands, the truth is that Cal has always been looking for The One.

He found her, too, not that long ago, and I expect to be attending Cal and Macy's wedding in New York before too much longer.

"I guess I don't understand the big deal," Cal says thoughtfully. "She loses the case. So what? That happens."

"Apparently not to her," I mutter. "But that's not the problem. The problem is that she's tied to this case emotionally. She has some personal connection to the plaintiff. It's going to destroy her if she loses."

"What's the connection?" Cal asks curiously.

"No clue," I admit with frustration.

He's silent a minute, then he gently says, "Reeve, how much do you even know about this woman?"

I understand what he's saying. How bothered can I be when I don't even know what the true stake is to Leary? I don't know this because she hasn't opened up to me. He's saying that maybe I'm still in fuck buddy–dom and don't realize it.

Taking a deep breath, I let it out slowly. "I know enough about her to know I want to know more."

"Got it," Cal says in immediate understanding, then hesitantly, "If she's that important, maybe you should tell her what you know."

I shake my head and rub the bridge of my nose, because he has managed to zero in on the source of my anxiety. "I could lose my bar license if I did that," I tell him, which he already knows. "And honestly . . . she's not *that* important."

It hurts me to say that, but it's true. I like her . . . a lot. But not enough to ruin my career.

"Understood," Cal says. "Then maybe you should break it off."

Yeah, that's not going to happen, either. I'm too addicted to her right now. I'd sooner cut off my right arm. "I'm not willing to do that, either."

"Then you are well and truly fucked, my friend," Cal says sadly.

"Don't I know it," I agree.

So, Cal ultimately doesn't provide any insight that helps, but more or less validates the conclusion to which I had already come. I'm going to keep this information to myself, for the sanctity of my law license. I'm going to let this play out and see how things continue to develop with Leary and me. And if our feelings continue to grow stronger, I have to hope to God that Leary won't hold it against me when I destroy her case.

CHAPTER 13

LEARY

"I'm not sure how it's possible," Reeve says as he stares at me across my kitchen table, dinner having been fan-freaking-tastic. "But you actually get more beautiful every time I see you."

I snicker as I pick up my wineglass. Waving it at him, I laugh, "Save the flattery, Mr. Holloway. You're going to get laid tonight."

I expect him to laugh with me, because I think I'm witty and charming, and he usually thinks so, too. Instead, his face falls sober and his eyes burn into me. "I'm not flattering you, Leary. I'm telling you the God's honest truth. You are more beautiful every time I see you."

A stillness overcomes me and I swallow hard. I set the wineglass down and return his stare. "How do you do that?"

"Do what?" he asks, his head tilted to the side.

"Make me feel like the most beautiful woman in the world. The most special. The most desired."

"Because you are," he says, and the tight leash I've kept on my heart the last few weeks shudders, loosens, and then falls away.

His words are genuine, with not an ounce of ulterior motive in them. I can tell, because I've come to know this man fairly well during our time together. He truly believes that about me, and it's a fucking revelation. No one else has ever felt that way about me before.

"We're not in fuck buddy–dom anymore, are we?" I ask him.

Reeve stands from the table, walks over to me, and pulls me from my chair. Bending down, he sweeps me up in his arms and starts to carry me toward my bedroom. "I don't think we ever really were, baby."

He takes me to my room and somehow manages to remove my clothes and his before I even know what's happening. He does it slowly, turning it from our normal frenzied fumbling to something sweetly seductive.

Then I'm on my back in the middle of my bed, and he's on top of me, hard and heavy between my legs and content to just hold my face and kiss me softly. He does this for so long that I seem to lapse into a contented alternate reality, focusing on the feel of his lips and the texture and taste of his tongue. I imagine this is what a drug addiction feels like, so damn good that you would give up your very soul just to have a little bit more.

Reeve's lips move from my mouth to my jaw, down to past my collarbone, where he takes his time with my breasts. I know Reeve is a self-admitted breast man, which makes him an ironic choice to defend Jenna's case. But normally he's devouring me, biting and pinching to get the most arousal out of me. Tonight, however, he's gentle and careful, softly swirling his tongue with a humming noise in the back of his throat. It makes me want to arch my back and purr like a kitten in his arms.

His fingers work like butterflies between my legs, pulsing flutters across my most sensitive parts. He builds me up slowly, like a dull fire catching its first big flame from a tiny gust of wind. Then the fire takes hold, leaps, and fans, and with one perfect touch of his thumb against me, I come apart in a slow burst of magical fireworks within my body.

It's the most beautiful orgasm I've ever had, and I know I'll never forget it.

Pushing up on his elbows, Reeve hovers above me. His eyes are serious, a deep ocean of unstated emotion. "Tell me it's okay not to put on a condom," he says quietly, his voice husky with desire. "Tell me it's okay to fuck you bare."

"It's okay with me," I tell him quietly as my hand comes up to touch his face. My fingers graze along his temple, push back into his hair. He turns his head slightly, pushing it against my palm in a display of needful affection.

Nothing else needs to be said about the condom issue. The minute he asked me if it was okay, I trusted him enough to know he's telling me that he's clean. When I told him it was okay with me, that meant I was protected and clean, and he took me at face value, because he proceeds to fill me with his massive length in one sweetly sublime thrust.

Reeve slowly moves within me, leaning to the side on one elbow, his other arm locked out straight to give him more leverage. His face hovers over me, lips just inches from mine. I can smell the wine on his breath and hear the ecstasy rumbling in his chest.

We stare at each other, boldly, candidly, leaving no room for walls or barriers to the feelings that have developed. I feel, in this moment, closer to him than any man before in my life.

Reeve rolls his hips, pumps into me carefully, drawing out every bit of feeling and nuance as our flesh slides against each other. He makes love to me, all the while staring into my eyes. It's a connection that starts to cement us together hard, and I know when both of us come, it won't be broken.

At least not by any ordinary means.

My climax starts building again, and I can tell Reeve's is, too, as his hips move a little faster. He lays his weight down on me, grabbing my hands with his and pulling my arms above my head. His fingers lace with mine, and I raise my knees up to his ribs to accommodate him deeper.

Both of our bodies now undulate against each other, slick with moisture, our chests heaving from exertion. Because Reeve's body is flat against mine, every grind of his pelvis against me causes deep pulses of pleasure to fire throughout my body.

With one extradeep push, the buildup of pressure tears free, and I'm falling apart. I do so with a soft cry, arching my neck and biting at my lip.

I hear Reeve say, "So fucking perfect," and then with one more hard thrust, he starts shaking. His head falls to my shoulder, and he lets out a soft groan of release while his cock jerks inside me as he comes.

My arms wrap around his neck, and I hug him tight as we continue to shiver against each other. This has been the most perfect sexual experience of my life, because I actually opened up my heart, and it made all the difference in the world.

I think I should have figured out after that first night we slept together at his house that Reeve could never be just a fuck buddy. It's one thing to have sex. It's quite another to sleep all night with a man. There's something intimate in drifting off to dreamland, wrapped up tight in someone's arms.

It's not something I had with Ford. Ford and I were truly about the sex. We were friends, of course, and could talk about many things. But we weren't snugglers. We didn't express ordinary affection, or tell each other our deepest secrets while sharing a pillow.

From that first night, I learned that Reeve *is* a snuggler. He likes to be wrapped around me when he sleeps. He claimed it was only because he was used to snuggling up with Mr. Chico Taco, but I seriously doubt that, as the massive dog has his own gigantic bed on the floor. And poor

Chico. On the nights that Reeve stays with me, he has to suffer with sleeping over at Vanessa's house. This I feel bad about, for Mr. Taco's sake, but secretly I'm pleased, because every time Reeve asks her to take him, he always tells her he's staying at my house for the night.

Petty, I know, but I love it.

Right now, we aren't exactly in full snuggle, time-to-go-to-sleep mode. Instead, Reeve is flat on his back and I'm pressed into his side, my head lying on his shoulder. My right leg is twined with his, slightly bent and raised so I can feel his softening cock against my knee, still wet with his release. His arm curled under me strokes my hip while my fingers play with the patch of trimmed hair that surrounds his dick.

"Looks like we're back on the battlefield tomorrow," I say absently. It's the first time I've willingly brought up Jenna's case to Reeve.

"Yup," he says. "We should probably do a lot of glaring at each other across the table. You know, just so people don't think we're fucking each other."

I snicker and give a playful tug on the hairs my fingers are skimming through. "I'm sure we'll both conduct ourselves professionally."

Reeve is silent and I concentrate on the thrum of his heartbeat under my ear. Tomorrow is the court-ordered mediation for Jenna's case. All cases filed in superior court are ordered into mediation, where the parties sit down and try to settle the case voluntarily. If that doesn't work, we start preparing for trial.

"I've recommended they make an offer to settle," Reeve says, and my fingers still because he's giving me information he probably shouldn't. I don't say anything, though, because I don't want him to feel any obligation to divulge anything to me.

"Even if they take my advice, the amount they put on the table won't be enough," he says as an afterthought.

"Is there any amount of money that will make it right for Jenna?" I ask rhetorically.

"Not for what she's been through," he says with compassion.

My heart zings in joy that Reeve has said that—not because I think it will help my case, but because he's a truly good guy and despite the fact he's working for the Antichrist, he has a heart. I saw it when he looked at Jenna's deformities with compassion, and I can't help but think someone like him would be better serving the cosmic universe by working on our side of the law rather than doing insurance defense.

"Tell me about Midge Payne," Reeve says out of the blue, changing what was a precarious subject for us anyway. "I'm dying to know if she's real or an urban legend."

I chuckle softly. "I can assure you she's real."

"There are so many rumors floating around the bar," Reeve says.

"Well, I know a mixture of truth and rumor, probably. Let's see . . . she started working for Grant Knight in 1977 when she graduated from law school at Duke. She was twenty-four and he was forty-four. Even though he was married, he seduced Midge and they became lovers. She made partner in 1978 and the firm became Knight & Payne."

"Saucy wench," Reeve says with a chuckle.

"Right?" I agree. "Anyway, this I do know to be true, because Midge has told me on more than one occasion. Grant taught Midge how to use all of her assets, especially coming up in a legal world when women were the minority in our profession. That included not only her legal knowledge but her wit and her sensuality."

"That was very progressive of him," Reeve butts in.

"Agreed," I say with a smile. "Unfortunately, Grant died eight years later at age fifty-two from a heart attack. Rumor is Midge was having sex with him at the time."

"What a way to go."

"The best way to go. Rumor also has it that Midge was devastated when he died, that she truly loved him even though he never divorced his wife to be with her. It's said she's never had a serious relationship since then but that she does take a lot of lovers—some men, some women. There's a really kinky rumor running around that she's actually fucking one of the law clerks in the criminal division. He's only twenty-four or something, but apparently hung like a racehorse."

"She sounds unbelievable," Reeve says. "Although much of that is rumor, so how can you know?"

"Well, what little interaction I've had with her, I can believe every bit of it. She's the most progressive, enlightened female attorney I've ever met. I aspire to be like her."

"Hopefully not the part where she takes a lot of lovers, right?" he teases.

"Definitely not," I tell him. "I'm very satisfied with my current man."

That earns me an affectionate squeeze from Reeve, and I squeeze him back for good measure.

"I will tell you a true story about Midge, though." I'm in a sharing mood for some reason. "She didn't interview me for the job at her firm. Her cousin Danny did. But Midge was watching from a video monitor and feeding him questions. They had one special question they asked each applicant, and apparently I gave the best answer, and that earned me the job."

"I suspected you were brilliant," he says as his hand slides down to caress my ass.

Mmm. Nice.

"I'll never forget meeting her on my first day. I looked horrible, so dowdy and uninteresting. Midge encouraged me to explore my feminine side. To use my other attributes to help get me further in the game."

"Well, first, I can't imagine you ever looking dowdy, and second, you're saying I have Midge Payne to thank for your little striptease in the elevator?"

"You should send her flowers or something," I mutter.

"I definitely should," he replies. Then as an afterthought he asks, "What was the interview question that you nailed?"

"Oh, that," I say as I lean up on my elbow so I can look at him. He's grinning up at me, completely enjoying my loose lips, because I normally reveal very little about my life. I find I like this sharing thing. With great flourish, I say, "Danny asked if there was ever a scenario in which I'd be willing to put my law license at stake. Apparently, every single candidate answered with a resounding no."

Reeve's smile fizzles and dies. His jaw goes tight. "And how did you answer?"

He clearly knows I answered the opposite, but he wants the details. And for some reason, I feel like he's not going to like my answer. It was a simple question, but the answer was a bit more complex. I spent a lot of time and money earning my law license, and there are very specific things I can do to lose it. Law schools pound into their students the fear of letting their ethics waver and getting in trouble with the bar. The loss of my law license would be catastrophic, so this is something I do take seriously.

But as with most everything in life, there are exceptions. Even though I know he really won't like my answer, I give it to him anyway. "I laid out several scenarios where I would jeopardize it."

"Like what?"

"I'm not sure of my exact words . . . it was so long ago. But I think I said I'd do it if someone's life was at stake."

For some reason, Reeve's body seems to relax with that answer, and his smile starts to form again.

"I also said I'd do it if justice could prevail, as long as it didn't hurt anyone else." His smile slides again, which presses me to ask, "Does that bother you?"

"No," he says hurriedly. "It's just . . . I don't like the thought of you putting your license at risk. That's your livelihood. Your life. It's never worth the risk."

Reeve's eyes are wide and worried, and yet he's not truly getting me. And that just won't do. After what we just shared when he was making love to me, I need to make sure he gets me.

I swing a leg over Reeve, straddling his pelvis. Placing my hands on his stomach, I peer down at him, his face lit up by the bedside lamp. "Remember I told you a little bit about my childhood? Grew up poor, yada, yada, put myself through school, blah, blah, blah?"

He nods at me, his hands coming up to stroke my knees resting at either side of his rib cage. "I expect there's a little bit more than yada, yada, and blah, blah, blah."

"There is," I tell him. "I lived in a dusty trailer park in a tin can with a leaky roof and feral dogs fighting in the dirt streets outside. We subsisted mostly on ramen noodles, and on a good day our elderly neighbor would throw us a few veggies from her garden to go with it. All my clothes came from the thrift store, and by that I mean I had one pair of jeans, a few shirts, and maybe three pairs of underwear. The lack of clothes meant doing laundry more often, and by laundry I mean using the kitchen sink to wash them. We didn't have money for birthday presents or Christmas, and I didn't even taste my first bite of steak until I was in college and my boyfriend took me out to dinner one night. I thought I'd died and gone to heaven. My childhood was rough. Wouldn't wish it on any child. I was teased and bullied because I was poor, and the only pleasure I really got in life was escaping into books through the school library."

Reeve doesn't say anything, but his eyes burn with anger and sympathy.

"I had it rough, but despite having hardly anything at all, the one thing I did have was love. My mom provided me with so much love, none of the other stuff really mattered."

"I don't know what to say," Reeve says in a raspy voice, his hands tightening on my knees.

I continue my story. "My mom worked odd jobs. She didn't have a high school education, having dropped out of school after falling in with a bad crowd who liked to party hard. She got pregnant with me, and I don't know my father because my mom doesn't know who he is. He was a passing face, a faded memory from a night when she was so high on drugs she didn't get his name and didn't insist he use a condom."

"Jesus," Reeve whispers.

"But she loved me. More than anything. She gave up drugs and alcohol when she got pregnant with me, never used again. But work was hard to find in eastern, rural North Carolina. We had good times that would provide the occasional mac and cheese. We had bad times, though, when she was out of work, and by bad I mean I would go days without eating unless it was a school lunch. My mom had choices to make. She'd have just enough money to pay the electricity bill, and during the winter, we had to have heat, so that meant no food. We were always giving up something to get something else."

Reeve's hands leave my knees and travel up my arms, stroking me with reassurance as I continue my story.

"I remember a few times that I was so hungry I couldn't stop crying, which would make my mom cry." I take a deep breath, push it out, and bare a very personal fact about my life. "She'd have men come over to our trailer. They would disappear into her back bedroom, and I would hear noises coming out of there and the bed knocking against the wall. I was too young to really know what it meant, but I know that when the men left, my mom would have money and she could buy me food."

"Fuck," Reeve mutters.

"You understand what I'm saying?" I ask him quietly.

He nods, his eyes swimming in sadness.

"My mom would have done anything, and I mean anything, to nourish me. There is nothing she wouldn't have sacrificed, nothing she wouldn't have risked, to try to keep me fed and sheltered. She did that because she loved me."

"She loved you very much," Reeve murmurs, lacing his fingers through mine.

"She taught me my most important lesson in life," I tell him so he starts to understand where I'm coming from. "There are some people you risk everything for. So going back to the question Danny asked me in my interview . . . yes, in a heartbeat I'd put my license at risk for my mother or someone I loved. It's a no-brainer to me."

Reeve knifes upward in the bed, his arms banding around me and pulling me close. His mouth crushes onto mine, and he kisses me so deeply I know I'll still feel it tomorrow. He seems desperate, as if he's trying to convey his understanding with his tongue and teeth. My arms wrap around his neck, and I feel him start to swell underneath my bottom.

Pulling away from the deep connection of the kiss, he leaves his lips resting gently against mine. "I think you might be the most amazing person I've ever met."

"Do you get me now?" I whisper, my lips moving against his.

"Yeah . . . I get you now," he says and then kisses me again.

CHAPTER 14

REEVE

I'm sitting in Leary's large conference room, flipping through my presentation. I was the first to arrive this morning for the mediation because I always like to take extra time to set up and skim through my notes. Any moment I'm expecting the others, including Leary and Jenna as well as Tom Collier and retired judge Peter Goetge, who will be the one who will direct and mediate any potential negotiations today.

I don't expect that Tom will offer much money, so this is probably all just a formality. After today, it's crunch time.

We're just shy of a month from the trial, and I'm starting to get stressed.

Ordinarily, trials don't cause me any worry. Some lawyers get physically ill, the prospect of standing in front of twelve strangers more than they can bear. Add in an irate judge, and the anxiety level increases tenfold. Add in high-stakes money, and some lawyers have to medicate.

Not me.

I love the adrenaline rush, the spotlight, and the competition of it all.

Normally.

Not with the *LaPietra* case, though.

I'm getting stressed because every day that the trial looms closer, it means that Leary is going to find out just how devious I can be in the courtroom. When she learns of my deviousness, and when it causes her case to fail, she's going to hate me for it.

There's not a day that hasn't gone by when I don't argue with myself over what to do. Half the time I think I should just throw my professional ethics out the window and divulge to her what I know about Jenna. The other half of the time, I keep hoping that something else will happen to save me from it all. Like, maybe a comet will strike the earth. Or TransBenefit will fold into bankruptcy. Or Jenna will hit the lottery and this case won't matter anymore.

Ironically, the only real thing that has kept me somewhat sane has been Leary herself. Every moment I'm with her is complete and absolute escape from the harsh realities of my job. I don't think about anything else. I concentrate only on her. I want to live in a world where there's only Leary and me . . . and Mr. Chico Taco, too.

All silly pipe dreams.

So I continue on, taking advantage of every precious second with this beautiful, sexy, and complex woman.

Luckily for me, there are a lot of seconds, minutes, and hours when we're together. We've fallen into a natural routine. Leary has started staying at my house every night, mainly so Chico doesn't have to go stay with Vanessa. This has been at Leary's insistence, and I thought it was very sweet of her to consider his feelings. But then she did something one day that I'll never forget.

I walked into my living room. She was sitting on my couch with Chico's head in her lap. She was rubbing his ears and making cooing noises at him. She bent over and whispered in his ear, "You love me more than Vanessa, don't you, buddy?"

I had to turn around and walk back into the kitchen and place a kitchen towel in my mouth so she couldn't hear me laughing. It had become clear to me that Leary was staying at my house to gain favor with my dog and turn his allegiance from Vanessa over to her.

Fucking adorable.

After that night several weeks ago when she told me about her mother and the things she did for Leary's well-being, things changed between us. She opened up to me, I accepted the gift, and from that moment forward, I entered into a committed relationship with her. Not just in a monogamous sense, but committed to this woman's emotional well-being.

Everything about her became important to me. Every touch from her, every sound out of her mouth, every nuance of her day. It all became mine. I possessed her and she consumed me. But for this stupid fucking trial, my existence would be absolutely perfect.

Unfortunately, Leary did not stay with me last night because she had work to do. So did I, for that matter. In fact, we were both holed up in our respective offices, working on the *LaPietra* case because we're holding the mediation today.

Fuck, I missed her in my bed last night. She's fast becoming a necessity to me. While I was working, I couldn't help reaching out to her.

I sent her a text around 10:00 p.m. Still working?

Her response was immediate. Yup. Hey. What page of the deposition of Dr. Summerland did he admit that he pulled a double on-call shift before Jenna's surgery?

I had to laugh before I responded. I'm not helping you prepare your case against me. Bad girl.

She wrote me back a smiley face but nothing more.

I went back to work, finishing up a few notes on my PowerPoint presentation for the mediation. I played around with font sizes and tweaked a few sentences. But something started niggling at me.

Why was Leary focused on Dr. Summerland's on-call shifts before the surgery? I mean, all doctors worked hard hours, went with little sleep. Even surgeons.

Clearly she was searching for some type of angle, and I guessed she was going to try to attack him at trial on not being fresh enough to do the surgery. But she needed more than just circumstantial evidence that he might have been too tired after the on-call shifts. I didn't remember her asking him any actual detailed questions about his stamina during his deposition, so maybe she'd found something else.

I put aside my mediation materials and pulled out a binder that held all of Dr. Summerland's surgical records, including the hospital nursing notes. I started flipping through them again. I read everything, word for word, yet nothing jumped out at me.

But then I saw it.

A small, barely legible note from one of the nurses: *12:18 p.m. Dr. S and R.V. step out.*

Then another note. *12:32 p.m. Dr. S back. Surg in progress.*

It was a bit odd. Could be nothing. I mean, sometimes doctors needed a break. As long as the anesthesiologist stayed in the operating room, there's nothing inherently wrong with that.

But what if it did mean something? What if Leary found out something?

I flipped through the notes and read all of the nurses' names that were involved in pre- and post-op, as well as the surgical nurses. *R.V.* was Rhonda Valasquez, one of the surgical nurses. I put a task on my calendar to try to interview these nurses and make sure there wasn't something going on of which I should be aware. We hadn't intended to call the nurses as witnesses, but I have no clue if Leary is going to.

It was probably nothing to worry about, but I needed to check it out so I wasn't caught by surprise at the trial. Surprises were not good, and yet . . . I was going to be springing a big one on Leary.

My stomach rolls and cramps.

The conference room door swings open, and my stomach unclenches and my chest starts to squeeze as Leary walks in. I mask my true feelings, instead standing up and shaking her hand professionally. So weird, acting like we're only professional colleagues, considering she gave me an amazing blow job morning before last.

Right after she finished swallowing that morning, knowing we wouldn't see each other again until today, she said, "That was just to give you something to dream about, baby."

I groaned and kissed her hard, but we were both running late, so I couldn't repay the favor.

I will tonight and told her as much.

Peter Goetge walks in right behind, and we all sit around and make small talk while we wait for the insurance adjuster, Tom Collier, to arrive.

Small talk continues for another fifteen minutes, and Peter regales us with a funny case he mediated last week. I keep half an ear on him, the other part of my mind occupied with Tom Collier. He's the guy with the checkbook and the final say-so if his company will offer any money. Not only that, he's required by law to be here. All parties are.

When Peter finishes his story, I pull my phone out and hold it up. "I'm going to give Tom a call. Find out when he'll be here. I'm sorry he's running late."

Peter gives a good-natured smile, and Leary just cocks a beautiful eyebrow at me, causing my cock to thump like a well-trained puppy.

I dial Tom and he answers on the third ring. "Collier."

"Where are you?" I ask in a low voice. "Mediation was supposed to start fifteen minutes ago."

"The *LaPietra* mediation?" he asks.

"Yeah, the *LaPietra* mediation," I growl. Fucking moron.

"I'm not coming," he says matter-of-factly. "I'm not going to offer anything, so no use in wasting my time with a trip there."

I glance up at Peter and Leary, who are watching me with curiosity. I cover the phone and apologize, "Excuse me a minute. I need to step out."

When I close the conference room door behind me, I walk a few paces down the hall and growl, "What the fuck, Tom? You have to come. It's ordered by the court."

"But I'm not offering anything," he points out.

"Doesn't matter. You know this. You have to come and at least sit down at the table."

"Well, I'm not. The weather's too nice today, and I've got a round of golf scheduled in an hour."

Sighing in frustration, I already start thinking about how I'm going to handle Leary when she blows her stack over this. "Tom, Miss Michaels is going to be livid. She'll file a motion for sanctions, and the judge will grant it."

"That bitch better not. I showed her courtesy by not filing a motion against her. We're even."

"That's what this is about? About you getting even with her?" I ask in astonishment.

"That's the gist of it," he says smugly. "Now, go in there, do your job, and tell them no offer."

He hangs up on me, which causes my blood to boil. Shoving my phone in my pocket, I walk back into the conference room, feeling the proverbial noose around my neck.

After shutting the door, I turn around and place my hands on the back of one of the conference room chairs. Looking at Leary, I say, "I'm sorry. Tom Collier isn't coming."

"Does he understand he's under court order?" Peter asks in a deep voice, letting no one forget he sat on the bench for twenty years before becoming a mediator and deserves respect.

"Yes, sir," I say apologetically, shooting Leary another glance. Her lips are flattened out and her eyes are icy.

Peter pulls out a form from his briefcase and uncaps his pen. "I'm assuming, then, that they are unwilling to make an offer?"

"That's correct," I say, my gaze flicking back and forth between the two of them.

"Well, I'll just go ahead and report that this case has been impassed," Peter says as he starts to fill out the form before him.

"With all due respect, Peter," Leary says as she stands from her chair. "You cannot report an impasse. An impasse only comes when the parties all meet and cannot come to a resolution. Mr. Collier did not show up, thus there has not been a meeting."

"But his counsel is conveying there will be no offer," Peter points out.

"And yet, he is doing so without having seen the benefit of my presentation. Who knows? Maybe I would have shown Mr. Collier something that would induce him to make an offer. We'll never know, though, will we, since he didn't bother to show up."

Peter sighs and puts the form away. Leary is right. Technically, all parties have to be here before an impasse can be called. Technically, she has the right to present her evidence to try to persuade TransBenefit to make an offer.

"Miss Michaels," Peter says with authority, "you are accurately stating the letter of the law, but what good will come of it? Judge Henry will just order Mr. Collier to the table at a later date, he won't make an offer, and you'll be in the same position you are in now."

"Again," Leary says with surety, "with all due respect, the difference is that I spent over fourteen hours yesterday preparing for this mediation to present my case. My hourly rate is three hundred dollars, so that is forty-two hundred dollars in legal fees I've lost out on when I could have been doing something else had I known he wouldn't show up. I also talked to all three of my experts on the phone yesterday to confirm their opinions, and trust me, doctors bill more than I do. I expect I'm out a good ten thousand just in one day's preparation for this mediation. I expect you to report Mr. Collier didn't show up so I can ask the court to sanction him for that amount."

Peter sighs again, this time without as much gusto, because he knows Leary is right. "Fine. I'll report he didn't show," Peter says as he grabs his briefcase and heads toward the door. "If you'll copy me with your motion for sanctions, Miss Michaels?"

Leary nods her head and starts packing up all of the materials she had just so painstakingly laid out. I know she's pissed, but I also know she's hurt. She's put so much energy into this case, has so much emotion tied up in it, I know she was relishing being able to lay it all out to us, hoping beyond hope that maybe it could get resolved today and prevent her client from going through a lengthy and painful trial.

Peter leaves, giving me a nod of his head, and the door shuts behind him.

"Leary . . . I'm sorry—"

"Don't," she hisses at me, her venomous gaze slicing and burning through me. "Don't say a fucking word."

Yeah, that won't do.

"Leary . . . I had no clue he wasn't going to show up," I tell her gently but firmly.

"You expect me to believe that?"

"I do," I say simply.

"You know," she says, an edge of hysteria in her voice as she slams items into her briefcase, "I actually do believe that. I guess what I can't wrap my head around is how you can work for someone with so little soul as to not see the merits of this case. Not see how badly your client has fucked up Jenna's life. Who doesn't even have the decency to show up and tell me to my face they won't offer a dime."

My heart twists over the anger-laced pain in her voice. But I'm also angered, because she can't blame me for my line of work. She knew it about me from the start. "If I'm such a terrible person for who I'm working for, then why are you with me, Leary? Why do you let me inside your body? Why do you even let me inside your world?"

She lowers her face and shakes her head. Her voice is whisper-soft and sad. "I don't know. I really just don't know."

My gut feels hollow. I'm losing her, and I didn't expect it would happen so fast. "Listen, let's go out and get an early dinner and talk about this. These things happen in cases, and you can't take it so personally."

"But I do," she says, her eyes raising to mine again. "I do take it personally, and that will never change about me."

"Then explain it to me," I coax her. "Let's go get a drink, something to eat. You can tell me why this is so important to you. I'll listen and I'll understand."

She stares at me a moment, indecision in her eyes. Then I watch as her spine stiffens and she picks up the last of her materials, putting them in her briefcase and snapping it shut. "I can't. I have plans."

"With who?" I grit out.

"Ford. We're going to dinner."

Rage flushes through me, white-hot and blinding. "You have plans with Ford?"

"Not yet," she says as she walks toward the door. "But I will in about fifteen minutes."

I grab her arm as she brushes by me. She looks at me in defiance.

"Are you doing this to punish me?" I ask menacingly.

She smirks at me, and while I've always loved Leary's honesty, I can't say I love it now when she says, "Yes. That's exactly what I'm doing."

My hand falls away from her. "That's the way of it, then?"

Her chin raises up and her eyes are frosty. "That's the way of it."

"So be it," I tell her, a deadly calm overtaking me.

Grabbing my briefcase, I open the door and walk out. I don't give her a backward glance.

CHAPTER 15

LEARY

Ford's car pulls up to the curb in front of my house. I stare at him through the living-room window as he gets out and walks up the sidewalk. Moving toward the door, I open it before he can knock.

"Thanks for coming over," I say softly, stepping back so he can enter.

"Of course I was going to come over," he says with a worried look on his face.

I wasn't sure he'd come. Not with him ignoring me for the past few weeks. I was surprised when he picked up my phone call as I sat behind my desk, trying to stop the frantic beating of my heart.

I was still pissed and hurt over what happened, but I was also scared. Reeve's last words had a finality to them, and after I took a moment to process, I realized that I think he was saying good-bye to me.

When Ford answered the phone, my voice instantly cracked and I barely managed to get out, "Hey, Ford."

"What's wrong?" he immediately responded, knowing that I rarely get emotional about anything.

"Oh, nothing," I said, my voice quavering.

"Leary, what's wrong?" he repeated, his voice strong and unrelenting.

"I need . . . um . . . I just really need to talk to you. I need a friend," I said, and had to bite the inside of my cheek to stop from crying.

"I'm at a hearing in Vance County. I can be at your house in about two hours," he said, and just like that, my friend was back.

And now he's here in my house.

Clasping my hands together, I chew on my bottom lip while Ford looks at me with eagle eyes. I open my mouth, not sure what to say. How do I pour my heart out when I haven't even been willing to admit my heart is involved with Reeve?

Ford's gaze turns sympathetic. He opens his arms and says gruffly, "Come here."

And I do.

I walk right into his embrace, lay my head on his chest, and give a heaving sigh. His arms wrap around me, solidly and with care and comfort only. He presses his lips on top of my head and says, "It's going to be okay. Let me just hug you a minute, then you can tell me all about your problems with Reeve."

I give a tiny laugh, a little on the maniacal side, and squeeze him around his ribs. "Deal."

Finally I pull away and pat him on the chest. Looking up into his handsome face, I say, "Come on. I picked up some fruit and cheeses at Fresh Market. We can crack a bottle of wine, and you can listen to me pour my heart out."

I lead Ford into the living room, where I have the food and wine laid out. He takes a seat on one end of my couch, and I sit on my love seat, curling my feet up under me. Pointing at the spread, I urge him, "Go on and eat."

"Aren't you going to?" he asks as he leans forward to grab a cracker and cheese.

"In a bit," I say, because right now, my stomach is churning too hard to handle food.

Ford pops the cracker in his mouth and leans forward to pour some wine while he chews. He pours two glasses and raises from the couch slightly to hand me a glass.

"So, is this weird?" I ask him as he sits back down and takes a handful of grapes.

"What?" he asks with a grin. "Talking to your ex-lover about your current lover?"

"Well, yeah, that's pretty much what I was going for."

"Not weird," he says with a smile. "We're friends, Leary. That's always been first."

"I guess I felt like you've been avoiding me lately," I say softly. "Have you?"

He swallows and nods. "A little."

"Are you hurt I'm with Reeve?" I ask gently, then amend. "I mean, was with Reeve, because I think this is totally a past-tense situation."

"We can talk about that in a minute, but no, I'm not hurt you're with Reeve. He's a good guy and I want you to be happy."

"But you're acting like you're hurt," I prod, because I can sense there's more.

"Saddened," he clarifies. "I guess maybe deep down, I thought maybe you and I would eventually . . . you know . . . just stick with each other."

"But we've been on and off for years," I point out.

"Yeah, but I knew it was different with Reeve. There wasn't going to be an on again after him. So I think I might just be mourning something that I'll never have again."

I blink at him in surprise. "Why would you say that? How could you possibly know that?"

Ford gives me a knowing smile. "Think back. Every other time you've wanted to pursue someone, I would ask you if you wanted me to back away, right?"

I nod at him, take a sip of my wine, and let it swirl briefly on my tongue before I swallow.

"Every time your answer was always, 'Yes, for now.' You always added on, 'For now.' I always knew you'd come back to me eventually."

I cock my head at him, confused at what he's trying to say. "I don't understand."

"This time," Ford says dramatically as he leans forward for a slice of cheese, "you didn't say, 'For now.' You just said you wanted me to back away. I could tell then, Reeve was different. I could tell then that you weren't coming back."

My gaze lowers down to my wine, my heart hurting over Ford's words. In a way, I'm now mourning my loss of Ford, because I hadn't really thought of that before. But it's true . . . when I told Ford to back away, I was going all-in with Reeve. It was the first time that had happened since I'd started working with Ford, and he saw and understood something then that I'm only getting now.

"I'm sorry," I say softly as I look back up at him. "I didn't mean to hurt you."

Ford shakes his head with a smile. "I'm not hurt, Leary. Again, just a bit sad. An end of an era and all that, so to speak. But you are now and always will be my friend."

His words are sure and true. He means it, and I feel immensely better.

"So, what did you do to fuck up this thing with Reeve?" he asks me out of the blue.

"What makes you think I did something wrong?"

"Because you have that shamed-dog look, and besides that, I know for a fact that Reeve is crazy about you. If you're sitting here talking to me, you did something to mess up what you two have going."

"Jeez, Ford," I whine. "How about give me a little credit? Maybe Reeve did something wrong, too."

"Probably," he agrees as he leans back on the couch and swirls his wine. "But I'm a smart guy. Reeve is a relatively calm guy and is the type to reasonably and maturely talk things out. I know you very well, and you are stubborn and have a terrible temper that makes you say things you later regret. I'm going to stick by my original feeling and say you did something to fuck up."

"I hate you know me so well," I grumble. And then admit, "I did fuck up. I got mad at him today for something that really wasn't his fault, wouldn't give him the time of day to talk about it, and then told him I was going out with you tonight."

"You're such a brat," Ford says. "Why in the hell would you tell Reeve you were going out with me?"

"To make him mad. To hurt him the way I was hurting," I defend myself. "At least I was honest about it. I told him I was punishing him."

Ford looks at me disapprovingly, then leans forward for more food. "What did he do?"

"He walked out on me. He said, 'So be it,' which in general breakup terms means 'Fuck you very much, it was nice knowing you.'" My voice cracks and takes on a panicked edge.

"Calm down, babe," Ford says gently. "Start from the beginning. Tell me everything that happened."

"Not much to tell," I say dejectedly. "We had the *LaPietra* mediation today. The insurance adjuster didn't show up. Reeve confirmed there'd be no offer. I went ballistic and blamed Reeve."

"Did he know the adjuster wasn't coming?" Ford asks.

"No. He was just as surprised as we were."

"Then why in the world would you be mad at him?"

"Because he works for Lucifer. He works for and makes a salary from these evil, evil men. He continues to defend this case when in good conscience he knows it's not defendable. He's nice and sweet and caring, and it hurts me that he's working in opposition to me." My chest is heaving from the oxygen it took to get out that angry outburst, but at least I laid out my true feelings. I really don't need to elucidate further, because Ford knows how I feel about big business. He knows that I view them as soulless corporations out to screw the little guy. He knows this is personal to me, because for much of my life, my family was the little guy.

"This case is more important to me than any case I've tried in my entire legal career," I say softly. "And Reeve wants me to lose it. He's going to try to make me lose it. How can I want to be with someone who wants bad things for me?"

Ford's mouth draws down into an empathetic frown. He stands from the couch and sets his wineglass down. He circles the end table and reaches out to take my glass from my hand. I easily let it go.

Kneeling down in front of me, Ford takes my hands and squeezes them. "You're not being fair to Reeve. You knew who he was and what he was when you started this. You had no problem sleeping with the enemy. Logically, you knew going into this there was going to be a winner and a loser. And I get it—now that feelings are involved, it's a tougher pill to swallow reconciling Reeve your opponent with Reeve your lover."

I nod at him, because he's spot-on.

"But what you're failing to understand is that Reeve does not want you to be hurt by the outcome, I can guarantee you. Is he very much aware that his efforts can cause you to lose? Yes. But he's just doing his job. Is he going to be happy if he wins? Maybe, because that means he did his job well. Is he going to hurt that you're hurt? I guaran-fucking-tee you that is going to be the case. So my question to you is, why can't it be enough that he doesn't want to hurt you? In this scenario, when that's the best you can hope for in this fucked-up relationship you have, why isn't that good enough for you? If you can't accept that about him, then you need to let him go."

My head spins and my jaw drops in guilty realization of everything that Ford just laid out to me. "I can," I whisper with sudden realization. "I can accept that."

Ford cocks a skeptical eyebrow at me.

"I *can* accept that," I say in a stronger voice. "I guess I just didn't realize it until now. I think I forgot that this may be hard on him, too."

Nodding, Ford says with a smirk, "Congratulations, I now proclaim you to be a reasonably mature woman."

I smack Ford on the shoulder. "Smart-ass."

Ford goes back to the couch. He takes a few more crackers and cheese. "So what are you going to do to fix this?"

"I'm thinking groveling may be involved," I say dejectedly.

"No time like the present. Give him a call now."

"Right now?" I ask hesitantly. Not because it's an insane idea, but because I'm still fresh off being embarrassed about making an ass of myself.

"Right now," Ford affirms, grabbing his glass of wine and sinking back into the couch.

"And . . . you're just going to sit there and listen in on my conversation?" I ask dubiously.

"Pretty much," he says with a grin. "I've earned it."

I roll my eyes and walk over to my purse, which rests on my foyer table, and pull out my phone. As I walk back into the living room, I dial Reeve's number. As it rings, I nibble on my fingernail—a nervous habit I've had since grade school—and keep my back to Ford, not wanting to acknowledge his penetrating look as I get ready to prostrate myself before Reeve.

His phone rings five times and goes to voice mail. His message is short, businesslike, and professional, slightly intimidating to me in this context. When I hear the beep, I take a deep breath and say, "Hey. It's me. Listen, I'm sorry for the way I behaved today. I was angry and took it out on you. I'm actually sitting at my house, eating cheese and crackers with Ford. He's pretty much told me I'm a dumbass for the way I acted, and I'd like the chance to apologize. So . . . um . . . call me. I can come over tonight if you want."

I pause, wondering if I should say something more, then realize, what more can I say? I apologized. I hope he accepts it. I really hope he wants me to come over tonight.

I tap on my phone to disconnect the call and turn back to Ford. He's smiling at me and making a thumbs-up sign. I smile back, content that I've done all I can.

Feeling a bit hungry, I walk back over to the love seat and grab a handful of grapes. Nothing to do but wait for Reeve to call me back.

It's midnight and I'm lying awake in my bed.

Reeve never called me back, and I wonder if he just didn't check his phone, if he's ignoring me, or if—worst-case scenario—he's seeking pleasure from someone else.

Like Vanessa.

To punish me the way I attempted to punish him.

Except mine would sort of be deserved.

The thought brings tears to my eyes, and I snag my phone off the small table beside my desk. The display is bright when I turn it on, temporarily blinding and hurting my eyes until I adjust.

I pound out a quick text to Reeve. Did you get my message? Are you ignoring me?

No hesitation before I hit Send. My anxiety over potentially driving Reeve away for good won't let me second-guess my desperate nature. I even briefly consider getting in my car and going over to his house to demand he talk to me.

But then the thought of what I might find when I get there scares the shit out of me, and I immediately discard the idea.

Ford stayed over for about an hour, cleaning me out of all my cheese and fruit as well as a bologna sandwich I made him. We actually talked about Jenna's case, focusing on how best to lay out the expert witness testimony. While I love my easygoing friendship with Ford, and while I can never adequately tell him how much I appreciated his friendship tonight, one other reason why I will always hold the highest respect for the man is his legal prowess. He's an amazing litigator and even more brilliant strategist. Most of what I know I learned from him. Most of the mistakes I've made in my career he's helped me work through and taught me how to avoid in the future. Ford will help me prep for the trial as we get closer, although I won't have him sitting at the counsel table with me. I want the jury to see just Jenna and me, the tiny little Davids up against the Goliath insurance company and their passel of attorneys I'm sure will be there, each individually billing out hundreds of dollars per hour.

Reeve doesn't text me back. I know he's awake because he's a night owl. Many nights we've spent together, he would make love to me, or fuck me, depending on his mood, and I would be so tired I'd go to sleep.

Not Reeve.

He'd get up and go into the living to watch TV, usually ESPN's *SportsCenter*, or he'd pull out some work. Sometimes I'd awaken at one or two in the morning and tiptoe into the living room. I'd find him wide-awake, surfing channels or reading legal cases. I'd crawl onto his lap, and with nothing more than a soft kiss on the side of his neck, I'd entice him to come to bed so he could get some sleep. It was almost as if I was taking care of him in that respect.

All the little things I shared with Reeve that I took for granted.

Until now.

Sadness that I haven't heard back from him washes over me. I can't waste an opportunity to let him know what I'm feeling.

I send him one more text.

```
I miss you.
```

Then I turn my phone off and try to go to sleep.

CHAPTER 16

REEVE

What a fucking day.

As I drive through my neighborhood, I heave an internal sigh over the work I need to get done tonight.

On my client's orders, I need to prepare a brief in opposition to the motion for sanctions against Tom Collier that Leary filed this morning and faxed to my office. She didn't waste any time, and as was my duty, I immediately forwarded it to Tom to review. In my e-mail to him, I explained that the law was on Leary's side, that he was under court order to attend the mediation, and by failing to do so was in contempt. I also explained that he would be best served to just roll over and pay the $10,000 she was asking for as recompense.

I'd like to say I took Leary's side in this out of some sense of guilt over what happened yesterday, but it's not that. Bottom line, the law's in her favor and there's no sense fighting a losing battle.

So why am I bothering to work tonight to get a brief prepared if the law is against me?

Because that douche Tom Collier is refusing to take my advice. We argued for thirty minutes on the phone, but he clearly doesn't care that he's going to lose this motion. Instead, he insisted I go ahead and file a motion for sanctions against her for what she did in Jenna LaPietra's deposition.

I spent another ten minutes trying to explain to the moron that technically, Leary didn't do anything wrong. Was it in poor taste for her to call him out like that on the record? Absolutely, but the only fix to that was to ask the judge to strike that portion from the record, which he would definitely do.

No judge would award sanctions for her behavior, and some judges—like Judge Henry, who was fond of Leary Michaels—would actually be amused.

Tom was having none of it and ordered me forward.

And because he is TransBenefit's representative, and TransBenefit employs me, I have to do what he says.

Within reason, of course.

I agreed to prepare the brief and followed up with a confirmation e-mail of same. I wanted it in writing that I was advising him not to do this and that he ran the risk of severely pissing off the judge and getting hit with harder sanctions than the $10,000. I did not agree to file the motion for sanctions against Leary. I told him it was frivolous and was pushing my ethical boundaries to do so, and if he had a problem with that, he could take it up with the partners at Battle Carnes.

He didn't respond, so I decided to wait the entire day to see if he would change his fucking mind.

Moron never did, so that's why I have to work tonight on a brief that will be an absolute waste of time and just piss Leary off even more.

Of course, I'm not sure I really care if I piss her off more. I'm still pissed at her, despite her apology voice mail. I'll admit, I warmed a tad when she texted me last night and told she missed me, but I held strong and didn't respond.

I wanted more time to think.

While logically I get why Leary was so upset, and I can even forgive her for trying to make me jealous by saying she was going out with Ford last night, the one thing I can't get past is the way my job and role in the *LaPietra* case trouble her. She's upset that I'm defending this case and is having a hard time reconciling that with her personal feelings for me. She's not easily handling that I wear two faces in this relationship.

And the truth of the matter is, if Leary was that upset over the adjuster failing to show at the mediation, what in the hell is she going to do when I pull out my surprise witnesses at trial, who will tear Jenna to pieces? She will never, ever forgive me for that. She'll never be able to understand I'm just doing the job that I'm not only paid for, but that my ethical duty demands I do.

So I didn't call Leary back because I'm not so sure we should continue. I'm not going to lie, I desperately fucking miss her. I couldn't stand not having her in my bed last night. Couldn't stand not waking up with her this morning.

But what's the point of going back to that?

I'm just going to lose it again in a few weeks.

I have a decision to make, and nothing about this day has given me any further clarity on the issue. I'm wondering if maybe I should call Cal and talk about it with him. Or maybe even Ford.

I didn't have a single qualm about Leary telling me she was going out with Ford last night. I trust her and him not to do anything. I know in my heart she was just trying to make me as mad as she was. And it worked for a bit, and then I recognized it for what it was—a failed attempt to hurt me so she could alleviate some of her own pain.

Just as I turn onto my street, my phone starts ringing. Because it's hooked up to my Bluetooth, I hit the Accept button on my steering wheel, and the call connects through my stereo speakers.

"Reeve Holloway," I say.

"Mr. Holloway, this is Rhonda Valasquez. I'm returning your call from last night."

"Yes," I say with immediate recognition. "Thanks for calling me back."

"You said on your message this is about Dr. Summerland and a lawsuit against him?"

"That's right. I represent Dr. Summerland and his insurance carrier," I say by way of further explanation. "I'd like to talk to you about the case if you have a moment."

She's quiet a moment and I almost prompt her response when I see my house coming into view and Leary's car sitting out front. Leary is sitting on my front porch steps.

Although my heart starts racing with a mixture of desire for her as well as anxiety over what we could possibly say to each other, I give my head a shake and turn my attention back to the phone call.

Pulling into my driveway, I stop the car and put it in park but leave the engine running. "Ms. Valasquez?"

"I won't help Dr. Summerland, if that's what you want," she says abruptly.

I'm surprised by the venom in her voice, and I go on high alert. "No, I don't expect that. I'm just doing some more investigation into this case and wanted to ask you about your nurses' notes."

"Is this about his surgery on Jenna LaPietra?" she asks hesitantly.

"Yes," I say, my throat suddenly going dry. I glance over at Leary. She's stood up from the porch and watches me as I sit in the car. "I'd love to talk to you. Maybe I can come by the hospital and we can meet on one of your breaks."

She gives a wry laugh. "I don't work there anymore. Dr. Summerland had me fired after that surgery."

"Fired?" I ask in confusion.

"Look, I don't have anything good to say about your client, Mr. Holloway. I'd appreciate it if you leave me alone."

The click in my ear is resounding as she hangs up on me. She made it emphatically clear that she wouldn't talk to me, and she was also equally clear that she has nothing good to say about Dr. Summerland.

That means it's imperative I talk to this woman, and I'm just going to have to keep after her. I'll get our investigator on it, find out if she's working somewhere else or, at the least, get an updated and accurate home address.

Sighing with fatigue, I turn my car off.

Now it's time to deal with Leary.

As usual, she looks completely stunning. It's a brisk day for early November in the Carolinas, and she has on a cherry-red wool coat with big black buttons down the middle. Her hands are in her pockets, and she's dressed casually, with a pair of faded jeans tucked into black riding boots.

I traverse the sidewalk toward her, and as I get closer she gives me a tentative smile and says, "Hey."

"What are you doing here?" I ask her, my tone bordering on polite but flat.

She gives me a chastising look. "When you wouldn't return my call or texts, did you honestly think I wouldn't come?"

I brush past her and trot up the three steps of my front porch. Mr. Chico Taco starts his booming barks from inside. Fingering my house key, I struggle to maintain some emotional distance, but when I turn to look at her, I know it will be next to impossible to do so. Her soft-brown eyes stare up at me in contrition, and I fully accept her regret over what she did.

"Listen . . . come on in and we can—"

"Reeve . . . hey, wait up," I hear from my left. Turning I see Vanessa jogging across her yard toward me, holding something in her hand. She's wearing workout clothes—skintight leggings that come to midcalf and a sports halter top that comes to midstomach. The fact that she's out in the cold wearing that tells me that it's calculated.

She pushes right past Leary, still standing on my sidewalk, and bounds up the steps, her long blonde ponytail swinging jauntily. Her hand extends. "Here, I'm returning the sweatshirt you let me wear this morning because it was so cold out."

I groan mentally over the insinuation in her tone, and based on the sly smile on Vanessa's face, there's no doubt she did this in front of Leary for a reason.

Movement out of the corner of my eye catches my attention, and I see Leary heading across my yard for her car. Her back is rigid and anger radiates off her.

Pushing past Vanessa, I leap off my porch, and in three strides I have Leary by the arm. Pulling her around, I immediately start walking back toward my house. "Oh, no, you don't," I tell her firmly. "You came over to talk and we're going to talk."

She tries to pull away from me and hisses, "I don't want to talk. It was a mistake coming here."

I don't let her go, and her attempts to struggle with me are futile. I don't say another word to her but lead her right up the porch steps to my door and past Vanessa, causing her to have to take a step backward or get plowed over.

Grasping my key solidly in one hand and Leary's arm in the other, I don't even turn around when I say, "Vanessa, you can go home now. Thanks for bringing my sweatshirt back."

I manage to deftly slide the key in, turn the lock, and open the door, all while keeping my hold on Leary's arm, who's still trying to twist and turn out of my hold.

Chico greets us at the door, but I push past him, dragging Leary along.

After the front door is slammed, I utter a curt "Sit" to Chico, who dutifully does so, then point to my couch and tell Leary, "You, too. Sit."

Her eyes narrow at me and I glare back at her, keeping my finger pointed toward the couch. She doesn't move.

"You can go sit, Leary, or I will make you sit. That will probably involve tying you up, but I'll make it happen one way or the other."

Her nostrils flare and I don't miss the subtle darkening of her eyes, but she stands her ground. Leaning in toward me so I catch her fragrance, she whispers, "You can go to hell."

She whirls away and heads for my door. My arm snakes out, and I once again grab her by the elbow. I think briefly about depositing her on the couch and sitting on top of her to make her stay, but one tiny whiff of her smell when she leaned in toward me, and that thought is abandoned.

Instead, I pull her toward me roughly, so hard she slams into my chest. One hand goes to the back of her head to hold her still while my mouth slams down to hers, my arm going around her waist to pull her lower body into me. I immediately start to swell hard with hunger for her, and I can't seem to give a damn that I'm angry with the woman.

Nothing seems to matter except her mouth against mine, my cock pressed into her lower belly and yes . . . right there . . . her hands slide up my chest and curl around my neck until she's trying to pull me even closer to her.

We kiss like starving fiends, breath coming faster, grunts and moans floating around our tongues. Spinning around, I pin her up against the wall with my body, shove my thigh in between her legs, and kiss her even harder.

I know we should be talking about something, but for the life of me I can't remember what was so important. What could be more important than this?

Than tasting Leary right now.

Possessing her.

Making her mine again.

Again? She's not mine now?

I rip my mouth away from hers, and my chest seizes when she gives a disappointed moan. Her eyes flutter open but they're clouded with lust.

My hands come up to grasp onto the sides of her face, and I lean in slightly so she can feel the true weight of my stare. Even though I'm slightly out of breath, I manage to tell her, "I did not sleep with Vanessa last night."

Leary blinks at me. A little of the fog dissipates from her eyes. Her pelvis tilts and seeks me out.

Shaking her head to make sure she understands me, I repeat, "I didn't sleep with Vanessa. You got me?"

She nods, her pink tongue sneaking out to lick at her lower lip. Her eyes focus on my mouth, and I know she's not fully engaged with me.

"She texted me at work today that she took one of my sweatshirts when she walked Chico. She was just returning it."

"Okay," Leary says testily. "I got it. Now can you just fuck me?"

I grin at her before leaning in to kiss her again. This time a bit softer. My fingers come up and work the buttons of her coat open, then I'm sliding it from her shoulders. She's wearing a simple cream-colored turtleneck tucked into her jeans with a wide black belt. It's amazing how, even in jeans, she can still look elegant and classic.

Bending down, I curl my hands under her ass and hoist her up. Her slender legs wrap and lock around my hips, and her head tilts to the side to kiss along my jawline. I walk her back toward my bedroom, giving a sharp "Stay" to Chico when he gets up to follow us.

Next follows a struggle between the two of us trying to undress each other. We fumble with buttons, zippers, and her bra clasp. Shoes get in the way; socks prevent a sexy disrobing.

None of that matters, though, because in moments Leary is on top of my bed and I'm on top of Leary, my cock resting heavy and pulsing with need across her pelvic bone.

I kiss her again, starting off slowly, but almost instantly, the lust flows hotly again between us. Her hips flex against me, rubbing her bare pussy all over my cock. Her wetness seeps through her folds, coating my shaft slick and driving me delirious with need.

Looping one arm under the back of her leg, I hoist it up and spread her wide. Fisting my cock, I line up, watching in fascination as I push just the tip in with a slight movement of my hips. I take a moment and marvel at the beauty of my thickness just nestled in between those pink lips, knowing that I'm getting ready to sink into her heaven.

My gaze comes back up to her, and her eyes are pinned on me with anxiety. "Are you okay?" I ask her, holding my body absolutely still.

"Do you forgive me?" she whispers, and it all comes back to me.

I pushed her right into my bed without giving any thought to resolving things between us. My mind scrambles . . . what the fuck am I doing?

Should I stop or should I push inside her?

Do I accept things the way they are and just wait for the day she truly hates me for what I'll do to her case?

Or should I man up and cut things off right now?

My cock jerks in rebellion over the thought of pulling away from Leary, at least physically, so I completely succumb to my lust and need for her and slam my way inside without answering her question.

Leary's neck and back arch off the bed, her head tilts back, and she groans in approval over my invasion. I pull out and thrust back in hard again, my entire body shuddering over how good her tight pussy feels around me.

Once more . . . slide out, slam back in, and Leary lets out a tiny whimper of pleasure.

My hand strokes up the side of her body, over her breast, past her collarbone, and I wrap my fingers around the front of her neck. Leary's eyes snap open, looking at me in curiosity. I give a small squeeze to her slender throat and grind against her, my breath huffing out with exertion.

I pull out and slam back in, hard and deep, my fingers squeezing just a bit harder so I know I have her attention.

"There's nothing to forgive," I tell her quietly. Slide free, almost to the tip . . . pump back in to the hilt. "But you need to promise me a few things."

She nods at me, her mouth open slightly, her eyes clouding over again as I keep tunneling in and out of her. God, she's so fucking sexy, and it's taking all my control not to just unleash a fury of need on her right now.

I pull out one more time, push back in, not so fast, but so deep that my pelvis grinds harshly against hers. I rotate my hips once more, grinding again. Leaning my face toward hers, I snag her lower lip between my teeth and give her a bite before letting go. I lick gently at her lip then pull back just enough so she can see my eyes.

I'm not sure what type of desperation they're showing, but before I can finish her and me off at the same time, I have to know I have a fighting chance with her for the long haul. I need to know that she accepts me for what I am, otherwise I'm dooming myself.

"You need to promise me you know—deep in your heart—that nothing I do on this case is done to hurt you personally."

"I do," she murmurs. "I know that."

I reward her with a few more luxurious thrusts of my cock.

"Promise me, Leary," I breathe against her lips. "No matter what happens during the trial, you know and accept I'm just doing my job."

I stroke deep inside her and she moans. I've lost her to the pleasure, so once again I still inside her body. Curling my hand, I now hold her by the back of the neck. I pull up, causing her head to rise off the pillow. A swift kiss . . . another bite to her lip. "Promise me, baby. You know I'm just doing my job. I'm not trying to hurt you."

"I know," she assures me, and she contracts her muscles around my dick, causing me to groan. "I know and I promise."

Leary's arms come up over my shoulders and wrap tightly around my neck. She pulls me to her face and kisses me deeply, sweetly swirling her tongue against mine. My hips start moving again, unable to hold still against this onslaught.

Our breathing picks up . . . our kissing turns deeper . . . our hips move in synchronicity, mating my cock with her pussy on the most profound level imaginable.

I have her promise. She won't hold my job against me.

I have her promise.

I hope she keeps it.

CHAPTER 17
LEARY

"Are you going to tell me where you're taking me?" Reeve asks me, for what I think—by last count—is the fourth time.

"No," I tell him, giving him a side glance as he sits in the passenger seat of my car. "Let it be enough that there's something important I want to show you, and you'll have to cool your heels until we get there."

It's been four days since Reeve and I made up.

Four days since I promised him that I wouldn't hold his job against him. That I knew and accepted that anything he did in this case was not designed to hurt me personally.

I made that promise willingly and with utter truth in my heart. I'm not willing to let this case stand in my way of being with this man. As a rational woman, I have to accept that Reeve is who he is. He's my opponent on this case, and we can't change that. He's going to fight me tooth and nail when we get in that courtroom, and I'm going to fight him back just as hard. That's the way our legal system works.

What I did with my promise is assure him that no matter how much blood we draw in the courtroom, I am not going to let it change my feelings about him.

And there are indeed feelings involved.

Deep feelings.

I realized it the minute Reeve walked away from me after the mediation. The finality of his words and his tone of voice immediately made me see that I was getting ready to lose something very good in my life. Now that I have him back, I'm going to try harder than ever to continue to cement this bond we've established.

And that's why on this Saturday morning, I insisted he get up, get dressed, and we go for a drive. I told him there was something I wanted to show him.

It's time for me to share more of who I am. It's time for me to pull the door open wider and let him all the way in.

"Duplin County?" Reeve says as we pass a welcome sign on Interstate 40.

"Yup. Where was I born and raised," I clarify.

Reeve's head turns toward me quickly, and I shoot him a quick look. His eyes are round and surprised. "You're not taking me home to meet your mom, are you?" he asks seriously. "Because we really need to stop and let me get some flowers or something."

I laugh and reach over to pat his knee. "Um . . . no. I'd give you a better heads-up if that were the case. And besides, my mom now lives on the coast, just below Wilmington. I bought her a small house down there about two years ago."

"Why the coast?" he asks with interest.

"She's always loved the ocean. And just . . . you know . . . for everything she did for me growing up. All her sacrifices. I wanted her to be at peace somewhere she loved."

Reaching over, Reeve takes my hand off the steering wheel and brings it to his mouth, where he kisses my fingertips. "You've got a beautiful soul, Leary. I can't imagine how proud your mother must be of you."

I smile and blink back the small prick of tears in my eyes over Reeve's lovely words. The validation he gives me is a comfort, because I haven't always been so giving to my family.

"So, if we're not going to see your mom, what are we doing?"

"Patience, my extremely hot and sexy man."

"Hot and sexy?" he asks with interest. "Like . . . would it be hot and sexy if I put my hand between your legs and got you off while we were driving?"

I take my eyes off the road briefly to shoot him a sharp look, just to see if he's kidding.

And holy hell . . . he's not. His eyes are dark and licentious as he looks back at me.

"Hands to yourself," I croak. "I'll wreck the car for sure."

He chuckles and turns his head back to watch the scenery go by.

We pull off the interstate a few miles down and head into my hometown of Kenansville. I show him the town square, point out the old redbrick hospital where I was born. As we pass through town, I point down a side street and say, "If you go that way about two miles, the trailer park I grew up in is down there."

"Want to go by there?" he asks softly.

"Nah," I tell him with a tiny smile. "I don't need that trip down memory lane."

We hit the outskirts of town, follow Highway 24 for a few miles toward Jacksonville, and then I put on my blinker to make a right-hand turn. Reeve looks out the passenger window, and I can see him sit up straighter in his seat in surprise.

I pull into Shadow Glen Cemetery and follow the main road. It winds around rolling hills studded with grave markers and pine-tree clusters. When I reach the correct spot, I stop the car, put it in park, and turn off the ignition.

Without looking at Reeve, I get out of my car and I hear him doing the same. It's relatively comfortable outside for November, and the small sweater I put on over my blouse is enough to keep me warm.

Reeve meets me at the front of my car, and I hold my hand out to him. He takes it, wrapping his large hand around mine protectively, and I turn to lead him up a small grassy knoll.

I weave my way past three rows of graves and come to stop in front of a large headstone of a deep, dark gray, which has a matching stone bench sitting alongside the grave. I point at the headstone and say simply, "My sister . . . Lauren."

Reeve is silent as he reads the words carved into the monument. I didn't spare any expense.

LAUREN RENEE MICHAELS

SLEEP WELL, OUR DAUGHTER AND SISTER.

TAKE THY REST FOR GOD CALLED THEE HOME

SO YOUR PAIN AND OURS IS NO MORE.

1990–2011

"She had just turned twenty-one before she died," I murmur, then bend to pluck a few weeds at the base of the granite stone, tossing them to the side.

"What happened?" Reeve asks softly.

I stand back up, feeling my knees pop, and turn to face him. "A drug overdose. Heroin."

He brings a hand up to stroke my cheek. "I'm sorry."

Leaning into him, closing my eyes, I say, "Me, too. She was a good person, a kind woman. She just had demons that she couldn't conquer."

Stepping back, I take Reeve's hand and pull him over to the stone bench. I bought this last year so Mom, Jenna, and I could have a place to sit when we came to visit Lauren.

After we sit down, Reeve's arm comes around my shoulder, and he pulls me in close. I lay my head on his shoulder and stare at Lauren's grave.

"You asked me a few times why Jenna's case is so important to me."

"Yeah," he says in a soft voice.

"She was Lauren's best friend. They grew up together, were inseparable, really. Lauren and Jenna partied hard, ran with a bad crowd, barely graduated from high school. They both moved to Raleigh when they turned eighteen."

"You would have been, what . . . twenty-three?" he asks.

"Yeah, just finishing up my last year at Stanford. Honestly, I was so busy with law school, I really didn't pay too much attention to what was going on with Lauren. The five-year age difference ensured we weren't overly close growing up. Mom kept me up-to-date on her. I knew she was partying. She was dancing to make a living, same as Jenna. Living a pretty hard life. But honestly, it was so far removed from me and where I was, I didn't care too much about it."

"Nothing you could have done anyway," Reeve says softly.

"Probably not. At least not while I was living out in California," I agree. "But within a year, I was back in Raleigh. Jenna got pregnant with Damien and she cleaned up her act. Stopped the drugs and partying. Lived with Damien's father for a bit, so he supported her. She and Lauren drifted apart a bit during that time, and Lauren got worse. Started using hard-core drugs. She would come to me often asking for money. I'd refuse to give it to her. Refused to reinforce her drug habit."

"That's exactly what you should have done."

"I know. But maybe I could have done more. I tried to talk her into rehab, but did I really try hard enough? Should I have been more proactive? I was just starting out at Knight & Payne, and I was so consumed with my new career that I just didn't give her a lot of thought and effort."

Reeve stays silent but his arm tightens around me.

"Eventually, Jenna left Damien's father and she and Lauren started to get close again. They lived together, both of them continuing to dance. Jenna stayed clean, though, and Lauren, well, she continued to party. Jenna spent a lot of time cleaning up Lauren's messes. Bailed her out of jail more than once. Got her to go to rehab once, but she relapsed a few weeks after she got out. Cleaned vomit off her after a hard night of partying."

"Jenna's quite a woman," Reeve says.

"I feel an obligation to her," I clarify. "She did things for Lauren, cared for her in ways that I never did. And in ways that my mom couldn't. She tried hard to get Lauren straightened out, but it was all in vain. She loved Lauren like a sister. Was closer to her than I ever could have been. And I watch as Jenna struggles to take care of Damien, and it reminds me so much of my mom and her sacrifices. So, yes, that's why this case is so important to me. Jenna deserves someone to take care of her now. It's my way of maybe paying her back for being so selfless in caring for my own flesh and blood. She never gave up on Lauren, when I think maybe I did."

Reeve's shoulders heave with a huge sigh. He tilts his head and kisses me on top of my head. "I get it now."

Pulling out of his embrace, I turn to face him and step forward, pushing my way in between his knees. My hands go to his broad shoulders, and his come to my waist. He tilts his face up to me, and the first thing I do is ply him with a chastely sweet kiss.

His lips are velvety soft, his breath warm against mine.

Leaning back, I say, "I will never have another case in my career as important as this one. I've put more effort into this case than any other, the stakes for me are higher than any other, and yet it's all out of my control. I know that I could lose it all. I accept that. I can only do my best. And I know, without a doubt, that you will do a good job defending the case. I know it's your job and that you're doing it out of duty to your employer and to our legal code of ethics. I'm at peace with that. I just wanted you to know everything about me before we go further. I wanted you to understand why I flipped out on you before, but also to reiterate my promise to you again that I won't take your involvement personally."

I can't gauge the look on Reeve's face as he listens to me tell him this. His eyes are almost blank, his facial muscles lax. He just stares at me, and for the briefest of moments, I think I might see a tinge of regret.

Maybe regret over what I've been through?

Or perhaps it's guilt.

Guilt for his role in opposing his lover on a case that's embedded in her heart?

I'm not sure, but before I can explore it, Reeve pulls me closer and presses his face into the center of my chest. He huffs out a deep, hot breath that seeps through my clothing and warms my skin. His arms band around me tight. He wraps me into an all-consuming hug, turning his cheek to rest right over my heart. My hands slip into his hair, and I hold his head against me tighter.

We stay like that for several minutes. A comforting hug of understanding and appreciation. My conscience is now clear. I'm not holding anything back from Reeve.

I'm all-in with him, and once this case is over, there will be absolutely nothing standing in our way.

I slip out of Reeve's embrace at first light and leave him peacefully sleeping in his bed. I'm the early riser, and since it's Sunday, I feel the urge to make him breakfast.

This says a lot, since I'm not the best cook, but I can manage bacon and scrambled eggs.

I first make a pot of coffee, pour a cup, and grab my phone. There's something I've been wanting to do since taking Reeve to Lauren's grave yesterday, and I haven't had the opportunity to do it. Now that he's asleep and I have a tiny bit of privacy, I turn my phone on and dial Jenna.

Because she's an early riser like me, I have no qualms about calling at this hour. She answers in a cheery voice, "Hey, Leary. Please don't tell me you're already working on a Sunday morning."

"No work today," I assure her with a laugh. "I was just checking in to see how you're doing."

"You mean am I pissed about the mediation and that they didn't offer anything?" she teases.

"Well, are you? Pissed?" I venture tentatively.

"No, babe. I told you I'm not expecting a damn thing from this case. Anything you can get for me is something I didn't have yesterday. If you don't get me anything, I'm the same as I am today."

A gust of breath pops out of me as I sigh into the phone. "Why can't I be as calm and centered as you are?"

"Trust me," she says with a tinkling laugh. "Have a kid with autism. You learn how to be centered very quickly."

I smile to myself, because Jenna has indeed mastered that.

"Actually," I tell her as I take a seat at Reeve's kitchen table, "I'm calling you about something else."

"Shoot," she says simply. "Damien's watching TV, so I have a bit of quiet time."

Toying with the handle on my coffee cup, I shoot a quick glance down the hallway that leads back to Reeve's bedroom. His door is still shut tight, and I'm all alone.

"I went to visit Lauren yesterday," I tell her softly by way of starting out not at the beginning but sort of near the end.

"Oh, you did?" she asks with a hint of disappointment. "I would have gone with you."

"It was spur-of-the-moment," I assure her, my mind drifting back to the memory of Reeve hugging me graveside. "Something I had to do."

"Hey," she asks softly, "are you okay? You sound a little funny."

Clearing my throat, I assure her, "Yeah, I'm fine. Actually . . . really good, in fact."

"Oh my God," she gushes into the phone. "You met someone."

I laugh, because ever since Lauren died, and especially since I started representing Jenna, we've become pretty close. She's always lamenting that I don't have a boyfriend.

"Yes," I tell her softly, cutting my glance back down at Reeve's bedroom door. I want nothing more than to just crawl back in bed, snuggle into his warmth. "I met someone."

"Tell me everything," she says in a whisper, I know, for Damien's benefit. "And don't hold back a single sexy detail."

Giggling, I push my hair behind my ear and raise my feet to plant on the bottom of the kitchen chair. Wrapping one arm around my knees, I go ahead and come clean. "Jenna . . . the thing is . . . um . . . I'm actually kind of involved with Reeve Holloway."

She's silent . . . not even a tiny breath. Then she says, "Holy fucking shit."

"I know this is unconventional—"

"Holy. Fucking. Shit," she repeats breathlessly. "That guy is H-O-T. I mean, really freakin' hot. Jesus . . . how long has this been going on? Before my deposition?"

"Um . . . yeah . . . not long after that first motion to dismiss I had to argue," I say hesitantly. "And the thing is, Jenna—"

"Oh my God . . . this is fantastic. You're a tough nut to crack, but he definitely looks like the type of guy that could totally crack you," she says with a mercurial laugh.

"But Jenna, the thing you have to consider is—"

"Is he good in bed? Please tell me he's good in bed. It's been so long that I can't remember what good in bed feels like," she chatters away at me.

"Jenna!" I exclaim.

"What?"

"You need to listen to me for a minute," I say with exasperation.

"Jeez. I'm listening," she snaps.

"What I'm doing . . . being involved with the opposing counsel in your case . . . it has certain ethical implications," I begin, choosing my words carefully so she has no misunderstanding over what I'm saying.

"Have you shared any info on our case with him?" she asks quickly.

"No, but—"

"Are you going to throw my case because you don't want it to impact your relationship?"

"Of course not," I say adamantly.

"Is anything about your relationship going to negatively harm my case?"

"No," I say quietly. "I swear to you we do not discuss the case outside the normal bounds of professional communication. But I had to let you know what was going on. You are more important right now, and if you want me to break it off with him until after the trial, I will do it in a heartbeat. Reeve would understand, too."

"Oh, sweet girl," Jenna says, and I can hear the smile in her voice. "I trust you implicitly. I'm not worried about it, and I know if you think it's a problem, you'll do what's right."

"Are you sure?" I ask, chewing on my bottom lip.

"Positive," she validates.

I breathe out a swift gust of air, and with it my anxiety, and I close my eyes in thanks. I would break things off with Reeve—temporarily, of course—if Jenna was uncomfortable with this. But I'm immensely happy that she trusts me to do what's right.

That means I can still have my cake and eat it, too.

CHAPTER 18

REEVE

I step off the elevator onto the twenty-first floor and turn left toward the civil superior courtrooms and the judges' chambers that are ensconced in the hallway behind said courtrooms. Leary and I are supposed to meet with Judge Henry this afternoon for our pretrial conference to go over our final list of issues for the jury to decide as well as the witnesses and exhibits. The judge will also try to lean on us to settle the case, but good luck with that. Tom Collier is barely speaking to me, but there's one thing he relayed loud and clear.

There will be no settlement offers made to Jenna LaPietra.

Not ever.

I take a quick peek through the glass cutouts of the wooden doors to courtroom 21C and see that Judge Henry is still on the bench, listening as an attorney stands at counsel table and makes his argument. Judge Henry's secretary sent word over to my office—as well as Leary's, I assume—that he got called in to an emergency restraining-order hearing and would be running about fifteen minutes late to our pretrial conference. I still show up on time, mainly hoping Leary would, too, and I could just hang with her for a little bit. She left my house seven hours ago and will be back at my house tonight, yet I still want to take as much opportunity as possible to be near her.

During the trial I'm going to destroy Jenna's case and Leary in the process. It's a thought that keeps me awake at night, makes me snap at the tiniest of provocations at work, and makes me desperate to steal every precious moment with Leary that I can.

She's promised me that she won't hold my job and what I have to do in the courtroom against me, which I might have believed at one point, but not after she took me to Lauren's grave.

Not after she shared with me the nature of her relationship with Jenna.

Not after I learned what Jenna did for Lauren.

Turning away from the courtroom, I head through a set of double doors and enter into the back halls of the civil superior court division. Pulling out my phone, I try to call Rhonda Valasquez again.

As expected, I get her voice mail.

"Ms. Valasquez, this is Reeve Holloway again. I'd really, really like to talk to you. I do represent Dr. Summerland, but even if you know something that could hurt my case, I'd still like to hear it. It could help settle the case, spare Jenna LaPietra a stressful trial. Please call me back. You have my number."

I hang up, knowing deep down that this woman won't call me back. I have no clue what she knows about Dr. Summerland, but she knows something. The funny thing is, I'm not seeking the information hoping I can use the knowledge to protect Dr. Summerland. I think I'm really hoping she'll tell me something that would help Leary's case. Not that I could ever disclose that to Leary. That would be as big of an ethical violation as if I told her about the rebuttal witnesses I'm going to call to attack Jenna. I have no clue what I'm hoping to accomplish, but I feel that Valasquez is important for some reason.

I walk into Judge Henry's office suite and smile at his secretary, who sits at a small cherrywood desk outside the judge's chambers.

"Good afternoon, Mr. Holloway," she says with a warm smile.

Sneaking a quick look at the nameplate on her desk, I say, "Good afternoon, Mary."

"Judge Henry is still hearing a motion right now, but Miss Michaels is already in his office. You can go in. He shouldn't be but ten more minutes or so."

I nod at her and head into the interior office, knowing that in about two seconds I'll be looking at Leary's beautiful face, and my oxygen will feel a little sweeter once I'm in her air space.

I've been in Judge Henry's office before. It has typical dark paneled-wood walls, commercial-grade burgundy carpet, and dark-cherry furniture that matches his secretary's desk. He has two leather wing-back chairs, also in burgundy, that sit opposite his desk, and at the sound of my entrance, Leary leans to the side and peeks her face around the side of one. Her eyes rake over me quickly, and her lips curve upward in a sinful smile.

I close the door and she says, "Hey, stud."

Striding over to her, I don't bother with a response. Instead, I place my left hand on the back of her chair and lean over the top. Her face tilts up and I give her an upside-down kiss. "Hey, beautiful."

She snakes a hand up, and it curves around the back of my neck, pulling me back down. She kisses me this time, slipping her tongue deep in my mouth, and the sweet sensations of pleasure and peace run through me.

This woman riles me up like no other, yet makes me entirely calm at the same time.

Unreal.

I pull slowly away from her, loving the way her eyes are closed and a satisfied smile is left behind.

Stepping to the side of the chair and squatting down beside her, I bring my hand up and rest it on her knee. "What are you doing the rest of the day after we finish this conference? Want to knock off early and go do something?"

"I have a partners' meeting at four p.m. We're voting on next year's partnership candidates," she says, a wistful tone in her voice.

"Bummer," I say with a sad smile. "Are you coming over tonight?"

"You know I am," she says, and the promise in her voice has me wishing for time to go wonky and fast-forward by about five hours.

Looking back over my shoulder at the closed office door, I slide my hand up just a little higher on her leg. When I turn back toward her, I lean in a little closer and squeeze her leg. "Why don't you give me a peek of what you have under that skirt? Give me something to think about the rest of the day?"

She snickers at me and tries to bat my hand off her leg. "We're sitting in a judge's office, Reeve. Show some decency," she admonishes without any real censure in her tone.

Grinning, I slide my hand up a little higher. "I have no decency where you're concerned."

Her hand slams onto my wrist and grips it tightly, trying to halt my momentum. "Stop it," she growls—or is that a purr?

"Just a peek, baby," I cajole. "Black lace, right?"

"You're not looking," she says primly.

I straighten my fingers out, turn my wrist slightly, and they find her bare skin just above the lace of her stockings. "If you won't let me look, how about a touch?"

"No," she hisses and attempts to slam her legs together. I anticipate this, though, and shove my hand all the way in between her thighs until I cup her pussy. Grinding the heel of my hand on her, I whisper, "Touch or look, baby? What's it going to be?"

"Reeve," she says in a moan, "Judge Henry could walk in any moment."

"Maybe," I say. "And that would be really awkward. So quit fighting me and give me just a look or a touch and I'll leave you alone."

Leary's eyes flash hot at me with both annoyance and lust. "Fine," she snaps. "A quick touch."

Chuckling, I pull my hand back a tad so I can angle a finger under the elastic band that rests in the crease of her leg. Just as I get the tip of my index finger inside, I hear Judge Henry's booming voice out in the office area. The walls must be paper-thin, because I can hear him tell Mary, "Here are my notes on the restraining order. Go ahead and type me up a rough draft and print it out double spaced."

"Reeve," Leary says in panic and starts to push at my hand lodged between her legs.

Mary's voice comes through the door, "Right away, Judge Henry. But first, can I ask you a few questions about your accommodations for the judges' conference next month? I'm having trouble booking your flights."

Leary continues to push at my hand, but I hold it rock solid.

"Move your hand and get away from me," she whispers harshly.

Shaking my head, I give her an evil smile, working my finger under the elastic. "I want my touch first."

"He'll be coming in any second now," she protests.

"Just give in, baby," I urge her with a grin. "Five seconds, I'm in and out and then I'll leave you alone."

My heartbeat is slamming so hard against my chest, I'm sure Judge Henry and Mary can hear it outside the door. But for some reason, I don't want to give in. My need to touch Leary, to feel what's between those silken lips, has become imperative to me.

"Fine," she grits out, and her legs spread for me.

Fuck, yeah.

I slide my finger all the way in, swipe it through the lips of her pussy, and immediately find her practically dripping. I consider my options. A quick flutter over her clit or a bit of a deeper invasion?

Sawyer Bennett

Fuck . . . I want her to remember this all day while she's sitting in her stupid partner meeting. I opt for deep invasion.

I shove my finger inside her, easily sliding home because she's so wet. All the way up to my third knuckle and curl it upward. "Oh, baby. Fuck me . . . so damn wet."

Leary does nothing but moan and jerk her hips. I smile big but sadly as I pull my finger out. The conversation outside the door seems to be wrapping up. Tugging the edge of her panties back in place, I remove my hand from between her legs and stand up.

Leary's face is flushed pink, and she hastily scrambles to smooth her skirt down. When she looks up at me, I stick my finger in my mouth and suck it clean. "Mmm, baby. You are delicious."

"Oh God," she mutters and then adds in a complaining tone, "you are so going to fuck me good tonight to make up for that."

Winking at her, I reach down and adjust the semi I'm sporting and stride over to the chair beside hers, sitting down and crossing my legs in gentlemanly fashion. She slides a glance at me, shooting me a look of exasperation.

Before she can turn away, I say, "Hey."

"What?" she whispers.

"I adore you."

She smiles at me, not with just her beautiful lips, but with every prism of color in those fantastic eyes, and then Judge Henry opens the door and walks through.

We both start to stand up, but he shoots an impatient wave at us as he starts to unzip his black robe. "No. Sit, sit. No formalities here."

Both Leary and I say a quick hello as he removes his robe and hangs it on a hook on the back of his door. As he walks to his desk, he cuts us both a quick look and nods a greeting.

Then he does a double take at Leary. "Are you feeling all right, Miss Michaels? You look a little flushed."

She's as smooth as silk when she says, "Thank you for asking, Your Honor. I'm fine. Just decided to take the stairs rather than the elevator."

"Oh, good, good," he says absently as he sits down in his chair. Pulling his glasses from his face, he takes a moment to clean them with his tie and then puts them back on.

"Okay, so we're here for the pretrial conference for *LaPietra v. Summerland, et al.*, correct?"

"Yes, Your Honor," we both answer simultaneously, but Leary reaches into her briefcase and pulls out a multipage document. Handing it over to him, she says, "Mr. Holloway and I worked out a proposed pretrial order. We've been able to agree on all of the issues for the jury except for a minor disagreement on the wording of the causation issue."

Judge Henry takes the order and starts reading it. He pays careful attention to the wording issues. These will be the exact questions the jury will have on their verdict sheet when it's time for them to deliberate.

"Before I let you argue about the wording of the causation issue, is everything else accurate on the order? Witnesses? Evidence? You both agree on all this stuff?"

"Yes, Your Honor," Leary says quickly. "Everything is on there."

Massive guilt pours through me, because not everything. My three surprise rebuttal witnesses aren't on there, but under the law, I don't have to provide those. Just another reminder of the weight I'm carrying on my shoulders by keeping this secret from Leary.

Judge Henry nods and turns back to the jury issues. "Okay, Miss Michaels, tell me what the problem is with the wording here."

For the next ten minutes, both of us argue until we turn blue in the face. Our disagreement isn't a minor one, and it's something we tried to work out on our own one day through e-mail correspondence. It was weird having a spirited argument with her over the law and rules of procedure. It was a good thing we did it via e-mail and from our respective offices, because she was so sassy to me, I wanted to bend her over my knee and fire her ass up. I wanted to fuck her hard and make her come all over my cock.

Of course, none of that happened.

That night, though, when she came over to my house, I told her that it turned me on, and she proceeded to pick a fight over our respective positions on tort reform. She lit into me good, didn't hold back, and was about as disrespectful as you could get. Turned me the fuck on, and she got her spanking and a hard fucking to boot. I went to bed with a satisfied smile on my face as I pulled her into my arms.

Judge Henry finally makes a decision and actually comes up with a middle-ground compromise on the issue. I'm satisfied with it; Leary isn't. She wanted to win and she didn't, and I have to wonder what mood she'll be in when we leave here, since she didn't get exactly what she wanted.

"Is there anything else we need to discuss before the trial?" Judge Henry asks as he takes his glasses off and puts them on the table.

"I don't think so," I respond.

Leary says, "Nothing other than some standard motions in limine that I'll need to present before the trial starts."

"Sounds good," Judge Henry says. "We'll address those at the appropriate time. Now, I need to ask, is there any chance of settlement? I see in the file that Miss Michaels has filed a motion for sanctions against Mr. Collier and TransBenefit for failing to show up at the mediation."

His hard gaze is pinned on me, and he's giving me a little preview of his feelings about that motion. "I'm sorry, Your Honor. Against my advice, TransBenefit is refusing to make an offer."

"You know I don't like these insurance companies not playing by the rules, Mr. Holloway. This motion that Miss Michaels had to file does not make me happy. Is your client aware that the law pretty much demands I award her the money she's asked for?"

"Yes, sir," I say quickly. "I've advised Mr. Collier to pay the amount rather than have me argue the motion, but he doesn't want to take my advice."

"Well, maybe pass on to your client that I might just tack on a little more to what she's asking for not only wasting her time but mine as well."

"Duly noted, sir," I say with an apologetic smile. "I'll pass the message along."

"Okay, then," Judge Henry says as he stands up from his desk. Leary and I also stand, and we all take a moment to shake hands. "I'll see you two in my courtroom week after next for the start of the trial."

Leary and I wish Judge Henry a good day, grab our briefcases, and head out the door. After waving good-bye to Mary, we hit the back hallway.

"How mad are you about the jury issue?" I ask with a teasing smile.

"Not mad enough to avoid you tonight," she says saucily. "You owe me a good fucking, remember?"

I do a quick look behind us, don't see anyone, and spin on Leary. Dropping my briefcase, I grab her by the shoulders and push her back into the wall. She doesn't even get out an outraged gasp before my mouth is on hers and I'm giving her a good, hard kiss.

I make it quick because I don't want to get caught, but before I pull completely away from her, I ask, "Do you adore me, too?"

Her eyes light up, go a shade warmer, and she places her fingertips on my jaw. "Yeah, I adore you, too."

CHAPTER 19

LEARY

The trial has started.

It's on.

We're in our third day of jury selection, and it's almost complete. Contrary to what many people think, a case is either won or lost in jury selection. There's evidence and witnesses and then the pomp and circumstance of compelling closing arguments. While that's all important, none of it matters unless you have the right jury.

The law says the jury should be fair and impartial.

I say horseshit.

Every attorney who has ever conducted an effective voir dire has done so by stacking the jury with people who are biased in his or her favor. To do this, the judge gives us latitude in asking a wide variety of questions, designed to pick at and expose a juror's true feelings and philosophies. Mix that in with body language, tone of voice, and eye contact, and there's a true art to homing in on those jurors who can make or break your case.

So far, Reeve and I have agreed on ten of the twelve spots. The clerk has called in two more people from the jury pool to fill the empty seats, and I begin questioning them, starting from the top once again. Basic background information, marital status, current job, educational history, et cetera. Then I dive into meatier issues, like how they feel about tort reform and people who bring lawsuits against doctors.

So far, I've been pleased with the jurors. I've tried to stack it male heavy, because they'll be more sympathetic to an attractive woman with deformed breasts. Women, naturally, will not be sympathetic to Jenna being a stripper. I did exercise a few of my challenges on two men who, despite what might be a natural affinity for boobs, had other things about them that made them unattractive to me. One was a schoolteacher, and they're notoriously conservative, and the other was a minister. Now, I've had my share of liberal ministers on juries before, but there was something about the way the man looked at Jenna that had me on edge. All of his answers made him come across as completely fair and impartial, but I noted censure in his gaze. So I went with my gut instinct and released him.

Turning to the first applicant in one of the empty seats, I say, "Thank you for the background information, Mr. Harmon."

He beams back at me. He's young, maybe twenty-five or so, unmarried, and employed as a graphic designer. His blond hair is long and he sports a scraggly beard. He's wearing a pair of khaki pants and a blue flannel shirt, and I was absolutely charmed by his surfer-stoned-on-pot lingo. He even called me "dude" twice but, again, in a charming way.

"Can you tell me how you feel about the type of lawsuit that my client, Jenna LaPietra, has brought against Dr. Summerland and his practice?"

Mr. Harmon leans back, places one ankle on his knee, and grins. "Nothing wrong with it. It's what our country is about, right? Equal access to the judicial system and all."

I'm surprised he didn't add on a "dude" to that, but the guy is surprisingly smart. He has a college degree, after all.

"And in particular, when the trial is over, I'm going to be asking the jury to award Jenna a large sum of money. Part of that award will be for pain and suffering. Can you tell me what you think about the concept of paying someone money for intangible things like pain and suffering?"

Mr. Harmon leans forward, shoots a quick look at the judge, then brings his gaze back to me. He dramatically sniffs the air in front of himself and says in his best stoned-out voice, "Ah, nothing like the sweet scent of money to drive the stink of pain and suffering away, dude."

For the first time in my legal career, I've been struck dumb by a juror. His answer is absolutely fucking perfect, but was given in such a way as to border on disrespectful to me. Not that it bothered me, but I turn to look up at Judge Henry, wondering if he'll chastise the juror. I find him staring bug-eyed at the blond-haired young man, his jaw slightly agape.

Before he can collect himself, I turn back to the juror and give him an appreciative smile. "Thank you, Mr. Harmon. Those are all the questions I have right now."

I actually have a ton of other questions, but I'm not going to bother. After that answer, there's no way Reeve is going to let that kid stay on the jury. Mr. Harmon all but agreed he'd be the type to award big bucks for pain and suffering.

Fucking bummer. That dude—yes, dude—was the dream juror of all jurors. I give him one last almost-sad glance and turn to the other juror who was called into the box.

The courtroom has emptied out and the bailiff has turned out the lights. He patiently waits at the back doors for Reeve and me as we pack up our stuff. Reeve's cocounsel, Gill Kratzenburg, and the insurance company representatives—four in addition to Tom Collier—all made a break for the doors when Judge Henry recessed for the day. Jenna also hightailed it out of there, but that was so she could smoke a cigarette.

Reeve finishes up before me and comes to stand by my table. In a low voice so the bailiff doesn't hear us, he says, "Please stay at my house tonight, Leary."

I look up at him briefly, loving the needful look in his eyes, but then go back to packing up my materials. "I can't. I have too much work to do to get ready for opening statements and my first witness."

"Baby," he murmurs and tingles shoot up my spine. "Please."

Snapping my briefcase shut, I pick it up and look at him with a sympathetic smile. "Missing my body that much?"

He takes a step closer and leans down. He doesn't touch me, though, because that would be stupid, what with the bailiff waiting on us.

"I miss you," he says simply. "I just want you to sleep in my bed. It's been three days."

My heart melts and puddles warmly, and I really, really want to say yes, because I've missed him, too. We've both sort of wordlessly agreed not to stay with each other the last few nights, and I figured it was because we'd both be so busy there'd be no time to do anything.

Didn't stop me from missing him every single night, though. I was having a hard time sleeping even though I was exhausted after a full day in trial and then several hours of work each night in order to prep for the following day.

"I really have to go over my opening statement and tweak some direct exams," I say regretfully.

"Tell you what . . . come to my house. I'll cook you dinner and you can spread out in my dining room to work. You can eat and go back to working. I'll leave you alone and be waiting in bed for you when you're done."

The sweetest feeling of warmth and security flows through me. He wants to take care of me. He wants to be near me. I don't move a muscle but say, "If Mr. Nosy Pants wasn't in the back of the courtroom watching us right now, I would kiss the hell out of you."

Reeve smiles at me. "Is that a yes?"

"It's a yes," I say.

We nod good-bye to the bailiff and share an elevator down. Unfortunately, there are a few straggling jurors heading down with us, so Reeve and I stand on opposite sides of the elevator and keep our gazes lowered to our feet.

I follow him home, and while he starts dinner—just some soup and sandwiches—I head back to his room and change out of my monkey suit. I pull one of the soft white T-shirts he wears under his dress shirts out of his drawer and slip it on.

Back in the dining room, I go ahead and unpack my briefcase, pulling out the things I'll need to work on tonight. I'm not going to spend much time on my opening statements. I know the facts of this case inside and out, and the opening statements are nothing more than a forecast of the evidence I'll present to the jury.

No, I'm going to spend most of my time working on the questions I'll have for my first witness. Now, most attorneys would want their client to take the stand as the first witness in a trial. If you want to present a chronological case, it's a good and effective way to start. I know Jenna will do a fantastic job. We spent a majority of this weekend going over her testimony.

But I'm going to do something a little different. I'm going to call Dr. Summerland to the stand.

He won't be expecting it and neither will Reeve. Normally, the defendant would be called to testify during his case in chief, which follows mine. But the defendant isn't required to take the stand, and I can't afford to trust that Reeve will put him up there. I mean, if this douche were my client, I wouldn't put him on the stand. He's too arrogant and cocky, and the jury will hate him.

So I decided to take the bull by the horns and call Dr. Summerland during my case in chief. As I said, they'll never expect it because it's not a very common practice, and that will also ensure that Reeve will not have bothered to prepare Dr. Summerland for it as well.

I almost give out a maniacal, evil laugh, but suppress it. I don't want to have Reeve pressing me over what I find so fucking funny.

"Dinner's ready," Reeve calls out, and I turn from the dining room table and pad into the kitchen. He's laid out soup and grilled-cheese sandwiches at the center island and is pulling two bottles of water from the fridge.

"Looks fantastic," I say, and realize how starved I am. I haven't eaten since a quick bowl of cereal this morning. I'm always too wound up to eat during the lunch recess while a trial is in progress, preferring to stay at counsel table and work while it's quiet. Reeve, I've noticed, goes to lunch each day with Kratzenburg and the insurance cronies, but I didn't expect different. They would be analyzing every nuance of what happened in the courtroom.

"Eat up," he says as he puts a bottle of water in front of me, leans over to kiss the side of my head, and sits down on one of the stools. I hop up on the one next to him and pick up the sandwich, taking a small bite.

"Mmm," I moan in relief. "Best sandwich ever."

He grins at me and dunks his in the bowl of tomato soup in front of him. "It's basic but filling."

I nod, too hungry to answer him. We eat in silence for a few moments, both lost in our thoughts, which should be focused on our opening statements, but I'm not right this second. I'm thinking about how great this food is, how sweet Reeve is for cooking for me, and even from my peripheral vision, how damn good he looks sitting next to me.

Visions of me pushing my bowl away, crawling onto his lap, and dry-humping him at the kitchen counter fill my head. Blinking, I try to clear my thoughts. We both have work to do after we eat. No sex . . . at least not until we've finished our preparations for tomorrow.

"Glad jury selection is over," Reeve says out of the blue.

I expect my body to tense up over his comment, because it leads us into dangerous territory talking about the case, but then I realize I don't feel awkward at all. I don't think Reeve will reveal any dark secrets he might be harboring, and I sure as hell have no compulsion to share my game plan. Instead, I find it intriguing that we can talk about something in the trial that's already been concluded and maybe see what the other person is thinking.

"Are you pleased with the results?" I ask.

He shrugs his shoulders. "It's an okay jury for me. I think it's a fantastic jury for you. You did a good job stacking it male heavy."

I nod because he's right. It's a pretty damn good jury. Especially with Mr. Harmon on the panel.

Jerking in my seat, I snap my head toward him. "That reminds me . . . why didn't you excuse Mr. Harmon from the panel? You know he's absolutely pro-plaintiff."

Reeve doesn't look at me but takes another sip of his soup. "He's okay. I just had a gut feeling about him that maybe he'll be a little more impartial than you give him credit for."

My eyes narrow at him. "Uh-uh. No way. Not buying it. You totally should have kicked him off the panel, but you didn't. Why not?"

He just ignores me, taking another sip of soup.

I reach my hand out and lay it on his forearm, halting his movements. He turns to look at me.

"Reeve, why didn't you excuse Mr. Harmon? He's bad for your case."

With a blank face, Reeve just stares at me, a tiny muscle in his cheek pulsing. He swallows hard and covers my hand with his own. "Don't ask me that question, Leary. Just leave it be, okay?"

I open my mouth to argue because I'm pretty sure I know why he did it, but then I snap it shut. I don't want to hear him say it. I don't want him to admit that he's done something to help my case.

While part of me is sweetly overwhelmed that he'd do that, another part of me is horrified. Oh, not that he would do something unethical. As I've told him before, there are certain things I would sacrifice my law ethics for. But I don't want to accept he might have thrown me a bit of a bone, because I don't want there to be any expectations that I would ever do the same.

Because I wouldn't.

I wouldn't lift a single finger to help him in this case.

"I would never expect you to return a favor in this case, Leary," Reeve says. "I didn't do it expecting anything in return."

My mouth gapes open, because he's a fucking mind reader. His hand comes up, his knuckles chuck me under the chin, and my mouth closes. He smiles at me in understanding.

"I don't get it," I say, awash with confused feelings.

Reeve leans toward me, resting one hand gently on my thigh. He presses his lips against mine, and my eyes flutter closed over the gentle touch.

He pulls away, and I feel his hand curve around the back of my neck. My eyes open and he's looking at me so seriously, I feel the weight of his stare pinning me down.

"Leary," he says softly, "I want you to win this case."

"What?" I gasp, but his other hand comes up to press his fingers to my lips.

"Shh," he admonishes. "We're not going to speak about this again, but put everything between you and me aside. I don't believe in my case. I believe in yours. Unfortunately, I'm still stuck defending it. But that doesn't mean I'm not hoping like hell that you and Jenna get everything you deserve. And here is what we won't talk about again. I might do things to throw you a bone every now and then, and that's not going to change. Just know that I'm doing this because I want to and because I can, and not because of anything you do for me in return."

I blink at him in astonishment.

"We clear?" he asks softly.

I blink at him some more.

"Leary?"

Finally, I nod my head. "I don't know what to say."

He smiles at me, his fingers squeezing my neck. "Tell me you adore me."

"You know I do," I say from a place deep within my heart.

"Tell me you're going to fuck me silly after you finish working tonight," he says, now grinning big.

"You know I will," I say as warmth spreads through me.

Reeve presses a quick kiss to my lips and releases me. He points at my food. "Good. Now hurry and eat, and hurry and get your work done. I'm kind of in a mood to play with my toys tonight."

His voice rumbles over me, and there's nothing I want more in this moment than to push my plate away so I can play with Reeve. But I can't. My priorities remain in order. This trial is too important, so food first, then work, and then I'm going to let Reeve do whatever he wants to me.

CHAPTER 20
REEVE

Leary's standing in front of the jury, having eschewed the wooden podium that sits off to the right. Instead, she prefers to pace back and forth in front of the jurors as she makes her opening statement. She does so without memorization or even written bullet points. Her entire story pours forth from her soul, and while opening statements are merely supposed to be a dry foretelling of the evidence, Leary talks to the jury with so much passion about Jenna's case, the jurors are all hanging on the edges of their seats as they listen to her.

She's fucking amazing at this shit.

Looks fucking beautiful, too, in a custom-tailored taupe skirt and matching suit jacket with a high mandarin collar. The skirt comes to just below her knees, and because it's a fairly brisk fall day, she decided to go with buttery golden-brown boots with a high heel. She's wearing her chocolate-brown hair loose around her shoulders, and I get it—with a jury that's predominantly male, she's going for a little sex appeal as well. There's not even a hint of a stuffy, uptight attorney in her form before the jury.

Her words start to fade as I can't help letting my gaze drop to her ass every once in a while. When I think of her ass and the things we did last night, well, let's just say it's a good thing I won't have to be standing up in front of the jury anytime soon. My opening statements went off without a hitch, although I'm pretty sure three of the jurors started nodding off during my speech.

Fine by me.

I don't want them to connect with me or my client, and I might have even flattened out the tone of my voice a little to help make what I was saying super monotonous. Anything, anything at fucking all I can do to give Leary a leg up without actually sacrificing ethics, I'm going to do. The guilt over calling rebuttal witnesses is so thick and pervasive, it's almost suffocating me at times.

Last night after Leary finished work, she came back to my bedroom and slid into bed. I had finished well over an hour before and entertained myself by watching *Chappelle's Show*.

Turning the TV off, I turned toward her, wrapping an arm around her waist and pulling her in close.

"Tired?" I asked her softly.

"Actually, a little wound up," she murmured, leaning in to kiss and suck along the base of my throat. It felt so fucking good that I immediately started to swell for her.

"Can I play a little bit?" I asked her, my hand slipping under the back waistband of her panties and palming her ass.

"What did you have in mind?" she asked in a husky voice, her hand going underneath the sheets and in between my legs, where she found me naked and hard as a rock.

Pushing my finger down in between her ass cheeks, I lightly rubbed over her tight bud, which caused her to jerk in my arms. "I was thinking about playing back here a bit."

"You're too big," she said immediately, even as her hips started gyrating against my finger as I gently massaged her sensitive hole.

"Yeah . . . I am too big," I said, not with any arrogance, but because I knew she couldn't take me back there right off the bat. "But I have a toy that I just know you'll love."

"Hmm," she purred low in her throat. "Okay."

And just like that, she submitted to me and my dirty little fantasies. And fuck, it was spectacular.

I didn't go for my butt plug right away, but rather stripped her bare and ate her pussy first, making her come twice so she was nice and loose. Then I flipped her over on the bed, brought her up on her knees, and pushed her chest down to the mattress so her ass was raised high in the air. Stroking her skin, I spoke dirty words to her that caused her to moan. She held her breath when I spread her ass cheeks and dribbled lubricant over her. I used my finger on her first, almost busting a nut when she groaned in satisfaction as I went three knuckles deep on her. I massaged and played gently with her, slowly building her up. When she was ready, I said, "Okay, baby, I'm going to ease this in. I promise it will feel good."

She didn't even tense. She was so loose and trusting that when I placed the tip of the plug to her ass, she actually pushed back against me a little. I worked it into her slowly, tilting my head to the side so I could see it as it slid into her body. When I had it in to the hilt, I twisted the base and she cried out.

And fuck, I was done playing. I grabbed my cock, rubbed it through her slick folds a few times, and then slammed into her until my pelvis pushed hard against the plug in her ass. Leary shrieked, not in fear or pain, but in absolute pleasure, and I know this because she immediately demanded, "Do that again."

So I did.

Again and again and again.

I fucked her hard and fast, she came really fast, and I didn't lag behind. So different from the sweet and slow lovemaking three days prior on our last night together before the trial started. There was a quiet desperation to the way I performed with her that night, and I hope when everything finally shakes out from this trial, Leary remembers how great every single action in my bed or hers has been between us.

"When you've heard all the evidence"—Leary's voice cuts back into my thoughts, and I shift in my seat, because my trip down memory lane just now has given me a hard-on under the counsel table—"I'm going to come before you, and I'm going to ask you for compensation. It's going to be a large amount. Be ready for it. It's going to be an amount to compensate Jenna for her past medical bills, the reconstructive surgeries she still faces, her lost wages, and her pain and suffering. All I ask is that you listen to everything with an open mind and reserve your judgment until you've heard all the evidence. Thank you."

Leary stands a moment more and takes time to look each and every juror in the eye. It's an impressive and brave way to make a connection with them.

Turning from the jury, Leary walks back to her counsel table and stands in front of her chair. She doesn't bother sitting down but rather waits for the judge to say, "Thank you, Miss Michaels and Mr. Holloway for your opening statements. The jury is now with Plaintiff. You may call your first witness, Miss Michaels."

I pull my yellow pad closer to me, prepared for Leary to call Jenna to the stand. I even write Jenna's name across the top sheet and underline it twice.

"Thank you, Your Honor," Leary says cordially. "At this time, the plaintiff would like to call Dr. Garry Summerland to the stand."

I freeze with my pen tip resting against my legal pad. Dr. Summerland curses beside me and then leans over to whisper, "What the hell is going on?"

Looking up to the bench, I hold up one finger on my hand. "Just a moment, Your Honor, if you please."

"Make it quick," Judge Henry says.

I put my arm around the back of Dr. Summerland's chair and lean in toward him. "She's allowed to call you during her case if she wants."

"This is fucking great," he hisses at me.

"You'll be fine," I assure him. "Just tell the truth and nothing will go wrong."

He glares at me and I think to myself, *I hope you lie, you cocky son of a bitch, and I hope Leary wipes the floor with you.*

Dr. Summerland stands from the chair, buttons his suit coat, and makes his way to the witness stand. The bailiff holds a Bible under his hand, and the clerk puts him under oath.

If I actually gave a shit about this case, this would be very bad for me. Leary pulled a brilliant move, and I admire the fuck out of her for it. She took a gamble, knowing the chances of me preparing him for this were nil. And now I want to laugh over the green tinge to Dr. Summerland's face.

"Good morning, Dr. Summerland," Leary says politely as she sits back down at counsel table. In North Carolina, attorneys are not permitted to stand while questioning a witness unless it's to hand them an exhibit.

He doesn't respond but just nods at her, his lips flattened in a grimace. Stupid fuck. It's common sense that if you *act* like an ass, the jury is going to *think* you're an ass. On top of that, the jury clearly likes Leary, so if he treats her hostilely, they're not going to like that.

I hope he's a supreme asshole to Leary. She can handle herself, and any animosity she builds up against Dr. Summerland will help ease the blow I'm going to deliver later on in the case.

Leary doesn't waste any time in laying out the history of Dr. Summerland's treatment of Jenna. She goes right in for the kill. "Dr. Summerland, can you tell the jury your educational background?"

His chin goes up and superiority oozes off him. "Yes. I did my undergraduate degree at UCLA, medical school at Vanderbilt, and my internship and residency at Emory."

"And you're board certified, correct?" she asks politely.

"Yes."

"In general surgery?"

"Yes," he says, not willing to elucidate.

"You're not, however, certified in plastic surgery, are you?" she asks him as she leans back casually in her chair.

"No, I'm not."

"Plastic surgery is very different from general surgery, wouldn't you say?" she asks demurely.

"In some respects, but in others we do some similar procedures."

"Like what?" she asks, tilting her head and sounding generally intrigued and curious.

"Like mastectomies," he says firmly.

"But the types of mastectomies you do are very different from a plastic surgeon's, correct?"

"Well, the concept is the same," he starts to say, but she cuts him off.

"When *you* do a mastectomy, it's for women who opt not to have reconstruction, correct? They just want the offending tissue removed?"

"I suppose that's one way to look at it," he grumbles.

"And plastic surgeons . . . when they do mastectomies, it's for the purposes of reconstruction so they can build back up the woman's breast through implants, correct?"

"Yes, that's what they do."

"Dr. Summerland, do you recognize the *New England Journal of Medicine* as an authoritative medical periodical?"

"Yes, I do. I read it faithfully," he says confidently. "In fact, there's an article in a 2009 issue that discusses mastectomies performed by general surgeons."

Leary dramatically raises her eyebrows in delight and smiles at Dr. Summerland. "Well, isn't that terrific?" she says jovially as she waves a document in her hand. "I just happen to have that article here. May I approach the witness, Your Honor?"

Judge Henry nods and Leary stands up smoothly from her chair. She walks up to the witness stand, the jurors all following her with avid interest. She hands Dr. Summerland the document. "I'm handing you what's been marked as Plaintiff's exhibit one. Does this look like the article you mentioned?"

Dr. Summerland flips through it and nods. "It does."

"And on the last three pages of the article, it gives photographs of acceptable results from a nonreconstructive mastectomy, doesn't it?"

Dr. Summerland leans in and peers at the pages she referenced. "Yes, it does, although they're in black and white and it's a little hard to see, since this is a photocopy."

"Well," Leary says dramatically as she walks back to her table and reaches over the low wall that separates the main seating area of the courtroom. She pulls back a huge thirty-by-forty-inch piece of foam board, keeping the front of it concealed. She walks over to me and turns it so only I can see it. I give it a quick glance, trying hard not to start laughing hysterically now that I see what she's doing, and give her a nod of acceptance. Leary's required to show me any demonstrative exhibits before she uses them.

She carries the board back up to Dr. Summerland, keeping it concealed until she reaches him. She stands in front of the witness stand and says, "Dr. Summerland, I took the liberty of getting the original photos from the *New England Journal of Medicine* and had them blown up so you can see them more clearly. Now, I'd like to know . . . do these photographs accurately represent the results of a typical mastectomy that you would perform as a general surgeon, and without hope of having reconstruction done?"

Leary turns the large board around so both Dr. Summerland and the jury can see it, and the two female jurors actually gasp.

It's a huge blowup of a woman's chest after her breasts have been removed. Horrid, angry scars line the bottom, her nipples and areolae are gone, and most obvious are several large, pitted areas left behind.

Dr. Summerland doesn't understand where Leary is going with this, so he gives a confident smile and says, "Yes. This is what a typical nonreconstructive mastectomy would look like that I would perform in my practice."

"And your patients, you would actually have them prepared for these types of results, right?"

"That's right."

"They wouldn't be shocked to see something like this, because they really hadn't intended to have reconstruction and implants put in, correct?"

"Yes, correct."

"Thank you," she says and tactfully places the board against the edge of her counsel table so the jury can still see it. She turns away from Dr. Summerland and walks back behind her table and reaches over the low wall again, grabbing another foam board. She walks it to me, I glance at it and nod my head, and she heads back to Summerland.

"Now, Dr. Summerland, you performed a breast-reduction surgery on my client, Jenna LaPietra. Correct?"

"Yes, I did," he says confidently.

"And as we discussed, you're not a plastic surgeon, are you?"

"No, I'm not." Another cocky grin.

"You don't have any advanced training like plastic surgeons do, say, in the contouring or shaping of tissue, do you?"

"No," he says, his smile sliding just a tad.

"You know what my client does for a living?"

He nods but doesn't answer. She doesn't press him but instead asks, "You know she's a topless dancer?"

"That's right," he says and actually sneers a little.

"Let me show you what I've marked as Plaintiff's exhibit number two."

Leary turns the board so Summerland and the jury get a simultaneous look at the huge color blowup of Jenna's chest. Summerland isn't affected by it. He's seen this picture before, so his face remains bland.

The jury, however, is horrified. They wince and grimace, and one woman covers her mouth and turns her head away. Dr. Summerland still doesn't understand how horrible the results are.

"Now, Dr. Summerland," Leary says politely, "what is this a picture of?"

"That would be your client's chest postsurgery," he says calmly.

"And is it just me," she asks sarcastically as she points to the other board that's resting against the table, "or do these results look a lot like those of the mastectomy photo we just showed the jury?"

Now he gets it. I see understanding filter in.

He starts stumbling. "Well, actually, you can see I left a lot of breast tissue in Miss LaPietra's case. She didn't want them totally removed, you see—"

"And yet, the results look eerily similar, don't they?" she prompts, but doesn't wait for him to answer. Instead, she attacks. "I mean, look here at the craters left in Jenna's breasts. Same as on the mastectomy photo. And the scar contractions pulling the skin? Same as well, right?"

"Yes," he says angrily. "Those do look similar, but there are a lot of differences if you want to—"

"Dr. Summerland," Leary snaps at him, and his eyes widen in surprise, "can you honestly look those jurors in the face and tell them that these are acceptable results for a topless dancer? Well, for any woman, really, who wants to keep her breasts?"

I look over at the jury and they're all glaring at him, daring him to say Jenna's results were acceptable.

Leary will go on to grill Dr. Summerland for another three hours and twenty minutes, but this moment will mark the beginning of Dr. Summerland's breakdown into the worst testimony in the history of forever. He takes her attack so personally that he starts arguing with her. The judge has to reprimand him four times, even once calling a recess to dress him down in private.

By the time Leary gets done with Dr. Summerland, I have to restrain myself from not standing up, putting my fingers in my mouth, and giving a wolf whistle, followed by a slow clap of respect. By the time Dr. Summerland gets off the witness stand on shaky legs, I know every single juror hates the man with an undying passion.

I just hope they hold on to that feeling, because we still have days and days of trial to get through. This trial will go on for at least two weeks, maybe more. It's a lot of time for them to forget what an utter douche my client is. I hope they remember how badly he fucked up and don't focus instead on the testimony they'll end up hearing last.

Because my witnesses will say that Jenna LaPietra was a paid prostitute.

CHAPTER 21

LEARY

"Thank you, Dr. Calloway," I say politely as I sit back in my chair. "I have no further questions."

Judge Henry looks over to Reeve. "Any re-cross, Mr. Holloway?"

"No, Your Honor," he says with a polite smile. I didn't expect he would. Dr. Calloway is my expert witness, a general surgeon from Duke. During my direction examination of him, he told the jury in no uncertain terms that Dr. Summerland had no business whatsoever in attempting a breast reduction. He told the jury that general surgeons are not qualified to do that type of surgery. He told the jury this after he made it clear that he taught a course in advanced medical ethics for general surgeons at Duke, and that Dr. Summerland actually took that course a few years ago as part of his continuing-education requirements. I tried hard not to look at Dr. Summerland when Dr. Calloway actually pointed at him from the stand and said, "Dr. Summerland should remember that we specifically discussed the boundaries that general surgeons are not to cross."

It was freakin' glorious.

As expected, Reeve's cross-examination of Dr. Calloway was short. He did his best to poke holes in his firm stance, even getting Dr. Calloway to admit there was no law or rule against what Dr. Summerland did. It was an effective cross, as much as he could expect against this type of expert, but he knew not to push more when Judge Henry asked him if he had any further questions.

The judge releases Dr. Calloway, who gives a polite smile to the jurors as he steps off the witness stand. I start to stand up to call my next witness, Dr. Franklinton, who's a plastic surgeon at Duke. His testimony is going to focus on how complex a breast-reduction surgery is, and how it's imperative to gently and delicately remove the tissue, paying fine attention to sensitive shaping of the remaining breast. I expect it will highlight just how inept Dr. Summerland was when he butchered Jenna.

"Your Honor," Reeve says as he stands up and I turn to look at him in surprise, "may we take a small break before the next witness?"

Judge Henry looks at me. "That's fine with me."

"Then we'll take a ten-minute recess," Judge Henry says, and rises from his seat to probably take a potty break of his own. The bailiff escorts out the jury members, who look grateful for the slight reprieve in testimony.

Reeve doesn't leave, though. Instead, he huddles at his table with Dr. Summerland, Tom Collier, and two of the other insurance representatives. I can't hear what they're saying, but it doesn't matter. I'm flipping through my notes to make sure I'm up to speed on everything I want to get out of Dr. Franklinton when he takes the stand.

I get so immersed in my work, I jump in shock when Reeve taps me on my shoulder. I look up at him, immediately covering up my notes with my hand. It's not that I don't trust Reeve—it's just a habit I've developed in the courtroom. And to prove how much I do trust him, I remove my hand just as quickly.

He gives me a tight look and says, "If you have a moment, I need to talk to you and Judge Henry privately in his chambers."

Surprised but curious, I get up from the table and follow Reeve into the back hallway and to Judge Henry's office. Mary is not at her desk, but the judge's door is open and Reeve knocks lightly to announce our arrival.

Judge Henry is sitting at his desk and looks up with a smile. "Come on in."

We enter and Reeve closes the door behind us. He doesn't waste a moment's breath when he says, "Your Honor, in light of Dr. Calloway's testimony just now, as well as expected similar testimony from Miss Michaels's next two experts, my clients, Dr. Summerland and TransBenefit, have given me authority to make an offer to settle this case."

My eyebrows raise in surprise.

Not that an offer is coming in general. That often happens in the middle of a trial when the case is going especially well for the plaintiff.

No, I'm surprised that an offer is coming in *this* particular case, since TransBenefit has been so adamant they won't discuss the possibility. I don't respond but wait for Reeve to lay out the terms.

"They're authorizing me to offer five hundred thousand dollars to settle the case in its entirety—two hundred thousand in up-front money, and the remaining three hundred thousand in the form of an annuity administered by TransBenefit. Of course, they will also want Miss Michaels and Miss LaPietra to sign a confidentiality agreement."

"That's quite a jump," Judge Henry says, and I couldn't agree more. It's a serious offer, but it's not the amount I want for Jenna. I'm prepared to also call to the stand a vocational-rehabilitation expert to discuss Jenna's unemployability, as well as a life-care expert and an economist to discuss the economic damages her inability to work will project out over the future. Their preliminary figures are in the seven-figure range.

So, while $500,000 isn't anything to sneeze at, it's also a zero shy of what's really fair for Jenna.

"Miss Michaels," Judge Henry says, "this is a good offer. Go talk to your client and discuss it. I think it's something she needs to seriously consider."

I nod at the judge and Reeve and turn toward the door.

"Oh, one more thing," Reeve says, and I can tell by the look on his face that he's hesitant to say what comes next. "TransBenefit wants me to make clear this is a one-time-only offer. If it's rejected, there won't be a counteroffer and the current offer will be pulled from the table."

Wow. Hardball bastards. "Understood," I say, then I head out to find Jenna. I'm sure she's downstairs smoking.

After a quick bathroom break, I catch her in the hallway outside the courtroom doors. I pull her away and am relieved that no one else is around, the jury having been called back in and seated in the box. I'm sure Judge Henry has advised them that the break has been extended, but he won't tell them we're discussing a settlement. He wouldn't want to bias the jury with that information.

"We have an offer," I tell Jenna quietly, and her eyes widen.

"How much?"

"Five hundred thousand, with two hundred up front and three hundred paid in installments. But trust me, they'll pay the five hundred thousand in cash if we push them."

Jenna nibbles on her lower lip while she stares at me. "That's a lot of money. What do you think we should do?"

And here is where my job gets tricky. If it were my breasts that were mangled and my autistic son who was suffering because of my inability to earn a living, I would want more. I'm a risk taker by nature, and I'd tell them to shove it. I feel good about this jury. I feel great about this case.

I would tell them to go fuck themselves.

But this isn't my case. Those weren't my breasts, and I most certainly don't have an autistic child. I will go home every night, comfortable and secure, not having a worry in the world when it comes to paying my bills or covering medical expenses.

"I can't tell you what to do, Jenna. I think this amount is unfair. It doesn't adequately compensate you. Hell, a good chunk of that money would be eaten up by reconstructive surgeries."

Jenna shakes her head. "I don't need the surgeries. Every bit of that would go for Damien."

I nod in understanding. And she will get every bit of it. When Jenna first came to me about this case, I immediately got Midge's approval to handle it pro bono so I wouldn't be taking a legal fee from the offer. But I still need to make sure that Jenna is properly advised. "Even so, five hundred thousand is not going to last your and Damien's lifetimes. It will provide you with less than half of what you're going to need to survive and pay for his treatment."

Jenna turns away from me and walks a few paces. Her hands come to her head and she rakes her fingers through her hair. Giving a sigh, she turns to me. "What's your honest opinion about how it's going?"

"It's going well. The jury is with us, I believe. Summerland was horrible. Your testimony was fantastic. The experts are clear. I think they're going to find that Summerland was negligent in causing your injuries. The question, though, is what they'll compensate you. It could be more, it could be less. It just depends on how inflamed they are toward him."

"Such a crapshoot," she murmurs to herself.

"It is."

Jenna walks up to me and takes my hands. "I can't repay you for all the hard work you've put into this case. Without you, I would have never been able to tell this story to a jury."

"Jenna," I say quietly, "this is nothing. I would do this a million times over for you, because you deserve it. And let me tell you now, no matter what happens in that courtroom, I swear to you that I will not let Damien go without. If we lose, you do not have to worry about your child. I will always be there to help."

Jenna shakes her head, denying my offer, but I squeeze her hands and tell her urgently, "Yes. I will always be there. Don't be afraid of the future."

Tears spring to Jenna's eyes and she pulls me in fast for a hug. As she clings to me, she whispers, "Turn down the offer. Let's see what the jury will do."

As I pull away, I search her eyes to make sure she's clear on what she's telling me to do. She looks back at me with resolute courage, and I give her a nod.

"Can I go smoke another cigarette?" she asks.

"Sure," I tell her. "It's going to take a few minutes to convey this to opposing counsel and the judge, and see if they stick to their guns and don't make a counteroffer."

Jenna heads toward the elevator while I head for the side door that goes to the back hallway. As soon as I swing it open, I see Reeve standing there by himself, leaning with his back against the wall.

His head swings my way and his eyes are worried. "What's she going to do?"

I walk up to him, giving him a small smile, and say, "I'm sorry. She won't take it."

Reeve turns his face away and mutters a curse. When he looks back at me, he reaches out and grabs one of my hands. Leaning in, he says in an urgent voice, "You need to take this offer, Leary. It's good money. It will give her a new life."

I'm a little surprised by the hint of what could be hysteria in his words. Giving his hand a gentle squeeze, I pull away from him. He watches me like a hawk. "I'm sorry, but Jenna's made her decision."

Reeve swallows hard, and I see a wave of sadness overcome his face. It makes me feel strangely uneasy and something cold settles inside my chest. But then it's gone, and he gives me a resolute nod of his head. "We better go tell Judge Henry."

He turns away from me and that unsettled feeling remains. Reaching out, I tug on the sleeve of his suit jacket. "Wait."

Reeve turns back to me, his eyes clouded and fatigued.

"Is there something I should know? Am I missing something here?"

Lifting his chin up, Reeve blinks a few times and clears his throat. "No, why do you ask?"

"I'm a little surprised you're bothered I turned down the offer. I feel like my case is going amazingly well, and the jury is going to give Jenna more than your client is offering. Yet you seem truly troubled by this."

I look closely at Reeve, waiting to see if anything surfaces to give credence to the uneasy feeling within me. Instead, he looks back at me with clear and confident eyes. "No, you're not missing anything. I just happen to think it's good money and you're risking a lot to turn it down."

"I understand the risks well," I tell him calmly, my eyes still flicking to his to see if his countenance reveals anything. "I never think a verdict is guaranteed. I understand Jenna could lose, no matter how good I feel about it right now."

No reaction but a slight tightening of his jaw, and Reeve gives me a small smile. "Well, that's good. If you're comfortable with the risks, then so am I."

I follow Reeve back to Judge Henry's office. We convey that the offer has been declined. Even though Reeve advised us there would be no counteroffer, the judge makes us go through the motions and exhaust negotiations in a formal manner. He demands that I send a number back to them, and I tell Reeve that Jenna will settle for two million. Our bottom line was actually a bit less than that, but I wasn't going to shortchange us in case TransBenefit has more money.

Reeve talks to his clients and is back in less than two minutes.

No counteroffer is forthcoming, and true to their word, the $500,000 is pulled from the table.

This shouldn't have bothered me.

I felt fine just minutes ago out in the hallway with Jenna's decision to press forward. I felt confident, and again, understanding there's no guarantee, I had no qualms about turning our nose up at that money.

But something doesn't feel right to me, and it all boils down to Reeve. I can't put my finger on it and I really can't ask Reeve about it, either, because we promised not to discuss this case. While I feel pretty strong in our evidence and know exactly how the rest of the trial is going to play out, I can't get over the feeling that I'm missing something critically important.

Judge Henry resumes the trial. I call Dr. Franklinton to the stand and he's brilliant. The jury eats up every word out of his mouth. Reeve can do nothing to shake his testimony. Dr. Summerland sinks lower and lower into his chair, and the jurors all take turns leveling glares at him and fond smiles toward Jenna.

Dr. Franklinton does so well that by the time he gets off the stand and the judge is recessing court for the day, all of my earlier feelings of unrest have disappeared. I only have three more witnesses left, the ones who will forecast the economic damages. Then I'll be done and Reeve will have a chance to put on his case. That will probably take another four to five days, and then Reeve and I will be arguing our cases to the jury. I'm more than halfway home. I can taste the victory on the tip of my tongue, and I'm not only excited about getting justice for Jenna, I'm excited to put this case behind me so Reeve and I can be together with no secrets or battles to wage between us.

CHAPTER 22

REEVE

This morning I was awake long before the sun rose, and long before Leary stirred next to me. Normally she's the early riser, the one pushing me out of bed.

I didn't get up, though.

Instead, I loosened my hold around her. Her face was turned so her cheek was pressed into my chest. One arm was curled under her, the other slung over my waist. I inched backward a bit and stared at her shadowy form in the gloom of the predawn hours.

As the sun rose, I watched as her features came into focus. The way her face was utterly relaxed, her lips slightly parted as she slept, her hair falling forward over her right eye. I tentatively reached up, pushed it back with my fingertips so I could have a completely unobstructed view of her. When my skin touched hers, I reveled in the sensation.

Then my chest squeezed in anxiety, as I was afraid our time was almost up.

I acted then on pure need, pulling her back against me. She moaned in her sleep, and when my lips pressed against hers, she opened her eyes to blink at me.

I felt the curve of her mouth against mine as it went from relaxed slumber to a welcoming smile.

I kissed her passionately, making sure she understood that this was far more than just a good-morning kiss. This had the potential to be a good-bye kiss, so I didn't hold a fucking thing back. I poured everything that I am and will ever be into the kiss, hoping it would speak volumes and she wouldn't doubt me later.

Kissing turned to stroking. Soft pants turned to rough gasps.

My hands wandered across her skin while hers did the same to me.

We made out like two teenagers in the backseat of a car on prom night, and when I couldn't stand it anymore, I rolled her onto her back, pushed in between her legs and made love to her.

She arched her back, giving me access to her slender neck, where I murmured gentle words against her skin while I pumped slowly in and out of her. It was beautiful and damning all at once. The memory of how I made love to her will haunt me, I'm sure.

I'll never forget how when I came inside her, she moaned, "I adore you."

I answered her, "And I you," and then I kissed her again.

"Okay, Mr. Holloway, Miss Michaels, it appears you both have concluded your cases before this jury. Are there any other matters we need to handle before we move on?"

I jerked and blinked my eyes as Judge Henry's words penetrated my poignant memories of this morning. Leary stood up from her table and answered, "No, Your Honor. I believe that's everything."

Of course, she would think that's everything. Last night she chattered at me like a little puppy, happy and relieved that all of the evidence was finished. Her case was wrapped up, and it took just a little more than three days for me to put on my expert witnesses. They, of course, gave testimony that was completely contradictory to Leary's expert witnesses. They didn't come off well because they weren't as qualified and there was personal bias. I rested my case late yesterday afternoon, and Judge Henry adjourned us until this morning.

Rising slowly from my chair, my chest cramped with fear, I button my suit coat and say, "Your Honor, the defense actually has two more witnesses to call to the stand. I expect their testimony won't take very long."

"I'm going to have to object," Leary says, and I don't look over at her. I can hear the shock in her voice. "There are no other witnesses listed on the pretrial order."

"May we approach the bench?" I ask Judge Henry, and he waves us both forward.

Leary's head turns toward me as we both slide out from behind our tables, but I can't even look her in the eye. Instead, I lower my gaze to the floor and motion with my hand for her to precede me.

I follow her up to the judge's bench, feeling like I'm walking to my own execution.

"What's this about?" Judge Henry asks me in a low whisper when we're both standing in front of him.

"I have two rebuttal witnesses," I murmur, the words tasting like ashes on my tongue.

"Rebuttal to what?" Leary hisses.

I still refuse to meet her gaze and instead look at Judge Henry. "Jenna LaPietra answered my requests for admissions, which were filed with the court and admitted into evidence yesterday. Request number nineteen specifically asked her to admit or deny if she had solicited and performed sexual acts on the customers in exchange for money. She denied the request. My two witnesses are prepared to offer evidence to rebut that."

Leary is surprisingly calm when she says, "Your Honor, I object. This is highly inflammatory and prejudicial. On top of that, it's absolutely irrelevant. It has nothing to do with the facts of this case, and Mr. Holloway is doing this to slander my client in front of the jury."

"It's relevant, Your Honor," I say flatly. "It not only goes to her character but it also goes to her veracity. The jury has the right to judge those traits when determining whether or not to give credence to her testimony."

Judge Henry looks back and forth between Leary and me while he considers our arguments. Finally, he gives a regretful sigh and says, "I'm going to allow the witnesses—"

"But Your Honor," Leary pleads, and I hear panic in her voice.

"Your objection is noted, Miss Michaels. It's now an issue for appeal. The testimony will be allowed. But Mr. Holloway, keep it narrow and do not attempt to go into sordid details. You're only offering this evidence to rebut her denial of your request for admission."

"Yes, sir," I say quietly, not feeling like I've won a damn thing. Doesn't matter if I keep the questions short and limited—the damage to Jenna and her case will have the force of a sonic boom.

We turn away from the bench, and again, I don't have the courage to look at Leary. I'm afraid if I do, I'll drop to my knees in front of the judge and the jury and beg her forgiveness.

Looking out into the gallery, I see the two witnesses I plan to call. The investigator originally interviewed three witnesses, but one of them called me just last night and left a voice mail that said she wasn't going to show up. Her message was short and cryptic, but essentially she said, "I just can't go through with it." I took that to mean that she didn't want any hand in the sordid actions of calling a woman a whore in front of a group of people.

Didn't matter. Two witnesses are just as effective as three.

When I get back to my table, I say, "Your Honor, the defendant calls Holly Wharles to the stand."

Then I bite the bullet and I do it.

I take a quick glance over at Leary.

Her back is to me and she's leaning in toward Jenna, whispering into her ear. Her arm rests across Jenna's back, and her hand is squeezing her shoulder. I can't see Leary's face, but Jenna raises her eyes and looks at me directly over Leary's shoulder.

They're filled with tears and my heart cracks farther open while my stomach cramps in shame. I swivel my head to look behind me at Tom Collier, sitting in the first row. His face is triumphant and filled with haughtiness. I look back to the jury, and they all watch Holly Wharles as she comes through the low swinging gate and walks toward the witness stand.

The clerk puts her under oath, she takes a seat, and I start to destroy Leary's case by destroying the credibility of the plaintiff.

Easy as pie.

If I've calculated correctly, Leary has about a forty-five-minute head start on me, and I can't imagine she'd be anywhere else other than her home. I'm prepared to grovel mightily.

The testimony of my rebuttal witnesses didn't take long, and because they were a surprise, Leary wasn't able to do an effective cross-examination. They were powerfully effective, and the jury was highly interested in what they had to say.

The minute they both testified, the jurors' sympathetic looks toward Jenna turned skeptical and condemning. I doubted at this point that any of them remembered what a douche my client was.

Judge Henry insisted on dismissing the jurors and giving them a bit of a long weekend since it was just before lunch on Friday. He reasoned that closing arguments would take at least half a day, and he didn't want the jury having to wait a weekend to begin deliberations. So instead, Leary and I stayed in the courtroom, and Judge Henry conducted the charge conference where we went over the jury instructions, that body of law that the judge will read to the jury to help guide them through their deliberations.

After that was finished, Judge Henry dismissed us and Leary jetted out of the courtroom. I went immediately to my law firm, where as I expected, Kratzenburg and Collier were in Kratzenburg's office drinking scotch and gloating over those last two witnesses. Both of them were riding high, like hunters off a fresh kill.

I, on the other hand, was worried sick about Leary as well as Jenna. I'd come to admire her through the course of this case, and I hadn't realized how much it would affect me when I hurt her.

Just before I entered Gill's office, I heard Tom say, "I'm glad we sent the investigator back out to push at those witnesses."

"Yeah, well . . . let's keep that between us," Kratzenburg said with a chuckle.

I gave a light knock on the door to announce my presence, and both men spun toward me.

"Reeve, you are a fucking rock star," Kratzenburg cackled when I stepped into his office. "Come have a drink with us to celebrate."

Collier just smirked at me. My fingers curled tightly into my palms, balling into fists that wanted to punch the ever-loving fuck out of his smug face.

Reaching into my pocket, I pulled out my key chain. Calmly removing one from the coil, I stepped forward and laid it on Kratzenburg's desk. "Consider this my notice. I quit."

Gill's eyes rounded and his mouth popped open in surprise. "You quit?"

"I quit," I repeated. "I'm going to clear out my office now."

I turned to leave, but Gill snapped out of his fogged surprise. "You can't quit. You're lead counsel in this case. You have a duty to show up and finish this."

Turning back around, I say, "I don't owe you shit. You've sat through this trial with me. You can handle the closing arguments."

Realizing that I was dead serious, Gill tried another tack. "I don't understand, Reeve. You did brilliantly. I'm sure you'll get a raise after this. Why would you want to quit the firm and this case?"

All of the anxiety, guilt, and sadness permeating my being morphed in a white-hot flash. It curled inward and when it exploded out, it was molten rage. I stalked around his desk, got right in his face, and snarled, "You want to know why I quit? I quit because you and your greedy, scum-sucking clients took pleasure today in hurting a woman whose worst crime was loving her son so much she'd do anything to protect him. You make me sick, and working for you makes me sick. It's a stain on my soul I can't bear anymore, so that's why I quit."

I didn't give him a chance to respond. I didn't look at Tom Collier, preferring to let time and distance hopefully start to fade him from my memory. I turned away and slammed out of his office, going to my own to pack up my belongings. I was out of there in fifteen minutes flat.

Pulling up in front of Leary's house, I see her garage door down but a black Mercedes sedan in the driveway. If I have to take an educated guess, Ford is in the house with her right now, marveling over my evil ways.

I walk up to Leary's front door. Before I can clear the top porch step, it opens and Ford is indeed standing there with his arms across his chest. I expect him to be thundering at me with rage, but his eyes are knowing and sad.

"She doesn't want to see you," he says softly.

"She needs to let me explain," I counter as I take a step closer. Past his shoulder, I can see the inside of Leary's house . . . her living room, part of her sunroom on the back . . . but no Leary.

"She doesn't want to hear it," Ford says evenly.

"Come on, man," I plead with him. "I just need a few minutes. I have to tell her—"

A delicate hand comes around Ford's shoulder, pushing him to the side. Leary appears from behind him, dressed in a pair of black yoga pants and a T-shirt. Her eyes are bleak and red tinged.

"Leary—" I start out, but she cuts me off.

Her voice is deadly calm. "Get off my porch. Get in your car and drive away. Don't ever contact me again."

She slowly turns away and starts walking back into her living room. Her shoulders are sagging, and from this angle, it looks like she's aged a hundred years.

"I'm sorry," I blurt out, needing to get the words out while she can still hear them. "I'm sorry for what happened. I didn't have a choice, and you have to believe me, it killed me to do that."

Leary stops for a moment. When she turns back to look at me, her eyes are blazing in fury. She takes two steps back up to the door and pushes Ford even farther out of the way. "You're sorry?" she whispers with barely controlled rage.

"Yes," I say emphatically.

"What exactly are you sorry for, Reeve?" she asks sarcastically. "For ruining a beautiful woman who did nothing to deserve the shit storm you just piled on her? Or are you sorry because you didn't have the balls to prevent that shit storm?"

"My hands were tied," I grit out.

"Bullshit," she snarls as she steps out onto the front porch and stands on her tiptoes to get in my face. "You had a choice."

"Fine. I had a choice. I chose to stay within the boundaries of the law," I defend myself, even though it feels so very wrong to do.

I expect her to retaliate. To attack. To call me every dirty name in the book, and hell, for good measure, she might as well slap the shit out of me.

Instead, my knees nearly buckle when tears fill her eyes and her chin starts to tremble. "You chose to be a coward," she says as teardrops fall, leaving silvery trails down her cheeks. Taking a deep breath, she blinks her eyes and rubs the back of her hand over her cheeks to dry them. "Now, get off my property and please don't bother me again."

"You said you wouldn't hold my job against me," I say forcefully, trying to keep dialogue open. "You promised."

More tears spill, sticking in her lashes and cascading down her cheeks. "I did," she says quietly, her words filled with pain. "And I'm apparently breaking that promise right now. But I made that promise before you gave me your heart and I gave you mine. I didn't take into consideration how badly you could hurt me."

"I didn't do this to *you*, Leary. I did my job. I did this to *your case*."

Leary gives me a sad smile, shaking her head. "Do you really believe that, Reeve? Knowing my background and what this all meant to me, did you really not think this would hurt me personally?"

I close my eyes slowly, telling myself this is a bad dream. I close my eyes because I can't stand to see the accusation in hers, and because I know she's right. I did this knowing she was going to get personally hurt, and I could have prevented it. I could have stopped all of this by being truthful with her from the beginning. I could have told her about those witnesses. Yes, it would have crossed an ethical line, but why didn't I see it then the way I see it now? That Leary would have been worth risking my career. She was more important than my ethics or my law license.

I need to let her know that, but when I open my eyes to tell her what a fool I've been, she's gone. Ford is still standing there, though, looking surprisingly sympathetic.

I can't stand the look. It merely confirms what Leary just told me—it's over between us.

I spin on my heel and lumber down her porch steps. When I reach my car door, I turn and see Ford following me. He clearly has something to say, so I just stare at him.

"Listen," he says carefully. "I'm sorry . . . for both of you. I know you had something special."

"Apparently not that special," I murmur as I look back toward her house, knowing that I'm the one who failed to make the choice that would have preserved it. "Do you think I chose wrong?"

"Doesn't matter what I think," he says, doing nothing to inflame or assuage my guilt. "But do me a favor—Monday in court, don't try to harass her into talking to you. You know the chances of her winning are very low now, and it's going to be hard on her as it is. Just keep your distance, okay?"

I open my car door and step into the driver's side. Shooting him a quick look, I say, "I won't be there. I quit Battle Carnes this afternoon after court was over. Kratzenburg will finish up the trial."

Sitting down in the driver's seat, I close the door and take a quick glance at Ford. He's staring at me thoughtfully, both of his hands tucked into his pockets. Giving me a nod of his head, he turns away and heads back toward Leary's porch.

As soon as I back out of the driveway and put the car in drive, I pull my phone out. I might have lost Leary for good, but maybe I can still do something to help salvage her case.

I dial Rhonda Valasquez's number again. As per usual, it goes right to voice mail, and I don't hesitate in my message.

"Miss Valasquez, this is Reeve Holloway again. I wanted you to know that I quit working at Battle Carnes today. I no longer represent Dr. Summerland. I really need to talk to you about this case. It's taken a bad turn, and if there's anything you can do to help Jenna LaPietra, I need you to do it. I am begging you to call me. Please."

Hanging up my phone, I drive back home. There's nothing to do but wait and hope that she calls me back, and then hope that she has something worthwhile to tell me.

CHAPTER 23

LEARY

"Are we ready to begin?" Judge Henry asks affably from up on his perch.

I give him a confident smile. "The plaintiff is ready, Your Honor."

Turning my gaze, I look over at the defense table. I knew Reeve wouldn't be sitting there this Monday morning—Ford told me that he quit Battle Carnes. This surprised me, but past that, I didn't have time to give any credence to the feelings that welled up within me at the news. Instead, I tried to numb myself to Reeve and everything that we had.

Gill Kratzenburg showed up this morning, and we met in the judge's chambers. He advised Judge Henry that Mr. Holloway would not be making further appearances and that he would handle the remainder of the case. Judge Henry was surprised, and I managed to look the same myself. Regardless, there was no sense in holding up the show.

Kratzenburg stands up. "The defendant is ready."

"Then let's move on to closing arguments," Judge Henry says and then turns to the bailiff. "You can bring the jury in."

"Your Honor," I butt in politely, "I would respectfully request that you reopen evidence and allow the plaintiff to call one rebuttal witness."

Kratzenburg explodes. "I object, Your Honor."

"Of course you do," Judge Henry says drily as he looks at Gill in boredom. "Just as Miss Michaels objected to your rebuttal witnesses." Turning his eyes to me, he pushes, "Tell me what you have, Miss Michaels."

"Yes, sir. I'll be calling Miss Rhonda Valasquez to the stand. She was one of two surgical nurses who assisted Dr. Summerland during Jenna's surgery. She'll be offering rebuttal evidence to Dr. Summerland's testimony here during the trial, as well as to some statements he made to me in his deposition, which I admitted into evidence as Plaintiff's exhibit number twenty-four."

Judge Henry nods and says, "I'll allow it. Let's call the jury in, and then you can call your witness."

As I sit in my chair, I watch as Gill Kratzenburg leans over toward Dr. Summerland, who looks positively green right now. He knows exactly why I'm calling Rhonda Valasquez to the stand, and I'd bet he'd sell his right kidney to be anywhere but here in this courtroom.

I'd like to say she's a gift from God, but she's actually a gift from Reeve. I was sitting in my living room on Sunday afternoon, wearing a pair of faded jeans and a Stanford sweatshirt, when my doorbell rang. When I opened the door, I saw a middle-aged, heavyset woman with sandy-blonde hair and light-brown eyes. She looked me straight in the eyes and said, "Miss Michaels, my name is Rhonda Valasquez. I was one of the nurses involved with your client's surgery. I have something important to tell you."

My jaw dropped and I sort of stuttered when I asked, "I don't understand. How did you find my house?"

"Reeve Holloway contacted me yesterday. He thinks I can help your case. I know I can."

And just like that, Jenna's case was saved.

Rhonda and I talked for three hours on Sunday afternoon, and she agreed to testify this morning. She wasn't hesitant at all, only claiming hesitancy in talking to Reeve, who'd been trying to contact her for weeks. She confessed she finally broke down when he left her a message on Friday saying he was no longer working for Dr. Summerland.

The door to the jury room opens and I wait for them all to file in. None of them look toward Jenna and me. All rapport that I established over the last few weeks was obliterated by Reeve's rebuttal witnesses last Friday.

It was time to change that.

Judge Henry explains to the jury that I have a rebuttal witness, and then he turns to me. "The jury is with the plaintiff, Miss Michaels."

Standing from my chair, I say, "I'd like to call Rhonda Valasquez to the stand."

She looks professional in her navy-blue-and-gold-checked dress. Her hair is pulled up into a smart bun, and she's wearing eyeglasses that she didn't have on yesterday at my house.

After she's sworn in, I ask, "Would you please introduce yourself to the jury?"

I instructed her to always make eye contact with the jury, and she remembers well. Turning to them, she says, "My name is Rhonda Valasquez. I'm a registered nurse."

"And were you present during the breast-reduction surgery Dr. Summerland performed on Jenna LaPietra?" I ask.

"I was," she responds.

"As part of your duties, do you make entries into the medical records?"

"Yes. There are usually two surgical nurses. One of us usually provides immediate assistance to the surgeon, and the other may document things in the chart as they occur."

I stand up from my chair. "May I approach, Your Honor?"

Judge Henry waves me forward and I walk up to Rhonda. "I'm handing you what's been marked as Plaintiff's exhibit number thirty-eight. Can you identify that for the jury?"

Rhonda takes the paper and looks at it briefly. "That's a page from the nurses' notes that were created during the surgery."

"And is that your handwriting?"

"No. That's the other nurse's handwriting. I was doing the main assistance, and she was responsible for charting."

Leaning over the edge of the witness box, I point to the middle of the note. "Right there it says, '12:18 p.m., Dr. S and R.V. step out.' What does that mean?"

Rhonda looks over to the jury. "At 12:18 p.m., both Dr. Summerland and I stepped out of the operating room together."

I can hear the jury muttering, completely taken with this information.

"And right below that?" I ask as I point back to the note.

"It says, '12:32 p.m., Dr. S back. Surg in progress,'" she supplies to the jury.

"So, the notes reflect that you and Dr. Summerland left the operating room together, is that correct?"

"That's correct," she says calmly.

"Isn't that unusual?" I ask curiously.

"It is," she says.

I glance quickly over at the jury. They're all leaning forward, completely entranced with Rhonda's testimony. I can practically see the thoughts racing through their gazes.

Where did they go?

What were they doing?

Was something illicit going on?

It's time to let them in on the secret.

"Miss Valasquez, why did you two leave the operating room together?"

Rhonda takes a deep breath and turns to the jury. "I noticed Dr. Summerland's hands were shaking quite badly as he started the procedure. I asked him once if he was okay, and he told me he was fine. It seemed to stop for a few moments, but then his hands started shaking again."

"What did you do?" I prompt.

"I asked him again if he was okay, and this time he yelled at me to mind my own business."

A ripple of awkward movement comes from the jury as they shift and adjust in their seats.

"Did he continue to operate?" I ask her.

"He did," Rhonda says, "but I was extremely worried. His incision was irregular and I knew he wasn't physically able to perform surgery. So I told him that exactly."

"What was his reaction?" I ask softly.

"He was extremely angry. He barked orders at the anesthesiologist to monitor Jenna and that he'd be back. Then he ordered me out of the room with him."

"And did you go?"

"I did. I followed him out and into the scrub room."

"What happened?"

"He pulled off his gloves first, then his surgical mask, and started to dress me down for calling his capabilities into question in front of the other operating-room occupants. And that's when I finally realized why he was shaking."

This is a carefully orchestrated statement by Rhonda. We worked on her testimony for a long time yesterday, and I wanted the jury hanging on her every word.

"Please tell the jury what you observed," I gently command her.

"I smelled alcohol," she says matter-of-factly, and I hear a collective inhale from the jury. "It was strong. I'm not sure if he'd been drinking before the surgery, or if it was left over from the night before, but it was enough so I could smell it on his breath from a few feet away."

"What happened next?" I prod her further.

"He ordered me out of the surgical suite. Told me he was reporting me for insubordination."

"And did you leave?"

"I did," she says firmly. "And I went straight to my supervising nurse to report what happened."

"What did she do?"

"She said she would handle it. Told me to go home for the day and she'd call me later."

"And did she handle the situation?" I ask, taking a quick peek over at the jury. Their stares are all riveted on Rhonda.

"I'm thinking not," Rhonda says with derision. "The hospital administrator called me that night and told me my job was terminated."

"Terminated?" I ask in shock, turning my face to the jury. They all swing their gazes to me, and I can see they are pissed.

"Yes," Rhonda says quietly, and all twelve sets of eyes swing back to her. "Apparently no one confronted Dr. Summerland that day. They let him continue to operate, and the administrator called him at home that night. He denied my allegations and said I was being belligerent during the surgery, which is why he dismissed me."

"But surely the other people in the surgical room corroborated your story," I suggest to her. Although I know the sad answer to this already.

Rhonda shakes her head and looks at the jury with morose eyes. "They didn't. I think they were afraid of losing their jobs. Dr. Summerland holds a lot of power at the hospital. Plus, I'm not sure they smelled the alcohol the way I did. I only smelled it when he took his mask off."

I let those last words hang in front of the jury a moment before I return to my chair behind counsel table. After I take a seat, I close my notepad and cap my pen, subtly letting the jury know that I'm just about finished.

"Miss Valasquez," I say softly, but loud enough that the jury is with me, "is there any doubt in your mind that Dr. Summerland was impaired during that procedure?"

She shakes her head and spans her gaze across the jury box. "No. I smelled the alcohol and saw his shaking hands. His incision was irregular. I'm confident he was too impaired to be performing any type of surgery that day."

With a grateful smile and a nod of my head, I say, "Thank you, Miss Valasquez. I don't have any further questions."

Their next settlement offer came about five minutes after Rhonda Valasquez left the witness stand. Gill tried to attack her credibility, tried to pawn her off as a disgruntled employee who had a bone to pick with Dr. Summerland. She handled it perfectly, stating that she actually got another job pretty quickly, one that paid better and had a better work environment. She was extremely happy to be where she was and not at all upset over being terminated.

In fact, she told Gill on cross-examination, the only thing that did upset her was that no one bothered to stop the surgery so that Jenna wouldn't be harmed. That effectively shut Gill up—he knew he wouldn't be able to tarnish her.

Jenna and I spent a lot of time discussing the offer. They laid a million dollars on the table, and it wasn't something to sneeze at. I was hesitant in turning our noses up at it, because although I could tell the jury was now livid with Dr. Summerland, I couldn't be sure if they held anything against Jenna.

Ultimately, it was Jenna who decided not to take the money and let the jury decide her fate. I have no clue if it's right or wrong, but the decision is made and I need to put on my best performance right now.

After conveying to Gill that we're declining to settle, I run to the ladies' room to collect myself. Within five minutes I'll be back up before the jury giving the most important closing argument of my life. I won't see a dime of any money, don't give a shit about getting any accolades. My only thought as I stare in the mirror is trying to persuade twelve strangers to make this right for Jenna.

I wash my hands, dab on some lip gloss, and walk out.

Ford is waiting for me in the hallway, casually standing a few paces away from the bathrooms, checking his phone for messages. He hears me and his head pops up.

"You ready?" he asks with an encouraging smile.

Smoothing down my skirt, I walk toward him. "Yeah. Ready as I'll ever be."

Ford reaches a hand out and squeezes my shoulder. "Midge sent me over to watch and be your moral support. She wanted to be here, but you know . . . defeats her whole recluse thing."

I give a snort of laughter, grateful for Ford's humor. "I wouldn't expect otherwise."

Turning, Ford and I walk toward the courtroom doors. "Rhonda's testimony was fantastic," he says. "It's got the case back on track. You were right in turning down the million."

"You think her testimony was enough?" I ask curiously as he holds open one of the swinging doors for me. I can only hope it was enough to overcome the damage done by Reeve's rebuttal witnesses—thinking of them still burns me up.

"More than enough," he says emphatically. "It sealed the deal."

I give him a small smile and turn to walk up the aisle toward the front of the courtroom. Reaching out, he grabs my hand and I turn back. "You owe Reeve for that."

I blink at him in surprise and pull my hand away. "Don't," I warn him. "It's not the time or place."

"I know," he says quietly. "But when you're up there in front of the jury, channeling all of your emotion and rage against Dr. Summerland, let your feelings about Reeve flow into that. Remember what he did, the reasons he did it, and how it all makes you feel. Then when you're pleading with that jury to give Jenna justice, you remember that the reason they're going to give you justice is because Reeve handed you Rhonda Valasquez. Let it fuel you."

His words pack a punch. I get what he's saying—he's not asking me to forgive Reeve, and he's not asking me to go back to the way things were. He knows damn good and well that ninety percent of any jury argument is passion and only maybe ten percent is law and reason. He's telling me to tap into every bit of emotion I have, knowing that much of it has to do with Reeve and his involvement in this case, from betraying me to saving me, and most important, everything that I had with him that is now no more. I've suffered a loss, and he wants me to use it to prime my emotions.

I'm not sure if Reeve handing me Rhonda Valasquez makes up for what he did to our case in the first place. It's hard getting past hurt and betrayal. And yes, I was incredibly hurt that Reeve obviously didn't care enough about me to give me a heads-up over his rebuttal witnesses. Ethically he shouldn't do it, and yet I didn't think that was good enough reason to withhold from me.

I felt that way because I was pretty darn sure I was falling in love with him, and I thought he felt the same for me. I thought I meant enough to him that he would risk it. I was let down that he did not.

But when it ultimately boiled down to it, Reeve did in fact risk his license for me. Even though he quit Battle Carnes and the case, he still had as much ethical duty to Dr. Summerland as he ever did. By providing me with Rhonda Valasquez, he committed a serious breach of ethics, and that tells me that maybe I am more important to Reeve than I thought. Or maybe even more than he thought.

I nod at Ford and turn away, swallowing hard against the rawness of sentiment starting to build up inside me. Conflicting emotions surging and raging.

If it was his intention to get me riled up with fervor and passion, Ford just did his job very well.

CHAPTER 24

REEVE

I slip into the back of the courtroom quietly, hoping not to draw attention to myself.

Well, I hope not to draw the attention of one person—Leary.

I don't care if anyone else sees me, and to prove it, when Gill Kratzenburg and Garry Summerland hear the doors open, they both look over their shoulders and pin their stares on me. Summerland glares and Gill's eyebrows raise in surprise. I don't spare them but a second and slip into the back row of the gallery seating, behind the plaintiff's side to show them that I don't give a shit what they think. That I'm here, merely as a spectator, and I am clearly choosing the opposite side of the war I was seated on a few days prior.

I'm thankful no one else looked my way. The judge is watching Leary, as is the entire jury, their faces all riveted on what she's saying. I'm a few minutes late getting here, knowing I'd miss part of Leary's closing statements.

Ford texted me midmorning to let me know that Rhonda Valasquez testified on behalf of Jenna and it went fantastically well. It was the first

I'd heard from him since we had words in Leary's driveway last Friday. I was surprised that he even bothered but grateful for the update. I had no clue whether my impassioned plea to Rhonda would induce her to seek Leary out, but clearly it worked.

I didn't respond to Ford, but within a few minutes, he sent me another text.

Closing statements starting in twenty minutes if you want to watch.

I stared at my phone for a few minutes, trying to read something into his message. Did that mean Leary wanted me there? Probably not, because no matter what transpired between the two of us, I know Leary well enough to know that her mind was not on me. I know that her sole focus would be on that jury and what she was going to say to them.

It only took me about five minutes to decide to head over to the courthouse and sneak inside so I could see Leary in action. Although I was officially off the case, there was still something that was bugging me about the rebuttal witnesses, and it had everything to do with the conversation I overheard between Gill Kratzenburg and Tom Collier when I handed in my key. Tom had indicated that they sent the investigator back out to push at the witnesses, which means that their testimony must not have been helpful to begin with. Something happened to get those witnesses to change their minds, and because I had their numbers programmed in my phone, I had intended to call all three of them to poke and prod a bit more into their testimony. It just wasn't sitting right with me for some reason, and my insatiable curiosity needed to be appeased. I figured I could do that later this afternoon and would rather watch Leary's argument to the jury.

My chest aches when I first look at her, casually strolling back and forth in front of the jury box as she argues. She chose a conservative dark-gray suit with a pearl-colored blouse. Her hair is pulled back into a low ponytail that hangs sleekly down her back. Of course, she's wearing her sexy-as-shit mile-high black heels that made her legs look even more amazing than I know them to be, but otherwise, she's conveying to the jury by her look and demeanor that this is some serious shit she's discussing with them.

"The evidence is clear. If you want to look at this case boiled down into the finest of black-and-white detail, consider this. All three of our expert witnesses emphatically told you that Dr. Summerland had no business doing this type of surgery. Simply put, he wasn't qualified. Now, you heard Dr. Summerland's own experts—who we know had some personal bias to consider—hem and haw over their opinions. They said they disagreed with my experts, but remember this: The two general surgeons you heard from admitted to all twelve of you"—and here Leary sweeps her hand out toward the jury—"that they had never attempted to do a breast reduction surgery in their careers. They all admitted to you that they would refer those cases out to a plastic surgeon."

I watch the jury, noting that every single one of them is listening avidly to Leary. They're not allowed to take notes, which I find to be a good thing because I often feel like they could miss something important. Several of the jurors are nodding in agreement.

"The medical opinions are clear. Dr. Summerland breached the standard of care by doing an operation he was clearly not qualified to do," Leary says to summarize the causation issue to the jury. She pauses, looks down at the ground, and takes a deep breath. When she looks back up, her face is troubled.

"But I imagine there are many things that aren't so clear to you," she says softly to the jury. "I imagine you have confused feelings over some of the things you've heard over the last few weeks. Things that don't have anything to do with science or medicine or expert opinions."

She pauses, slowly looks at each juror with open honesty. "Salacious things," she says ominously. "Dirty, nasty, sordid allegations."

Leary turns away from the jury, walks over to Jenna, and stands behind her as she sits at counsel table. Placing her hands softly on Jenna's shoulders, she gives a squeeze and looks back to the jury. "What do you see when you look at Jenna LaPietra?" she asks the jury.

She doesn't expect an answer. In fact, they can't give one, but she lets the question lie heavy and pregnant in the air.

"Do you see a whore?" she asks, so quietly I almost have to lean forward to hear her. "Is that what you see?"

Not one of the jurors moves a muscle, and none of them lower their gazes. They all stare right back at Leary.

"That's what the defense wants you to see," Leary says, her voice rising a little in pace and tempo. "They want you to be so sidetracked by their smoke and mirrors that you'll forget all about what you're really here to decide. They hope you get so incensed over their allegations that you'll just happen to overlook what this case is really all about."

The courtroom is so silent you could hear a pin drop. Dropping her hands from Jenna's shoulders, Leary tucks her hands in the pockets at her hips and strolls back up to the jury, her gaze cast downward. When she reaches the center of the jury box, she looks back up at them.

"Let me ask you this," she says, again in a softer voice. "If you do believe the defense experts and you do look at Jenna and think she's a whore, does it even really matter? I mean, in the grand scheme of things, if a woman would go to any lengths to provide for and support her autistic son, would you really hold that against her?"

Leary turns slightly to the left, walks down in front of juror number one, a middle-aged man who, if I recall correctly, is a bank-teller supervisor. She leans in close to him over the box rail and says, "Mr. Vartles, I remember you're married and have two children. Is there anything you wouldn't do for your kids? Is there anything your wife wouldn't do for them?"

Then Leary walks down the entire box and addresses each juror with like questions.

Is there anything you wouldn't do, Mr. Priest?

What about you, Mrs. Cranford? Any line you wouldn't cross for a sick child?

How about you, Mr. Mason . . . I know you don't have children, but what about your mother? Is there anything you wouldn't do for her?

She does this over and over until she's asked every single juror to put himself metaphorically in Jenna's shoes. Not one of the jurors looks away, and several give a slow shake of their head although they can't answer verbally.

When Leary is satisfied she's made her point, she takes a few steps back from the jury, pulls her hands out of her pockets, and holds her hands out to the side.

"I'm here to tell you that the two witnesses who stood up in front of you and said that Jenna prostituted herself are out-and-out liars. They perjured themselves on the stand. Jenna has denied those allegations in her answers to the defendants' request for admissions. But I'm also here to tell you, it doesn't matter one whit if she did or didn't do it. Because I think we are all in agreement here that a mother's love shouldn't be held against her. At least not here, not in this courtroom, when it has absolutely nothing to do with this case. Has nothing to do with Dr. Summerland walking into an operating room and performing a surgery that he was not qualified to do, and while he was intoxicated. Has nothing to do with the fact that Jenna LaPietra was maimed and mangled by a heartless and arrogant man with a God complex, fueled on by alcohol."

The jury at this point is all unanimously nodding along with Leary. She has them practically eating out of her hand. I really don't need to see any more. I don't need to hear one more word out of Leary's mouth that could make me any prouder of her than I am in this moment.

As I quietly slide off the bench and stand up, I hear Leary's voice say, "Now . . . let's talk about how you, the jury, can help right this wrong. How you can help make this travesty a little more tolerable for Jenna and her son."

A small smile forms on my face as I walk to the rear courtroom doors, imagining that jury deliberations are going to focus on not *if* they should give Jenna something but rather how much they're going to give her.

Ford sends me a flurry of texts all afternoon.

> 11:23 a.m. Jury has been charged and out for deliberations

> 12:39 p.m. Jury has asked to see the economist report

> 1:12 p.m. Jury asked for lunch to be brought in rather than stop deliberations

> 2:07 p.m. Gill upped offer to $1.3 million. Leary refused

> 2:51 p.m. Jury asked judge to reread instructions on future economic damages

> 3:02 p.m. Jury has finished deliberations

I don't get another text after that. Instead, at about a quarter past three, Ford calls me. I answer on the second ring. "What did they give her?"

"Three and a half million," he says, his voice bursting with excitement.

A grin spreads across my face as I close my eyes in gratitude. "Fucking awesome."

"Yeah, it is. You should have seen Summerland. He exploded when the verdict was read and started ranting at the jury. Judge Henry was banging his gavel for order. Finally a bailiff had to come over and push him back down in his seat. It was classic."

"I bet," I say in amusement, so very thankful I wasn't sitting there having to endure that douche throwing a tantrum in open court.

"Well, I just thought you'd want to know," Ford says. "I mean, not sure that would have happened without Rhonda Valasquez."

"Would have happened if I hadn't called those rebuttal witnesses," I say, still bitter over having made a terrible choice that cost me the woman I love. Especially now that I know their testimony was manufactured, a fact that I finally verified by talking to the one witness who refused to show up in court that day.

Ford sighs into the phone. "Look, man, I don't know that your choice was wrong. It was ethically the right thing to do. You were following the law and the rules."

"Yeah, well, Leary doesn't think those laws and rules should apply in all circumstances," I remind him. "I let her down."

"You did, but that's also on her. Those are her expectations you failed, but doesn't mean that her bar wasn't set improbably high."

"Maybe," I tell him. "But in hindsight, I still ended up breaching my moral compass by sending her Rhonda Valasquez, so apparently I guess I subscribe to her philosophy that some things are worth the risk. I was just late in figuring it out."

"Maybe not too late," Ford says wisely. "Why don't you come out with us tonight and celebrate? A bunch of the members of our firm are going to get together over at the High Court and toss back a few."

The High Court is a popular downtown bar that caters to a good chunk of the legal community. It's usually jam-packed with lawyers and court personnel on weekends and weeknights and does a brisk happy-hour business, which usually includes lawyers celebrating victories or drowning their sorrows over losses.

"I think I'll take a pass," I say with a laugh, hoping to convey a bit of lighthearted acceptance of my current situation, despite the fact I feel like I'm sunk in a black pit of misery.

"You two need to talk," Ford says.

"Yeah, well, she made it pretty clear that she wanted nothing more to do with me."

"And you're just going to accept that?" Ford asks.

"For now," I say quietly. "Leary doesn't seem the type that's going to let go of that kind of hurt very easily, and frankly, I'm not sure she should. I let her down. Time to pay the consequences."

"I get it," Ford mutters. "Maybe she'll get her head out of her ass at some point."

"Well, I'm not going anywhere," I say. "I'm here when she wants to talk. Unless I move to New York. That's a possibility."

"It is?" Ford asks hesitantly.

"Yeah. I'm licensed there as well. Have a lot of contacts. I don't want to, but I could go there if I don't have any better job prospects here. I'm not in a rush, though. I've got a healthy savings account. I'm not hurting."

My phone starts buzzing and I pull it away from my head to take a quick peek. Muttering a silent curse, I bring it back to my ear. "Look, I've got to go. Gill is calling me."

"Good luck with that," Ford snorts, and then he's gone.

I wait for the line to completely disconnect and then answer Gill's call. "Reeve Holloway."

"It's Gill," he says in a tight voice. "Thought you'd want to know we lost the case and lost big."

"There is no 'we,' Gill. I quit, in case you forgot, and no, I'm not really interested in the outcome."

"You know," he sneers into the phone, "I find it interesting that your cell-phone logs show repeated calls to Rhonda Valasquez over the last several weeks, including one that was made to her Friday afternoon after you quit the firm."

This allegation does not surprise me. In fact, I'd been ready for it ever since I walked out of the firm on Friday, leaving behind my cell phone, which didn't belong to me. The number did, though, so I stopped at an Apple Store on the way home and bought a new phone and had the number ported over. Still, I knew they'd probably go through my logs and see my calls to Miss Valasquez.

"What's your point, Gill?" I ask calmly.

"My point is, I'm betting that you handed Rhonda Valasquez on a platter to Leary Michaels."

"Prove it," I challenge him.

"Oh, I intend to. I've got a call in to Miss Valasquez now," he says, and I can actually envision the smirk on his face.

I have no clue if Rhonda Valasquez will talk to Gill. I never asked her to keep secret that I communicated with her, or more important, that I sent her directly to Leary's house. If she tells Gill that, he's going to report me to the State Bar, and it's a good bet that I'll lose my license. I knew all of this when I made the decision to help Leary out. I knew this could be the ultimate price I end up paying for all of my choices, and yet I still couldn't muster up the energy to care.

What I do now, though, is pull out a bit of an ace in the hole that fortuitously came my way this afternoon. "I know the testimony of the rebuttal witnesses was fabricated," I say softly and am rewarded by a muttered curse from Gill. "I talked to Tammy Rhodes, and she told me everything."

"Everything" being that when our investigator, Marc Stephenson, first interviewed these witnesses, he was told emphatically that they had no knowledge that Jenna LaPietra was prostituting herself. They'd heard rumors that it was going on, but they didn't know anyone involved. Miss Rhodes then told me that the investigator called her back and strongly encouraged her to jog her memory, so to speak, and even offered a bit of a monetary incentive if said memory cleared up to the extent that they miraculously remembered that Jenna had admitted to accepting money for her body. This confirmed my suspicion that Gill Kratzenburg and Tom Collier had those witnesses paid off, and that's a criminal offense.

Gill is silent on the other end of the phone, and I can practically hear the gears in his brain grinding and clicking. I wait for him to say something, to deny it all, but he doesn't. Because he knows damn good and well he can't.

"Listen, Gill," I say with every bit of rationality I can muster, "I think neither one of us is happy with how things played out. My suggestion is we both just let it lie and walk away. Things will get very ugly otherwise."

He knows I have him by the short hairs and that he can't do anything but agree with me. He acknowledges that in a way I find to be typical of the arrogance of the people working at Battle Carnes.

He hangs up on me.

I pull the phone slowly away from my ear and stick it back in my pocket.

Then I start laughing.

CHAPTER 25

LEARY

"Well, I think this house is perfect, except for the fact it needs a new roof," Jenna says as we walk back to my car. "If they'll come down on the price, I think this is the one for us."

Two days after the verdict came in, we're out house hunting for Jenna and Damien. I decided to take a few days off and relax after the trial—well, Midge actually insisted I take a few days off. She lectured me—via e-mail, of course—about how brutal a trial can be on a lawyer's energy and stamina. She ordered me to recharge my batteries, so to speak.

Jenna asked me yesterday if I'd go look at houses with her. Her first order of business is to get out of the apartment I'm paying for and into a particular neighborhood in Raleigh that has a phenomenal charter school providing special education to autistic children.

"It's a great house," I concur. "I have a friend who's a contractor. I'll call him to find out what it would cost for a new roof, and that will give you a basis for how much to offer on the house."

Sawyer Bennett

We get in my car, buckle up, and pull out of the driveway, Jenna throwing a wave to the real estate agent, who's locking the house up. "Want to go get a late lunch before you have to pick up Damien?"

"Sure," she says with a smile and then leans over to pat me on my knee. "And since I'm still technically broke until the money comes in, you'll have to pay."

I laugh and pat her hand in return. "My pleasure."

Jenna is silent a moment and then she says, "But I want to pay you back for everything you've done for me and Damien over the last several months. I know you refuse to take a fee on the verdict, but I want to pay you back for the apartment, food, and clothes."

"That's not—" I start to say, but she cuts me off.

"With interest," she says firmly.

I grit my teeth and don't say anything. I know it's going to be pointless to argue with her, so I decide to change the subject. "I think you need to reconsider the reconstructive surgeries."

"What?" she asks in surprise.

"I get not wanting them done when they were only offering five hundred thousand, but with this verdict, there's more than enough for you to have the surgeries done to correct the problems."

"It's not important," Jenna scoffs at me, and in my peripheral vision I can see her wave an impatient hand.

"It *is* important," I insist. "I don't mean this to sound trite, but as women, our breasts define us. They're an important piece of our femininity. You should get them fixed. You're young and beautiful. It will make you feel better about yourself."

She's silent, so I add on for a bit of levity, "Plus, you're going to want to start dating at some point. Your puppies need to be fixed to do that."

Jenna snorts. "You want me to start dating?"

"I want you to be happy, find love. It's important to have those things for yourself."

"I agree," Jenna says instantaneously, but something about her tone raises my warning hackles. "In fact, let's talk about the importance of love and happiness in regard to your life."

My head snaps over to her, and she's staring at me with a stern look on her face.

"Oh, no," I rebuff her. "This is not about me."

"Let's make it about you, then," she says right over me. "You need to fix things with Reeve."

"He betrayed us," I say irritably, mainly because Jenna is hitting on a very sore spot. I miss the man tremendously, but my pride seems to be standing in my own way.

"He saved us," she counters softly. "He gave us Rhonda Valasquez, and she saved our case."

"But it wouldn't have needed saving if he would have just—"

"Just what?" Jenna sneers at me and her tone brooks no nonsense. "The man did absolutely nothing wrong. And don't forget, Leary, this was my case, not yours. He played the cards he was dealt. He played by the rules. He didn't do it to hurt me personally. It was part of the game. So I want to know, if I can look at what he did and not have any bitter feelings, why can't you?"

My mouth opens.

Then closes.

I open it again and don't know what to say, so I close it once more.

Why in the fuck did it hurt me so badly when Reeve sprang those witnesses on me? Why did I have any expectation that he would clue me in on what he was going to do?

The only plausible solution I can think of is that I held him to the same standards I have for myself, and I have to wonder if that was fair. Should I have expected of Reeve an action that I would have gladly done for him had the situation been reversed? And if the answer is yes, does that mean that is so because I love him but he didn't love me?

Am I hurt by the fact that Reeve didn't care for me the way I cared for him?

I'm so confused, I continue driving on in silence. I have no idea how to answer Jenna's question. When she says it like that, it makes me seem petty and immature. But at the same time, I cannot deny it physically hurt deep in my gut when Reeve sprang those witnesses on me. My body physically reacted because it took his actions as personal, and was perhaps my first indication that maybe my feelings weren't being reciprocated.

And rather than discuss that with Reeve, I just cut him completely out of my life.

"Am I wrong to have been hurt by what he did?" I ask Jenna softly.

"No," she says gently, "because when the heart is involved, feelings will get hurt. But you were wrong to break ties with him without discussing it."

"What could he possibly say that would make it better?" There's really not an apology I can envision that will take away the sting I'm feeling.

"He doesn't need to say anything," Jenna says, and I give her a quick glance. Her gaze is empathetic but there is condemnation there.

"Excuse me?"

"When he came to your door, he apologized, so frankly, Leary, he really doesn't have anything more to say to you. He's already said he's sorry. Now it's time for you to do the same."

Anger surges through me, but then it's overtaken by a flood of guilt.

He did apologize to me.

Profusely, in fact.

Then he went one step farther and laid his entire law career on the line by sending me Rhonda Valasquez.

He risked everything.

For me.

He not only met the high bar of expectations I set, maybe unfairly, but he hurtled over it.

And I was too stuck with anger and hurt feelings to even give him any credit.

As I pull into Reeve's driveway, I imagine myself giving a closing statement to the jury. Except this time, the jury is going to decide my fate with the man I'm supposed to be with. I've decided against overt pleading, thought about potentially using sex to get him back on board but then tossed that away, finally just deciding that honesty and a simple apology will appeal to Reeve the most.

I have no clue if he's pissed at me. Ford seems to think not, but I can't discount the possibility.

What I *can* bank on is that Reeve is a genuine person and doesn't have an intentionally cruel bone in his body. He's truly sorry for what he did to me, and I have to assume that is still the case. I also have to assume, then, that he will at least listen to me and let me get my feelings out on the table.

And I'm not going to hold them back.

As I put the car in park, his front door is open, and my pulse starts skittering madly. Then it comes to a complete halt, and I'm afraid I might have just died an early death when I see Vanessa walk out of his house with Mr. Chico Taco on his leash. I wait for feelings of anger and jealousy to wash over me, but they never come. Instead, I feel massive disappointment that it's not Reeve I'm looking at right now.

I get out of my car and Vanessa looks my way. Her nose scrunches up slightly, but she walks over to me as I close my door.

"He's not here," she says while eyeballing me up and down.

"When will he be back?" I ask, trying to keep a polite tone.

"Not sure," she says as she shrugs her shoulders. "He's in New York."

"Oh," I say dejectedly, my gaze dropping to the ground briefly. When I look back up, I give her a small smile. "Okay, I'll just try him later."

"Clearly you didn't even know he was gone," Vanessa says condescendingly. "I take that to mean you two broke up."

The small smile slides from my face, and I level a steely look her way as I open my car door again. "Not really any of your business."

"So that must be the reason he's interviewing for a job in New York, then," she says as if a great mystery was just unveiled to her. "That's just great. Way to chase him off, Leary."

Interviewing for a job in New York? What the hell?

I glare at Vanessa but don't bother to respond. Instead, the minute I get in my car, start it up, and put it in reverse, I'm dialing Ford.

"What's up, buttercup?" he asks amiably when he picks up.

"Reeve is moving to New York?" I screech.

"Easy there, Miss Pterodactyl," Ford laughs. "You about busted out my eardrums."

"Cut the shit," I snarl. "Is Reeve moving to New York?"

"I have no clue," he says, his voice not so humorous now. "He said he might look for work there when I talked to him the day of the verdict."

"And you didn't think to mention that to me?" I demand.

"Well, no," Ford says sheepishly. "I didn't think it would matter to you."

"Oh, come on," I gripe. "You know me better than that. You know Reeve is for me and that I needed to get my head out of my ass. If you knew there was a potential for him to leave, you should have pulled my head out of my ass two days ago."

Ford chuckles and I grit my teeth. "Sorry, babe. My bad."

I blow out a frustrated breath. "He's apparently in New York now. Interviewing for a job."

"So call him," Ford suggests.

"No," I emphatically deny. "What I need to say to him has to be done in person. It's too important to do by phone."

"Then just wait for him to get back. I'm sure he'll be home in a few days."

"No, it's too important," I argue with frustration.

"Then get on a damn plane and go see him," Ford says with exasperation.

"Exactly," I affirm. "Call him, find out where he is, and let me know. But don't tell him I'm coming."

"You're awfully demanding," he grumbles, but I hear the affection in his voice. "I'll call you back as soon as I know something."

Smiling, I drive out of Reeve's neighborhood, hit the beltway, and head toward my house. I call my secretary and ask her to book me on the next available direct flight to New York. She asks me if I'll need hotel accommodations, and I tell her no. I'm going to bet on love prevailing and that I'll have sufficient accommodations in Reeve's room tonight.

Then I call Midge's direct number.

I have a huge favor to ask her.

CHAPTER 26
REEVE

The bartender sets a glass of Woodford Reserve down in front of me, and I slide my credit card across the bar to him. "Start a tab. I'm meeting a friend for drinks before I head out to dinner."

He nods at me, glances at my card, and says, "Of course, Mr. Holloway."

Picking up my glass, I raise it in salute to him and take a healthy sip. It burns nicely but does nothing to settle my stomach.

Fucking Cal offered me a job today. I met him and his partner, MacKayla Dawson, for lunch, and by the time I made it back to my hotel, he'd called and offered me a position at their law firm.

And now I have a choice to make.

Take the job, move here to New York, and start a new career.

Or stay in Raleigh and hope to God that one day I'll find my way back into Leary's good graces.

Decisions, decisions.

Pulling my phone out, I shoot a quick text to Ford.

I'm here. Just ordered a drink.

He called me yesterday to chat, and ironically happened to mention he was in New York for depositions. I suggested we get together tonight for drinks before I have to meet up with Cal, Macy, MacKayla, and her husband, Matt, for dinner, which I expect might be an attempt to schmooze me more as an inducement to take the job.

I poured the rest of the sordid story out to Cal last night when we hooked up for dinner. Macy had other plans, so it was just me, Cal, and some good whiskey. We caught up on old times, and I bitched and whined over my Leary situation.

And while Cal was empathetic to said situation, he didn't have much advice to offer. Only sympathized with my plight and said that he hoped I got what I truly wanted.

Now I just have to determine what that is.

New York or Leary?

Fucking decisions.

My phone vibrates and I see Ford has texted me back. Running a bit late. Be there in about ten minutes.

Setting my phone back down, I swirl my drink and ponder the almost insurmountable wall before me.

Leary is hurt. She feels I betrayed her. The trust has been damaged.

The question is, how do I fucking repair all that shit?

I made an attempt with Rhonda Valasquez, but I never heard a word from Leary about it. I sort of expected her to call after the verdict to, I don't know, maybe thank me, or tell me to go fuck myself. Something. Anything.

Instead, I got nothing but silence, so I made an impromptu decision to head to New York and discuss job options with Cal. He's been hinting for months that he wants me to move here and has been telling me how great his and MacKayla's firm is. They do the same exact type of work that Leary does, and I've been in the game long enough to know I'm better suited to representing the downtrodden over the wealthy.

Didn't expect a job offer so fast, though.

I take a healthy slug from the whiskey and set it down, gritting my teeth as it travels downward. I should just accept the job. Get it over with. Cut ties with Raleigh and what could have been and move on.

Except that every molecule in my entire being screams at me, *Dumbass!*

Someone pulls a stool out to my right, and by the scent of perfume, I know it's a woman. Ordinarily, I would sidle a glance over her way, see if she's worth checking out. See if I can buy her a drink, let nature take its course. Get laid, in other words.

No interest now.

Leary completely fucking ruined me.

Twisting my wrist, I look at my watch and then turn my head toward the front of the bar. Ford picked this place and since it's close to my hotel, I agreed. It's nice and small, quietly cozy and filled with hip, young New Yorkers stopping by for a drink with friends after work.

It's actually getting a little crowded, so I take a quick glance around to make sure I didn't miss Ford walking in. My gaze drops first on the woman who just sat down next to me, and yeah . . . she's pretty hot. She gives me a coy smile and I move right past her. I look around— everyone's in smart business suits with harried expressions on their faces as they slurp at their overpriced drinks and complain about their workdays.

Did I mention that I really, really don't like New York?

My eyes roam the bar area, every person looking like the next. I do a complete 360 of the entire bar.

I pass over men and women, seeing but not really seeing them, because frankly I really only want to see one person.

And holy fuck, there she is.

I have to do an actual double take.

Walking in the door is Leary.

My heart seizes up in disbelief and shock, and I'm wondering, what are the chances that she would be in the same bar as I am in a city of almost 8.5 million people?

I wait for her to see me as she glances around, and almost like a magnet, her gaze is drawn to me. Her expression immediately morphs into one of relief, and in that instant, I know she's here for me.

Not by coincidence, but for me.

I have not an ounce of control over my eyes as they rove all over her, eating her up. She's stunning in black high-heeled boots, a taupe sweaterdress molded to her curves, and her bright-red wool coat.

I start to stand up from my stool, but she shakes her head slightly as she walks toward me. I feel my heart pumping hard with every step she takes.

When she reaches me, her look is almost shy, which I find utterly charming on this self-possessed and confident woman.

"I'm going to go out on a limb here," I say by way of breaking the ice. "Ford isn't coming to meet me for drinks tonight, is he?"

The corners of her mouth tip up slightly. "No. It was a ruse to find out where you were."

"And you flew here to see me?"

She takes a step closer, touching her fingers against my knee. So innocent a touch, and yet it hits me with the power of a lightning strike. "I flew here to see you," she affirms softly. "I had to see you."

Leary opens her mouth but I quickly cover her lips with my fingers. "If you're here, by some chance, to reconcile with me, I'm going to save you a lot of time and effort. Just nod your head if that's the case."

Her eyes go round in surprise and I can feel her smile under my fingers. She gives a quick nod and I pull my hand away, replacing my touch with my mouth. I kiss her fast and hard, my arms coming around her waist to pull her into me. She answers by sliding her fingers in my hair and holding on tight while we explore each other's mouths, sitting in a bar in New York City.

She tries to pull away from me, muttering against my lips, "I need to apologize—"

"Shut up, Leary," I manage to say before I kiss her again.

She submits fully, her hands going to my neck this time and holding me hard as we kiss and make up.

Finally, I let her up for air. I pull my mouth away and stare at her, my heart for the first time in days feeling peaceful.

Her fingertips come up and gently trace my lips. "We need to talk," she says softly.

"We need to fuck," I correct her and turn to get the bartender's attention. I motion him to cash me out and turn back to Leary.

"Reeve," she admonishes, "we've got some things to resolve—"

"Hold on to that thought," I tell her and pull out my phone. I shoot off two texts.

First to Ford: I owe you, buddy.

The second to Cal: Dinner's canceled. Leary flew to New York.

Both short and sweet with no other explanation needed. I expect Cal will understand this means I can't accept the job, but I'll call him later just to make sure.

Ignoring Leary, I turn back and find that the bartender has brought back my credit card and the receipt. I leave him a ridiculously large tip because I am fucking ridiculously beside myself right this minute.

Pocketing my phone and credit card, I grab Leary's hand and drag her out of the bar. I take an immediate right out of the door. Thank God my hotel is just three blocks away.

When we make it a block, Leary starts pulling on my hand. "Reeve, stop. Let me get this out."

I ignore her, plowing forward, completely intent on elbowing people out of my way if they think to impede the progress I'm making toward getting Leary into my hotel room and naked.

She tugs again on my hand, and I tighten my grasp so she doesn't slip loose.

"Reeve," she says with frustration, "you need to let me apologize."

"Apology accepted," I tell her quickly and then shoot her a wink.

She wrenches free of me, and I immediately stop in my tracks to turn back to her. Someone bumps into me hard and curses, but I ignore it. She's glaring at me, her hands on her hips with the throngs of New York rush-hour pedestrians swarming by us.

I lunge for her hand and growl, "I apologized; you apologized. It's done. Now let's get to the makeup-sex part. We can talk details later."

"Stop it!" she yells at me, loud enough that several people turn their heads as they walk by. "We need to talk."

Her face is determined.

Beautiful, regretful, angry, and so determined.

Sighing in my own frustration, I rake my hand through my hair and throw my arms out to the side. I yell right back at her, "Fine. Lay it on me. Do you want me to apologize some more for hurting you? Betraying you? Want me to get down on my knees here in the middle of a New York sidewalk and beg your forgiveness? Just tell me what you want, because I will give it to you. I'll give you anything to make this all better so we can be together again."

For the most part, we're ignored, although I swear I hear one woman call out as she walks by, "Make him grovel."

That gets a smirk out of Leary, but she shakes her head at me and takes a step closer. Her hand comes out and grasps my tie, just below the knot. She goes up on her tiptoes and plants a soft kiss on my mouth.

"I don't want you to do anything but listen to me," she says softly. "I know you're sorry. I'm sorry, too. And you're right, we can discuss the details of apologies and forgiveness later. But I have something more important to say to you."

"Like what?" I ask with a smile because, fuck, she's adorable right now.

"I need to say thank you for Rhonda Valasquez. You put your entire career on the line to help me, and I can never repay you for that."

"I don't want anything for that," I tell her quickly.

She gives me a knowing smile. "No, I suppose you don't. But the sentiment is still the same. It was a brave and courageous thing you did. You risked everything for me."

"I did," I tell her softly, not realizing how much I needed her to understand the lengths to which I would go for her. "I'd do it again and again for you."

She nods and steps in even closer. "But the most important thing I need to say to you, before you haul me up to your hotel room, is that I love you. It's scary how much I love you, and I couldn't go another day without seeing you and telling you that. That's why I came to New York. I simply couldn't let you go another minute without knowing that."

"You love me?" I ask, not quite believing I'd hear those words from her so soon. I figured maybe . . . one day . . . she'd get there. When she was really over what I did to her. One day I'd earn her trust back and get those miraculous words.

"I love you," she reiterates. "And you love me, too."

I blink at her, not because I disagree, but because she sounds so confident in her assessment. "How could you possibly know that?"

"Because of the risks you took for me. It told me all I needed to know about the depth of your feelings. Am I wrong?"

"You're not wrong," I assure her. "I love you very much, Leary. And I'm sorry for what happened—"

Leary's mouth finds mine again, and the sounds and bustle of New York melt away. I let her lips and sweet tongue possess me, and I forget about everything else that exists in the world except for this woman.

She pauses our kiss just long enough to mutter against me, "No more apologies. Let's move forward, okay?"

Leaning in, I touch my forehead to hers and nod. "Forward."

"Good," she says and presses her lips against mine again. I can feel the curve of her smile lying sweet against my own.

"And by forward, do you think that might mean toward the hotel?" I ask her deviously.

"Yeah, that would definitely be good," she agrees and then proceeds to kiss me deeply again.

Finally, I break the kiss, because otherwise I'm going to be sporting a massive fucking hard-on in the middle of lower Manhattan, and the longer we stand here kissing, the longer it takes to get her naked and in bed.

Grabbing her hand again, I look down at her and smile big. "Ready?"

"More than," she agrees, and we take off, practically running toward my hotel.

EPILOGUE

LEARY

One Month Later

"Okay, everyone . . . simmer down," Danny Payne says in dramatic fashion. He stands at the end of the conference room table, draws his height up—which may, impressively, top him out at five eight at this moment—and holds up his hands.

The chatter and laughter that had filled the room to buzzing just moments earlier starts to wane until there's total silence. I glance around, looking at all of the faces staring up at Danny. Partners, junior partners, and associate attorneys of the civil division of Knight & Payne. My crew, my posse, all of us warriors for justice. All of us working for the great Midge Payne so we can stamp out corruption and bring victory to those less fortunate.

My soapbox never looked taller or shinier in my life, and I love it.

"Midge asked me to gather everyone today before we let you out for the Christmas holidays and make an official announcement," Danny says with his chest puffed out. He's always loved the limelight of being the attorney in charge of this law firm. "This is a big one and deserves a little celebration, so if you'll hold up just a moment."

Danny brings his hands together for two sharp claps and looks expectantly at the conference-room door.

Nothing happens.

He claps twice again and leans forward to peer hard at the doorknob, but again . . . no movement.

"Oh, for Christ's sake," Danny grumbles and skirts around the end of the table. He stalks up to the door and whips it open, revealing a waiter wearing black pants, a white shirt, and a black bow tie. He's so startled when Danny opens the door, he almost drops the bottle of champagne he's carrying on a silver tray.

"You missed my cue," Danny hisses and then opens the door farther to admit the waiter.

Except it's not just one waiter. Five of them walk in, two bearing bottles of champagne and the rest with fluted glasses. They efficiently walk around the room, popping bottles and pouring glasses of bubbly until everyone has one in hand.

Taking his place at the head of the table again, Danny takes the glass sitting before him and holds it in front of his stomach while his other hand slides in his pocket. He's the picture of casual sophistication, just a little on the short side.

"As I said, today is a big day," Danny says as he cuts me a smile. "Midge would like me to formally announce that our own Leary Michaels has been offered a full partnership in the firm of Knight & Payne, and she has graciously accepted. As you know, she joins the ranks of Ford Daniels, Cary Peterson, and Wendy Fischer, who have already made full partnership along with Midge and me. This is a momentous occasion, and I remember the day that Leary started here . . ."

I immediately tune Danny out. I'm a little embarrassed this is being done, but he insisted on making a huge announcement, since it is indeed a rarity that someone is offered a full partnership. That means ownership interest, stock options, and a buy-in for partial ownership of the Watts Building if I want. Yes, it was confirmed—Midge actually owns the entire Watts Building.

This was something she divulged to me when she called me into her office a few weeks ago and offered me the partnership. It wasn't something that was taken lightly. It meant that I had to buy in, to invest in the business. It meant more responsibility. It made me responsible for the debt in equal shares to the other partners. It meant longer hours, tougher cases, and more travel.

I didn't need to think about it, but so as not to appear too excited, I gave her my answer the next day.

Swiveling my head to the right, I look at Reeve sitting next to me. He's watching Danny give his speech, but I can tell he's tuned out, too.

I wonder what he's thinking.

I bet he's thinking of that unbelievably awesome blow job I gave him this morning before we got out of bed. Tilting back in my chair, I pull in my chin and tilt my head, trying to get a good look at Reeve's crotch, which is partially hidden by the edge of the table. I can't tell if he's got a hard-on or not, so no telling what he's thinking.

My gaze swivels back to his face and I find his eyes directly on me. One corner of his mouth is tilted up in a "caught ya" grin, with a cocked eyebrow to mock my audacity. I give him a sheepish smile back and reach over to stroke his forearm before dropping my hand.

Reeve started at Knight & Payne the week after we got back from New York.

That was the big favor I asked of Midge.

I asked her to make room for him in our civil division—not because he's my boyfriend but because he's a phenomenal trial attorney with a heart of gold. He proved over and over again by the way he treated Jenna with respect throughout the case that he has what it takes to represent the people on our side of the fence. When I told Midge what he did with Rhonda Valasquez, she was so impressed she called him on the spot and offered him a job.

She said, and I quote, "I like the way you think, Reeve. I like that you push boundaries. The job is yours if you want it."

And just like that, Reeve was not only my lover but my work associate as well.

As an associate attorney, Reeve didn't rate an office. So he was out in the Pit. Tragically, his desk was all the way across the Pit, so it was hard to see him. This actually could be considered a good thing, I suppose, because I'm sure that if he were closer to me, it would be difficult to get any work done. Regardless, we've made use of the smoke walls in my office on at least two occasions when we wanted a little hanky-panky during the middle of the day.

"... and in conclusion, let's all raise our glasses and toast Leary for an amazing career here so far, and for many more years of her brilliance to come in and out of the courtroom."

I blink, hastily pick up my glass, and raise it. Shouts of "Here, here" and "To Leary" echo across the room. Ford is sitting opposite me, and he leans across the table and I do the same so we can clink our glasses together. When I sink back into my chair, Reeve leans over and kisses my cheek. "Congrats, baby. I'm so proud of you."

Turning my face, I let my lips find his, and in an uncharacteristic display of wanton public affection, I give him a deep kiss that causes a tiny rumble to tear loose from his chest. When I pull back, I say, "I love you."

"I love you, too," he says.

"Okay, everyone, gulp that bubbly down and get back to work!" Danny shouts, and just like that, the party is over.

Thank God!

Everyone stands to leave. It's the Friday before Christmas break starts and almost 5:30 p.m. I still have a ton of stuff to do before I leave, though, so I let my mind start churning through my to-do list.

I round the table with Reeve behind me. Ford is waiting for us, buttoning his suit jacket.

"Hey," he says genially. "Have y'all met the new associate attorney? Cary Peterson's daughter?"

"Her name's Emma," I mutter, and then add as a warning, "and try to keep it in your pants around her, Ford. She's just a baby."

"Don't I know it," Ford grumbles. "Besides, I like my women a little more experienced. I read a survey once that said a woman doesn't know how to give good head until she reaches her late twenties. Think that's true?"

I roll my eyes and push past Ford, but I hear him and Reeve behind me talking in low voices . . . about blow jobs, no doubt.

Working my way through the Pit, I head toward my office. A few of the staff are packing up, and I nod left and right, giving smiles and wishes for a good holiday.

Just as I reach my office, I feel a hand on my lower back and Reeve is pushing me through the door. He pushes me all the way in, closes the door, and herds me around my desk. Slapping his hand on my smoke button, he steers me right to the large windows that look over the eastern edge of the Raleigh skyline.

His hands grab mine and he raises them up, placing my palms against the cool glass by my head. "Don't move," he whispers in my ear.

"What are you doing?" I ask in a husky voice, but I know damn well what he's doing.

"I'm getting some of you now because I know you're going to work late tonight," he replies, his fingers going to my skirt and lifting it up my legs. He drags the material up, bunching it at my waist, and then brings his hands downward, hooking into my underwear to remove them.

He's so skilled at what he does, I just lay my forehead against the glass and sigh as he takes my panties off, then spreads my legs apart. I expect him to whip his cock out and go to town on me, so I'm caught a little off guard when I feel his hot breath between my legs.

"Oh God," I groan when his mouth makes contact with me. I rest my cheek against the glass and squeeze my eyes shut as Reeve eats me out like a champion. It doesn't take long before I'm bursting apart, and then he's up on his feet, his hard-as-hell cock out and pushing inside me.

Reeve holds on to my hips, fucking me up against the window. Resting his chin on my shoulder, he pants, "So we're doing it this weekend, right?"

"Right," I gasp because he slams into me super hard.

"Good," he grunts as he starts to tunnel into me. "Can't wait."

"Me, either," I manage to moan in between sucking oxygen back into my lungs.

And I can't wait.

This weekend, Reeve and I are taking the next big step in our relationship.

We're moving in together.

We decided to put my house on the market and move into his, mainly because of Mr. Chico Taco. Reeve's house is larger than mine, and with a behemoth dog like that, we need the extra space. Plus, his house is a little closer to work, and even though I hate to admit it, it's nice having Vanessa available to take care of Chico when we have to work late.

Ford thinks I'm nuts for taking this step so soon, but not me. I have never been surer of anything in my entire life. I trust Reeve implicitly with my heart, so I don't see the need to hold back on anything.

Dropping his hand between my legs, Reeve murmurs in my ear. "Want you to come again, baby."

"Going to," I gasp as he hits me right in that beautifully sensitive spot. "Like . . . oh, shit . . . right now."

I start to tremble and quake as Reeve pounds harder into me, his hand between my legs working me even harder to draw my orgasm out. Then he thrusts deep, stills for a second, and drops his head to my shoulder as he starts to come.

"Fuck," he moans as he continues to thrust shallowly into me, using my warm grip to milk him dry. I curl one arm backward and bring my fingers to the back of his head, massaging his scalp as we both start to come down off our high.

Reeve slips out of me but pulls me back into his body, wrapping both arms around my waist. We both silently stare out at the darkened, winter Raleigh skyline. It's our kingdom. Our playground. From inside the Watts Building, we'll wreak havoc on corrupt businesses. From just a few miles away, in our home, we'll continue to possess and dominate each other's bodies night after night.

And from right within our hearts . . . deep inside . . . we'll continue to grow our love.

It's a journey I'm eager to start.

ACKNOWLEDGMENTS

I'm sure when I went to law school nineteen years ago, my mother never envisioned I would use any of that knowledge to write a sexy romance. And yet here I am doing just that. I have to thank you so much, Mom, because I never would have chosen the legal field as my career without you as that role model. I had a glorious career as a litigator and hopefully will continue on just as gloriously as a writer. Just know that I would never have accomplished half of what I have without you showing me what a woman can really aspire to be.

ABOUT THE AUTHOR

Photo © 2014 Marie Killen

New York Times and *USA Today* bestselling author Sawyer Bennett is a snarky southern woman and reformed trial lawyer who decided to finally start putting on paper all of the stories that were floating in her head. She is the author of several contemporary romances, including the popular Off series, the Legal Affairs series, and the Last Call series. Her husband works for a Fortune 100 company that lets him fly all over the world, while she stays at home with their daughter and three big, furry dogs who hog the bed. She would like to report she doesn't have many weaknesses but can be bribed with a nominal amount of milk chocolate.